# CROW IN THE HOLLOW

# CROW IN THE HOLLOW

*written & illustrated by*

## BRIAN W. PARKER

INKWATER
PRESS

PORTLAND • OREGON
INKWATERPRESS.COM

*Scan this QR Code
to learn more about
this title*

Publisher: Inkwater Press | www.inkwaterpress.com

Paperback
ISBN-13 978-1-59299-968-2 | ISBN-10 1-59299-968-9

Kindle
ISBN-13 978-1-59299-969-9 | ISBN-10 1-59299-969-7

Printed in the U.S.A.
All paper is acid free and meets all ANSI standards for archival quality paper.

1 3 5 7 9 10 8 6 4 2

*For my family, who nurtured me*
*For my wife, who keeps me whole*
*And for my Lord, who shapes my world*
*I owe you everything.*

# TABLE OF CONTENTS

## MAPS

## PART 1
## WATCHED BY THE CROW

## PART 2
## THE SWORDBEARER

PART 3

# THE SONGS OF CHANGING

PART 4

# WHERE SPIRITS WALK

PART 5

# THE CROW'S FLIGHT

# MAPS

The Continent of **Kypaka**  The year 1382 of The High Kaelish Empire

The *Kaelish Colonies*

The Great Northern Woods

Orin's Hollow

Silver Lake

Midland Marshes

The Golden Plains

Vorhaven

The Camps

Vernon

Dale

Connersville

Chanter's Port

Brockholm Bay

Chancery

Mgorehaven

Augustine

Isles of Nogra

The *Scalan Sea*

Vederic
*The Island of Saul*

N  E  S  W

▼ To the Empire of Kael and Umbar

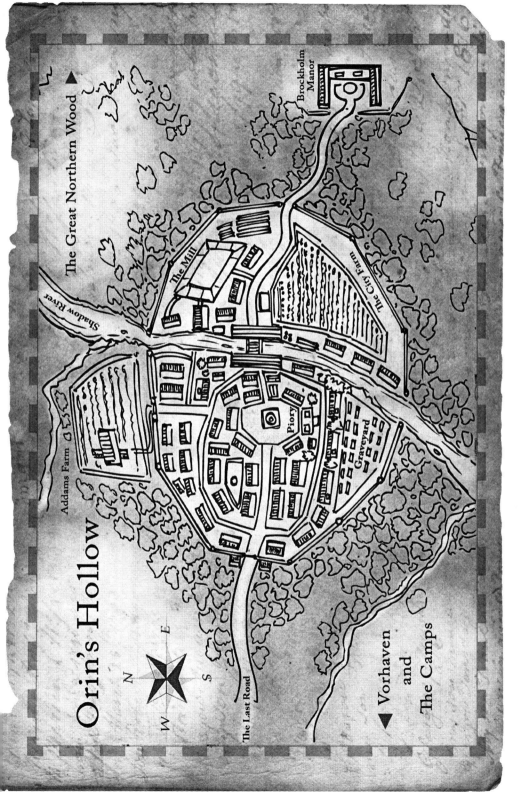

Orin's Hollow

The Great Northern Wood ▲

Shadow River

Addams Farm

The Mill

Brockholm Manor

The City Farm

Priory

Graveyard

The Last Road

Vorhaven and The Camps ▼

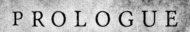

# THE STORYTELLER

IN THE BLUE COLD OF WINTER, THE PEOPLE OF ORIN'S HOLLOW SAT IN
the town square, talking excitedly amongst themselves—their
faces lit by the flickering orange light from the tall bonfires.

They sat and waited to see magic with their own eyes.

The man they waited for only came once every five years, and
always in mid-winter during the Sundering celebration. Now, as
they sat together, men, women, and children all breathless with
anticipation, the Storyteller walked quietly across the borders of
the town. He appeared, as always, on the old bridge that crossed
the Shadow River just as the last light of day left the frost-covered
branches. A wind began to stir, whipping the little flames of the gas
lamps in the square into a tizzy, and lifting clouds of ice crystals
free of the trees. It cast them about in an ephemeral dance that
swirled and twisted through the air, quickly taking the form of a
man. He stepped into the Waking World like a shimmering winter
breath made flesh and bone.

The Storyteller was a very thin man, with the dark, nut-brown
skin of the First People. He wore his long, silver-grey hair tied back,
and over his broad, bony shoulders was draped a dark cloak of rags
topped with a cowl of black feathers. He carried no bag or provisions, only a tall birch walking stick covered in strange markings
that few could understand. By most accounts he was a very normal,
albeit eccentric-looking old man—save for his ice-blue eyes.

The townsfolk would say that the wind moved differently when
the Storyteller was near, smelling of fresh pine smoke and spices,
and the very shadows held the promise of mystery.

He walked quietly down the cobbled street, past old houses he
knew, and some he did not, until he stood in the light of the bonfires. He raised his staff high in the air and sang out in a clear and
resonant voice.

*"Coy eya que-nashta u, ma ka la oy que-ookta sho."*

The flames instantly grew higher, and at their centers images began to take shape. Images of men in ancient armor, animals running free in the wild, and people of the tribes adorned in their ceremony robes dancing in the heart of the flame.

"What story would you have me tell, my children?" The Storyteller never raised his voice, yet it seemed to come from everywhere, and from nowhere at all.

"Tell us about when the outlanders came," one person said, while another cried, "Tell us of the Great War." Then, from amongst the din of voices calling for their favorite tale, a lone child's voice called out as clear as the ringing of a tiny bell.

"Tell us how Crow came to Orin's Hollow," a little girl said.

The Storyteller raised his hand, and there was silence once more.

"Well, my dear one, that is an unusual request. That is a story I haven't told in quite some time." He smiled, and slowly settled himself down before the crowd. He wrapped himself in his feathered cloak, and laid his staff across his bowed knees.

"Now, where to begin." And so, he started his tale.

LONG AGO, BEFORE THE OUTLANDERS *came on their ships across the wide ocean, and long before the colonists brought their new ways and weapons of fire and cold stone, there were the First People.*

*Their homes lay deep within the wilds, past borders of vine and branch. They were hunters, farmers, men, women, and children—proud and strong. But their ways were not as simple as some would have you believe. They made war with their neighbors and fought with spear and club and knife, for this is the way of man. When the One Voice sang the world into existence, he made men and spirits to live in it, and together they walked the shadowed paths of untouched nature. They were bound, you see, by power and lust and the magic that governed the ancient world's balance. The secrets of immortality and of the hidden places belonged to the great spirits,*

called the mahko, *and the power of change belonged to men. That power is
called* sen-wa—*The Songs of Changing.*

*The music of creation flows through all things, man and spirit alike.
The words were ancient beyond man's comprehension, and when sung aloud
they formed songs that possessed a great power. When voices were lifted to
its strange, undulating rhythm, all things were possible. A man could sing
down a spring rain, call mighty hawks from the highest tree, or even cause
flames to leap free from smoking pits and dance like children in the wind.
Some songs could create and bind, while others would rend and destroy, for
the power of change is both light and dark. And so, men made a pact that
this power was to be guarded and protected. Of the tribes, none were more
feared or more honored than the Chinequewa—the Silent Ones. It was
their charge to protect the ancient knowledge, and punish those who would
use it for evil. They were masters of the* sen-wa, *and it was said that they
never spoke unless required, fearing the power of their own voices. Legends
spoke of their warriors, gifted with great abilities, running effortlessly along
the branches of the king pines like silent ghosts and disappearing in the
blink of an eye, leaving only the distant hum of their songs. But when the
outlanders came, no songs were sung to defend against their fury. The Chinequewa had simply disappeared deep into their mountain homes. Instead,
the warriors of the other tribes set out to meet these strangers from foreign
lands. They knew defeat lay in their futures, but better that than to be
taken as slaves.*

*The outlanders had come from far to the east, blown to these shores on
sails as white as gulls' wings. Some came seeking adventure, others riches,
but all had come to find the freedom they had never known in their home-
lands. What they found were the First People. The warring years were
long, but in the end the outlanders declared lordship over the land. In time
they brought their women and children and began to build lives for themselves. Towns sprung up in places that had never known man's touch, or his
ambition, and with every stone that was laid the world began to change. It
wasn't until the outlanders came to this quiet valley at the border of the
great northern wood that the Chinequewa appeared again.*

*They came in the silent hours of winter, bounding through the skeletal*

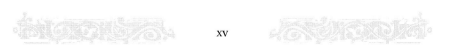

trees, *their weapons glinting with stark moonlight. They descended on the small settlement like vengeance from above. When the night was done, the Silent Ones had disappeared once again into the forest, leaving only quiet death in their wake.*

*In time, the people of the valley healed and rebuilt, but never forgot that winter's night, nor did they forget the Chinequewa. They were spoken of like myths and nightmares—one part truth and one part fantasy—feared by the outlanders, hated by the tribes, and lost forever to time. It was into this new world that a child was born. His name was Suqata, which in the ancient tongue meant "Watched by the Crow." It is an old name—one that conjures images of a troubled future for those given it.*

*This story belongs to him.*

PART 1

# WATCHED BY
# THE CROW

# CHAPTER 1
# SUQATA

Y OU COULD SEE THEM COMING ACROSS THE SNOW-SWEPT LANDSCAPE
from miles off, moving with the steady, weary plod of the
defeated. One by one, surrounded by men on horseback with shouldered muskets, the prisoners marched down unknown trails, bound
together by their hands; the men in front, followed by the women,
and lastly the children. Most kept their heads down, avoiding the
foreign eyes of their captors—all except for one boy near the end
of the line, wrapped in tattered skins. He was not a remarkable or
noteworthy child; skinnier than most, though they all were thin,
and darker than most, though they all had dark, autumn-colored
skin. His black hair had grown long in the weeks since he was
found and taken, and it now hung unkempt across his narrow face.
He had wrapped his arms close to his body against the cold, and he
held his hands balled in small, tight fists. Out of them all, only he
kept his oddly piercing blue-grey eyes set on the horizon. The boy,
Suqata, wanted to see what was coming.

He had survived weeks of the howling wind and freezing rain,
his body bent against the storms, watching as others fell along the
way. He had staggered past them on the road as they lay, left to
snow and wolves. Their captors never blinked an eye for the sick or
the wounded. There was nothing to do for them; it was their fate.
Now, after so many hard days, Suqata finally stopped walking and
their destination stood just over the next hill, still miles away and
yet obvious by the billows of black smoke rising from its center.
Suqata had heard the other children speak of this place before.
Through a dozen small comments, pieced together from broken
tongues he could barely understand, a picture had formed in the
young boy's mind—a picture of the place where the great king
pines were cut down and where the outlanders took their slaves.
They called it simply the camps.

They were brought in through two heavy wooden gates, banded with dark iron and topped with vicious points that looked to Suqata like the teeth of some ravenous animal. The streets were cold, wet mud that sucked at his hide shoes, and all about him he could feel the stares of the outlanders as they watched the new slaves arrive. Suqata couldn't stop himself from shivering no matter how hard he tried. Everything about that place felt alien to him, from the close, stale air filled with the ringing of hammers to the raucous sounds of men working. There were no children there, only men, horses, and the immense wood and stone longhouses. Wagons pulled by huge teams of oxen trudged down the caked streets, while teams of workers and slaves filled them with stacks of cut logs that rivaled the height of the buildings.

Suqata's mind reeled, his senses struggling desperately to keep up with the changes around him. Everything, from the flashes of light coming from the smithies to the harsh calls from the working men, filled him with pangs of fear. Even the smells of the place seemed hostile. It was a mixture of strong, acrid smoke, spices, and the copper tang from the forges that burned his nostrils and filled his eyes with small, stinging tears.

The encampment was built on the edge of the forest line just beyond the swaying tops of distant trees, over which Suqata could see the mountains. Even here, he could feel their inexplicable pull, as the forest beckoned to him from beyond the camps' high walls. The scraps of clothing he had wrapped around himself for warmth were now worn to threads, and his thin legs hardly had strength enough to stand. Still, at that moment there was nothing he wanted more than to stand amongst those tall trees again. Gone were the soft sounds of the wind, and the rustle of branches overhead. Every memory before that quiet forest had dimmed to the point of nonexistence. It was his home, as far as he knew, and now it felt oh so far away.

The new captives spent their first days in wooden pens while they were being sorted, but by sunup all the prisoners had been

4

separated from their kinsmen and mixed with other captured tribes. The Sandokee boatmen from the south, with their dark mahogany skin and tattooed faces, were placed side by side with Tonaskowa hunters of the golden plains. Few knew the other's tongue, so no one spoke. Suqata sat alone, his hands still clenched in tight fists, although more than one of the women had reached out to comfort him. Their faces were always drawn and tight with sadness until they noticed his eyes: his piercing blue eyes. "Silent One," they whispered. He had the eyes of the Chinequewa. Their hands would then withdraw, leaving Suqata alone again. In the night, as Suqata lay staring into the darkness, he would hear someone start to sing one of the old song-prayers. One that all the tribes knew, even in their separate tongues: "Oh Great Spirit, the One Voice who sang the world into being. Shield us from evil. Deliver us from the dark." They sang quietly into the night, though none of them heard a reply.

THOSE WHO WERE TOO YOUNG for heavy work were separated from the other slaves and moved through the muddy streets towards a tall stone building near the center of the camps. They were marched through its double doors and led down, down into a deep brick-lined chamber, the center of which was dominated by an immense stone wheel. There was a great deal of movement here as lines of boys pushed the great wheel in endless circles. Suqata was found a place along one of the wheel's spokes and tethered there while the outlanders pointed and yelled in their strange tongue, commanding them all to push. As they did, other slaves brought in carts filled with heaps of wheat and barley that were cast beneath the grinding wheel.

BY THE END OF THEIR first day, Suqata's shoulders ached and his legs felt like they would collapse beneath him at any moment. A larger boy named Mahatowa, who had been set to push beside him on the grinding stone, more than once had to reach over and pull Suqata back up into position. He grunted something in a hushed

and angry tone, though Suqata didn't understand. When he spoke again, he struck Suqata hard with his elbow, then pointed angrily to Suqata's hands, which were still clenched tightly into fists.

"He says you need to open your hands and push, unless you want to be beaten for moving too slowly," a hushed voice said from out of nowhere, causing Suqata to spin around in shock.

"Who said that?" he cried.

"I did. Down here." The voice had spoken again.

"I understand you! You can speak my tongue?"

"Of course I can. I am Chinequewa, too. Now hush, boy, and look down."

Suqata glanced down between the spokes of the stone wheel, to the space beneath where the women and elders gathered up and separated the ground grain. There he saw an old man's face staring back at him with pale eyes.

"Don't be frightened, young one. I want to help you, but you must do as I say. This thick-head beside you has a point, you know. Whatever it is you are holding in your hands is going to have to go if you are to push the wheel."

"No, I don't want to," Suqata replied, this time giving the other boy a hard stare. "Tell him to leave me alone."

"I would, but I think that would be unwise. He isn't very pleasant, trust me, and I don't think it would go well for you if you get him whipped on your account. Why don't you just let whatever it is go?"

"NO!" Suqata cried. This time his voice was stronger, and even in the din of the mill house it reverberated in air like the sound of a rung bell. From his place between the spokes, the old man's sightless eyes were wide for a moment. Quickly the surprise faded, and he let out a long sigh.

"Now you've done it. They'll be over here any minute to see what all the commotion is. I have another idea—I'll teach you a trick to hide your little treasures, how about that?"

Not far from where he was tethered, Suqata saw one of the

outlanders stand and start moving towards his place on the wheel. He was burly, and held a thick club in his hand as he checked amongst the boys.

"Tell me quickly, please," Suqata whispered to the old man.

"Open your hands first."

Suqata relaxed his fists, and resting on his palms were two perfectly smooth river stones, both white as bone.

"Say these words, like you were singing a song; *anashi na, da unuk cha.* Quickly!"

"*Anashi na, da unuk cha.*" Suqata sang the words.

"Again."

"*Anashi na, da unuk cha.*" Suqata sang again. This time, the words seemed to vibrate on his tongue when he spoke.

"Again. From deep down," he whispered urgently.

"*Anashi na, da unuk cha!*"

As he sang the last of the chant, he felt something change. He looked down at his palms and watched in awe as the two stones simply disappeared from his hands. The large boy beside him let out a strangled yelp and moved just out of Suqata's reach.

"Where did they go?" he said in a hushed, trembling voice.

"They are still there, boy, to be called back when you want them."

"How do I?"

"Push now, questions later—unless you'd rather take it up with the outlander's stick?"

Suqata grasped the spoke of the stone wheel with both hands and began to push again, though he never took his eyes away from his now empty hands.

"Are you a witch, Hopano?" Suqata said as he shoveled spoonfuls of thin root soup and hunks of hard brown bread into his mouth. The thin boy had stuffed himself almost to overflowing, and every word he spoke came with a spray of wet crumbs. The old man called Hopano sat quietly beside him, brushing the cascade of flying bits

away without a second thought. After their day of work the slaves had been set up in one of the outlanders' longhouses with hay mats to sleep on. From large cast-iron pots were distributed bowls of food, which the slaves took gladly. Already, pockets of familiar tribes had started gathering, segregating the slaves amongst themselves. Hopano had been sitting alone when Suqata found him, occasionally drawing a suspicious eye from others in their group. Soon Suqata began to realize he would be treated in kind. Even then, he could see Mahatowa glaring at him with his beady little eyes from beside one of the cooking fires. It didn't bother him much, though. Suqata hadn't eaten a hot meal in weeks, so that was his main concern, although he now had to split his excitement between his bowl and his mysterious new friend.

"A witch? Where did you hear that word?"

"One of the men with sticks said it today, when we were walking back to the longhouse. They were looking at you and pointing."

Hopano laughed into his bowl. "You don't miss much, do you, young one? Yes, some men have called me witch. Fools and lackwits, truth be told," he replied, continuing to sip down the last of his meal, holding the bowl lightly in his thin hands. He was an elder by any tribe's standards, with more seasons behind him than lay ahead. His warm red-brown skin was lined and spotted from the passage of years, and small scars along his brow and jawline seemed to tell a story of a hard life. Even though he was blind, there was fierceness in his gaze, and a quiet strength that lay coiled beneath a shell of age. Suqata noticed it in every flick of Hopano's arm as he swatted away the night flies, each movement punctuated by the distinct sound of beads clattering in his steely grey hair.

"What I am is a wordweaver; one who is gifted with a voice to sing the *sen-wa*."

"What is a *sen-wa*?"

"The Songs of Changing, boy," Hopano replied, this time sounding annoyed. "Did you not have wordweavers amongst your

tribe, boy? You are of the Chinequewa tribe. I should think you had quite a few in your village."

Suqata thought hard for a moment before answering, all the while thin lines of soup dribbling down his lip.

"I don't remember," he finally said.

"Truly? Not a thing of your people or where you come from?"

"I remember my name is Suqata."

Hopano raised one wiry brow. "Well, that's a start. Your name means 'Watched by the Crow' in the ancient words. Some considered that a curse, long ago when the world was full of more fools than you could count. Come now boy, I think you can do better than that. Think harder."

Suqata tried, but there were only dim memories—as if a wall of thick fog had formed in his mind that he could not see past, turning everything beyond it into shadows and ghostly shapes. "I can remember fire," he said, closing his eyes tightly in concentration, "and my feet in a little river. There was an old woman smiling at me. She smelled funny, too. Nothing else."

Hopano sat for long moment until a look of sadness came over him, but it quickly faded, replaced with a sly grin. "That's fine, boy," he said. "No use dwelling on the past anyway. Let's focus on the future then, shall we. The *sen-wa* are mankind's greatest gift. They are the words passed down to us from the beginning of time and the world, and with them we can change the very essence of the Waking World. When you sang today, your voice changed the state of your little treasures. One moment they were seen, the next they were hidden from all."

"Will you show me how to make them come back?" Suqata continued, undaunted in his questioning.

"You must sing a *sen-wa* of finding. The words are *die e unashi.*" Hopano said, "but I would not suggest you sing it now. You don't want your little treasures taken away, do you?"

"No. I guess not."

"Well, fine then. They are safe where you sent them, and there they will stay."

When Hopano spoke, there was a finality to the things he said, so Suqata decided not to press him about the stones. Instead, they sat quietly as Hopano attempted to finish his meal.

"So have you always been blind?" Suqata finally blurted out. He had held back on that question for about an hour, since the first time he had waved his hand before the old man's milky white eyes to no response.

Hopano set his bowl down. "Not always. Long ago, I was a boy with two keen eyes and a sharp temper the likes of which you have never seen," he said with a grin, "and what particularly set me off was troublesome fools waving their hands in my face. I was known for biting pretty hard."

Suqata was tempted to try again with his blind-test, but thought better of it, imagining the severe-looking old man moving forward with unexpected speed to take a bite of his hand.

"Before that, I was a hunter and tracker, a healer, and a great chief with many wives," he said flatly. "And long, long before that I was a bird."

Suqata didn't know if he was supposed to laugh or not. The old man, however, seemed quite serious.

"You talk kind of funny. Like you're telling fibs and riddles," Suqata said. "Are you trying to confuse me on purpose?"

"My words sound like riddles to you because you forget to understand. I hope you are not always such a blunt instrument, boy."

"There you go again."

Hopano sighed, closed his sightless eyes, and smiled. "Let me explain it then. In life, we are many things. Brother, son, father, lover. They are all the same person but with many names. The world is different for everyone, depending on where they are viewing it from. Is one person's view more real than another's? No. They all exist at the same time, and through them all moves the music of creation and change. That music sounds different to everyone, and

the words to Songs of Changing are never the same to all who hear
it, but sometimes there are those with a gift. They possess a connection to life, and an ability to hear the *sen-wa* as they were meant
to be. It is the true sound of the world. This knowledge allows
them to change the very essence of things. Do you understand?"

Suqata nodded his head, hoping he really did understand, or that
at least Hopano wouldn't ask him to repeat what he had just said.

"Good. Because I am about to show you something and I don't
want to waste my breath on ears that won't hear."

"Show me what?" he asked

"I am going to sing you a *sen-wa*. A very special *sen-wa*, and one
that will either prove my hopes in you, or will not." Hopano beckoned Suqata closer. Grabbing a woven blanket from his sleeping
mat and a small water skin, he led Suqata slowly away from the fire
and the prying eyes of the group. He then sat cross-legged, wrapping the length of his blanket around his shoulders. Spring nights
were crisp and chilly in the camps, and wind always blew through
the spaces between the boards of the longhouse. The cold didn't
bother Suqata, so he sat before Hopano in his loose britches and
hide vest, his long hair moving with the stir of the wind. Hopano
pulled the blanket tight around him and placed the water skin flat
on one knee. He then reached down with his wrinkled hands and
worked in the loose dirt to make a shallow hole no deeper than the
hollow of two cupped hands. Into it he poured the entire contents
of the water skin. The thirsty earth soaked most of it in while the
rest swirled in muddied circles.

"We are ready to begin," he said, closing his eyes. Hopano's
body immediately became very still. "Listen. Do you hear it?"

"No. What is it?"

"Breathe. Calm your heart. It's there if you would only reach
for it."

Suqata closed his eyes, taking deep breaths and placing his
hand over his chest to feel the rhythmic thrumming inside. With
each breath and each beat of his heart, the sounds of the world

became more distinct. The laughter of other slaves in the long-house and the crackle of the fires moved over his skin like the brush of fine spider's web. Then underneath all the other sounds he heard something different. It started out as just a feeling that grew and grew until it became unmistakable. Suqata could hear a voice. It rose and fell like a breeze and the words it sang were at once foreign and yet strangely familiar.

"You hear it now, don't you?"

"What is it?" Suqata could feel the tiny hairs on his neck rise. "Where is it coming from?"

"Questions later. For now, listen to its rhythm." They sat quietly for a very long time. The others in the longhouse had wrapped themselves up in their fur bedrolls and doused their fires, leaving Hopano and Suqata in darkness. The last wispy arms of smoke sur-rounded them in the deep aroma of hickory and pine nuts. Finally, Hopano began to sing.

The words were beautiful, and when he spoke them it was as if he was painting a picture with song. His voice rumbled like the stirrings of the earth, building slowly with each new line, and Suqata could feel the power in it. Next, before his very eyes he saw something astonishing happen. The dark water in the pool began to glow a brilliant blue. Small, luminescent waves moved through across the surface, and Suqata stared on in awe as images began to appear. Images of men and women, all slaves like him, walking for-ward towards the edge of a cliff overlooking a great valley. As they walked, their hide clothing fell away and was replaced with the garments of the outlanders. The beads fell from their hair and the bone jewelry from around their necks. By the time they reached the cliff's edge, they looked the same as the foreigners in almost every way. Amongst the crowd Suqata saw a vision of himself step forward. He was a few years older, and dressed in a blue uniform with bright and shining buttons down the front. While the others looked down to the valley below, the image of Suqata had his eyes to the sky. His face was without emotion. Then the blue-clad

Suqata opened his mouth wide, and sang out. In an instant, all were gone save for four figures standing in a rising fog. Two were old men, their features obscured save for their blazing silver eyes. They stood very close to each other, hands joined. Another figure was that of an outlander, tall and lean with a hungry, savage look in his eyes. In his hands he held a mammoth-sized fang covered in blood, offering it to Suqata. The last figure was a girl, her hands outstretched—a large hole opening where her heart should be.

Suqata stood before them. His blue uniform was now gone and replaced with a black cloak so dark it seemed to eat up the light. Each of the figures spoke in unison. "Choose," they said, and waited. Suqata then thrust his arms to the sky and let out a wild call like that of a bird, and immediately took flight into a sky full of shadows.

Abruptly the vision ended, and the light faded from the muddy pool, leaving the boy and old man once again in darkness.

# CHAPTER 2
# WORDWEAVER

SUQATA SAT BEFORE HOPANO IN TOTAL DARKNESS.

"I've never seen anything like that, ever," he whispered once his wits returned. "Was that me in the water?"

"Some version of you," Hopano answered. His white eyes seemed to stare right through the boy, weighing and testing something unseen within him. "Destiny changes, like a story with each new telling. It's like looking at a fish in the water. You may think you know exactly where it is, but if you grasp for it you will find it moved. Destiny is the slippery fish."

"I don't understand."

Hopano gave a long sigh. "It means, young one, that your future is not set," he said, deliberately selecting each word, "but there are some things that definitely must come to pass in it. Four guides you will meet on your journey."

Suqata's eyes were alight with excitement. "Show me how to do that!" he said.

"No." Hopano's answer was clipped, allowing no argument. "It is not a song I can teach you, but there are others. Oh, so many others. Some are simple, and are meant to be so." Hopano hummed a tune and spoke two words, slight and lilting, then raised his hand. Above his palm floated a point of pure white light that glowed brightly for a second and then disappeared. "Others can reveal secrets to you that are known only to spirits and demons." He flourished his hand. Suqata watched as Hopano's fingers faded into ethereal smoke, only to return to flesh and bone a second later, the corners of his mouth curling into a slightly wicked smile. "And you will learn *sen-wa* that will stay with you forever, the hum of them vibrating your very bones. They will give you abilities beyond that of any mortal man. But remember, boy, that all *sen-wa* are dangerous and should never be taken lightly or used to harm. Knowledge and power can be a knife with no handle, only two blades. One is pointing at you, while the other points away. For every time you use this power to harm, you will find that you cut yourself as well. Do you think you are ready for that kind of responsibility?"

"Yes, oh yes! I want to learn." The idea of danger did not dim Suqata's excitement.

"And for what? To what ends would you use this power?" Hopano asked.

"We could escape." It was the first thing to come to Suqata's mind. "We could use it to run through the walls, or flee towards the mountains. Anything."

"And yet here I am. I have been here for a season." Hopano closed his eyes and waved his arm in a wide arch. "This place is not a prison for people like you and me. This is where fate has placed us, and here is where we must be: for now. If you had not come to the camps, I might have never found you, and then to whom would I teach this knowledge? You have it in you, Suqata, to be something special. Something great. I knew that from the first time I heard your voice. But that is up to you. Can you be patient?"

"Yes. I'll do everything that you ask of me. I swear it," Suqata said with confidence.

Hopano was quiet for a long time after that. He did not stir and hardly seemed to even breathe. It was so long, in fact, Suqata thought to reach out and see if the old man had gone to sleep. Finally, he drew in a deep breath and opened his eyes. "I will hold you to that, boy, and don't you forget it."

"And then, once I've learned enough, then we can leave? We can go far away and never come back here again, Hopano?"

The old man didn't answer. Instead, he looked to the now drained pool: the place where he had seen the future.

FOR DAYS FOLLOWING THAT NIGHT, Suqata could think of nothing else but Hopano's promise. It was like fire to his mind, and suddenly everything

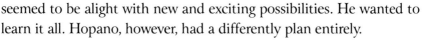
seemed to be alight with new and exciting possibilities. He wanted to learn it all. Hopano, however, had a differently plan entirely.

"FOR THE FIRST TWO MONTHS we will not even speak of the matter," he said one night over their meal quite matter-of-factly.

"What, why? I'm ready to start now. You've already taught me one *sen-wa*."

Hopano turned his empty gaze to Suqata and spoke again, this time without the slightest bit of humor in the pitch of his voice. "Patience is one of the greatest lessons a man can learn," he said, "and it is essential to a wordweaver. These powers are not be toyed with, and without a calm spirit they may be beyond your reach entirely."

"So, the first thing you are going to teach me is nothing at all," Suqata said with a sour expression on his face.

"Precisely. You are a quick study, aren't you?"

SO, FOR THE TIME BEING, Suqata waited. Life in the camps was mostly about waiting anyway: waiting for work to begin, or waiting for new orders to be given. As the days passed, Suqata tried his best to keep his mind busy and sharp, although the opportunities were sparse. Within weeks, Suqata had memorized all the names of the guardsmen in the mill, the overseers, and the boys he worked with, although he did still have a hard time pronouncing the Shenaski boy's: Tali'k ta'ulick. There were just too many clicking sounds. He had also learned a few words of the outlanders' language, though most of them were commands or curses. Every night by the fire, he would retell Hopano all the things he had heard and learned that day while Hopano listened. No matter how great the accomplishment, the old man would always say, "Good, but you must learn more. Much, much, more," and continue to eat his dinner.

On a bone-cold morning, the kind that only comes in the last days of spring when the sun hides its face till almost noon, Suqata was awakened by the guards along with ten other boys. They were told to dress quickly, and were then marched out in a line through the camps. Suqata followed as ordered, but was careful to listen to every

word the guards said, hoping for some clue to why they were being summoned. The streets were still, and the usual rumble of motion and industry was replaced with quiet and the distant call of magpies. The boys were brought to a half-finished structure near the old smithy and were all given long yokes with large buckets mounted on either end to carry. So arrayed, they were directed by another guard out of the great double gates of the camps that faced the shipping roads to the west. Again they were brought to a halt, this time just outside the camp walls near a pile of large stones and rubble.

"This is good enough. Have them start here," one of the guards said, while the others began roughly filling the buckets with stones. They filled and filled, until the boys were all bent over double from the weight.

"Now carry, you pack of savages," he said when he was done, and pointed back to where they had come from.

The orders were simple—carry, and don't stop. It was the kind of grueling task that was usually reserved for the men, but every now and again was given to the boys, "to help build some muscle," as the guards were known to say. Hard work, and tedious, but Suqata did as he was told. The fact was, no matter how demeaning the task, he appreciated the chance to be outside, especially beyond the gates. This was the first time he had stepped past the boundary of the camps since the day he arrived. That very thought awakened all kinds of notions in Suqata's mind. Dangerous notions. Just beyond the tall log wall, there were but a few yards of unbroken snow between him and freedom. It was almost unbearable. The idea was like a seed, growing in the recesses of his mind as he carried load after load of stones through those cursed doors, until he could hardly pull his eyes away from the forest. Finally, just as the first light of day began to break thought the grey dawn clouds, Suqata noticed something out of the corner of his eye. It was in the distance, just beyond the shadows of the king pines. It shimmered like silver, slight and barely noticeable unless seen at just the right

angle. Suqata paused in his work for a moment. He balanced the yoke on his narrow shoulders and tried to focus on the elusive light.

"You there!" the guard at the stone pile called out in a rough voice, "Stop dawdling and get back to work."

Suqata wanted to yell back, but instead he swallowed his words like burning bile and repositioned the yoke on his shoulders. He began to walk again slowly towards the gate, but once again saw the flash of silver. This time, it was moving. He squinted and watched as the shimmer turned and became two points of light, shining like twin moons in an immense shadow. Realization washed over Suqata like cold water. They were eyes, past the brush and branches, watching him intently. Then, as if his fear had summoned the beast to life, the grey shadow ripped free of the underbrush. Its fur bristled and its fanged muzzle lathered and dripped onto the ground before it. Suqata didn't need to hear the screams behind him to know what the creature was.

"Dire wolf! Dire wolf!" the guards called. "Seal the gate!"

All the boys dropped their yokes at once and ran for the open gates, followed closely by the guardsmen. Along the top of the wall, Suqata glimpsed the riflemen taking aim. Everything was happening so quickly around him, but to Suqata it was as if the world had frozen in its turning. His mind was frozen with dread, and his feet held in place under the shining stare of the beast before him. Nothing he could do would move his limbs, and the only sensations he felt were the thunderous thrum of his heart in his ears, and the hot sting of tears rolling unhampered down his cheeks. A volley of gunshots rang out behind him, all finding their mark in the wolf's grey fur, blood spouting from the wounds. The creature paid them no mind. It continued forward, stalking ever closer intent on his prey, growling deep and menacingly. It was close enough to attack now, and Suqata could smell the creature. The heady scent of pine needles, wet fur, and blood filled his senses. *I'm going to die.* It was the only thought Suqata's mind could muster as he tried to run, finding his body still frozen, his heart beating ever faster until

he felt that it might burst. Then, over the creature's snarls, Suqata heard something strangely familiar.

It was singing.

It started low, but grew stronger with each passing second, thundering in the air like the blows of a blacksmith's hammer. The sound was beautiful and terrible all at the same time, and sung by a voice so deep and resonant that it sounded like a thousand angry voices at once. Suddenly, Suqata staggered back, his body released from the wolf's spell. As soon as he realized he was free, he quickly turned and ran back towards the gates. He looked to the sentries on the wall and saw their entranced faces, dull and listless as if in a dream. Just behind him, the beast let loose a howl of pain that shook the trees, mingling with the mournful *sen-wa* on the air. It was almost unbearable to hear: so full of loss and madness that Suqata almost pitied the creature. He only chanced one look over his shoulder, and there the wolf lay, staggered to the ground as the undulating sound hammered its body likes waves against a weathered stone.

By the time he had reached the gate, Suqata was exhausted— but he never slowed. He ran as if death itself were snapping at his heels. When his hands met the coarse wooden doorway he pounded at it with all his might.

"Open!" he cried out, over and over again. It was one of the few words of the outlanders' he had learned. "Open, open, open!!" he cried for what felt like an eternity before the gates slowly crept apart, and he rushed through the space he was given. The guards grabbed him immediately and tried to calm him as he swung and thrashed with all the strength he had left, until finally they forced him to the ground. He lay there in the cold mud, his breath turning to grey wisps and his heart thundering so hard he could feel the blood course through him. Then, Suqata looked up through the open space in the gate. The wolf was gone. The only signs it was ever there at all were the pools of steaming blood in the thawing snow.

LATER THAT NIGHT, SUQATA SAT quietly with Hopano, drinking bowls of cabbage broth and staring into their small fire. He hadn't spoken all day—not since the wolf attack. Strangely, Hopano had been silent as well, sitting wrapped in his woven blanket. When his broth was done, he motioned to Suqata with his unused spoon.

"You've had quite the day, I hear," he said, wearily. "Anything you want to share with me?"

"Yes," Suqata answered plainly. "I know it was you today. That voice on the wind."

Hopano did not reply right away, instead taking a moment to set his bowl aside, smiling knowingly to himself.

"That wolf would have killed me if you hadn't stopped it. And that *sen-wa* you sang. It frightened me, and yet it was so beautiful. I could almost make out the words. *Uiek, kiyi, uiek nu …* "

"Silence!" Hopano said harshly. The others around them looked up for a moment from their fires, their eyes falling on the two Chinequewa with haughty suspicion, but just as quickly went back to their own discussions, leaving their strange neighbors to their affairs. Hopano's hands were shaking now, and he struggled to find the words to explain himself to the frightened boy. "Never sing or speak words of power unless you are prepared to deal with the outcome, do you understand me, Suqata? If you learn anything from me, learn this. We are all held accountable for the things we do or do not do. No act is without effect, especially when using power."

Suqata was quiet, as his teacher had commanded, but quickly Hopano's mood changed again to concern.

"Are you hurt, boy?" he asked. Suqata shook his head. "Good. That poor creature you saw today was touched by something not of this world. There was something inside it, driving it mad. I am glad it did not harm you."

"It stared at me, Hopano. It stared at me like it had come just for me," Suqata whispered. The thought had weighed on his mind, but saying it aloud sounded more ridiculous than he had originally thought it would.

"These are forces you don't want to trifle with, lad. Not yet. Let's just leave it at that. "

"Why? You said it was not of this world. It was just a wolf, right, Hopano?"

"Why! It's always 'why' with you, boy—always new questions! You should just accept the things I say to you as fact. Yes it was a wolf, but more as well. It was touched by a greater spirit—a *mahko*. Some think they are legends, myths, dreams, and nightmares. They are all that, and so much more. Needless to say, there are a great many things you know nothing about, Suqata, and this is but a piece of a finely woven cloak of mysteries. There are worlds beyond ours. Worlds where eternal spirits still dance in the deepest shadows, and places where creatures of malice and hunger haunt forgotten trails, waiting for those who might cross their paths. These places are real, though you cannot see them, and the powers within them have a great reach. They wait in silence, immortal and unchanging, testing the borders of the Waking World. Few things are beyond the power of the *mahko*, for they are the most ancient of all beings. So be vigilant. You never can be sure what is watching you from beyond those trees."

With that, Hopano rolled over onto his mat. "Now, to sleep with you," he said, and soon enough he was snoring soundly and contently.

Suqata sat up for a while longer, watching him—astounded at the old man's knowledge, but a little frightened by it as well.

"How can he sleep, knowing the things he does?"

Eventually, Suqata lay down as well, but close to the fire. It was hours before he could close his eyes.

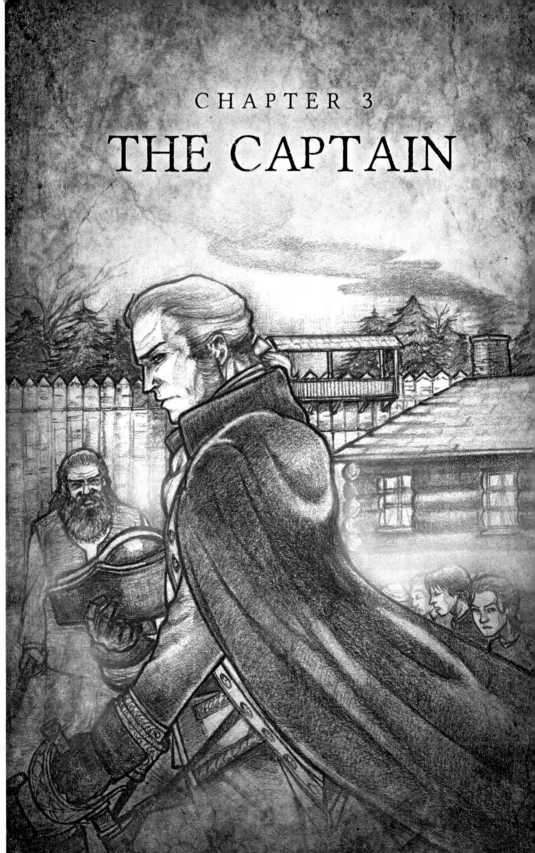

# CHAPTER 3
# THE CAPTAIN

THE COLD SEASONS ARE LONG NEAR THE GREAT WOODS. WHILE autumn feels like a run through winding forest corridors of red, yellow, and orange, winter was the long march. Months would pass in cold silence, the days growing ever shorter and harsher with each sunrise. Just when it seemed as though it would never end, winter relaxed its icy grip and yielded slowly to the green of spring and eventually summer. It is a cycle of birth, death, and rebirth. For the young, it could feel like an eternity. So it was for Suqata. As the seasons came and passed, he worked from dawn till dusk in the mill. He fetched and carried until his hands were as rough as tree bark. When the evening came, he sat at the fire and listened to Hopano speak. The old man was never at a loss for words, and never seem to tire of having a captive audience. Some nights he would tell Suqata incredible tales of monsters, spirits, and magic from times long forgotten—always with some hapless mortal caught up in affairs beyond his understanding. Suqata couldn't help but wonder how much of it was truly fiction. On other nights, Hopano would teach him more of the *sen-wa*. As time passed, there were fewer stories, but every night brought more ancient *sen-wa* to learn.

"Again!" Hopano yelled, snapping his fingers like a crack of lightning in the boy's ear. "You must repeat each song until you can hear it in your sleep. Once that happens, then you must learn it backwards." The old man was as hard a taskmaster as any outlander, and was less tolerant of mistakes, even from a child. Although Suqata had shown great promise with his first *sen-wa*, he soon learned that this power did not come quickly or easily. By now he could perform the Hiding Song at will, and found that the words came to him as naturally as speaking. This only made the fact that other *sen-wa* were so difficult all the more frustrating. After some months, he also learned the *sen-wa* of Tongues, which brought knowledge of any spoken language. This came in handy in the camps. Suqata quickly put it to use listening in on the conversations of all the different tribes—which sadly didn't make them any more prone to speak near the Chinequewa boy. Still, as time progressed, many of the simplest *sen-wa* still eluded him; *sen-wa* that changed element and form were as distant to him as the moon. Hopano never pressed the matter, just as long as Suqata continued to work hard and learn.

"Men have spent their entire lives trying to understand this art," he'd say. "The words. The rhythm. The control. They tried and failed. How can you expect to master all that in a day? How can you expect to master it in a lifetime?"

"So why am I learning it at all?"

"Because you must," was always his reply.

Once Suqata had learned enough of the ancient words, Hopano taught him more difficult songs, some of which were so dangerous Suqata was told never to sing them unless his teacher was present. These were the *sen-tal*, the Songs of Making, and the *sen-uk*, the Songs of Ending. They were mostly wards and protections, and some knowledge of summonings, but Hopano said they were forbidden for men to know. The fact he was willing to teach them to Suqata was no small honor. When Hopano sang them, the world took on a darker aspect, as if the old man had reached into the darkness and brought some of it back with him. When Suqata heard them, his mind always went back to the wolf in the woods, and the awe and fear he felt looking into its shining silver eyes.

"I can barely sing up a light bigger than a firefly without ruining it, Hopano. Why would you teach me new words and special songs?" he said as he watched the weak flicker emanating from a small globe before him. They were sitting together, just beyond the light of the camp fires, practicing as they always did before sleep. In seconds, the globe wavered and faded away.

"Because this is the basis of true mastery," Hopano said, placing his hand on the boy's shoulder. "*Sen-wa* of finding, light, and sight

are just the beginning to a wider world. There is knowledge beyond the Songs of Changing. Long-forgotten songs sung by spirits and demons before the world was made. With your combined understanding, one day you will be able to sing strength into your limbs, speed into your step. You will be able to change the very essence of the world around you."

Hopano picked up a small stone and showed it to Suqata, then sang in his deep, resonant voice. *"Indashi, mi yee, qui do-a, fiyee."* The stone's surface shimmered, like a pool disturbed by the wind, then swirled upward until it became a glistening spiral of crystal. Within the crystal, he could see light moving and sweeping with Hopano's voice, taking the shape of a small, delicate creature dancing in the glow. Suqata watched in wonder, and when Hopano's voice was still, the stone shrank back to its dull, grey beginnings and was cast aside.

"And once I've learned enough, once I have become strong, then we can leave this place. Right, Hopano?" Suqata always asked the same question, his eyes bright with the hope of escape.

"When you have learned what you must, and fate has finished with us here, then perhaps," Hopano said. He never said more than that. So, everyday Suqata learned. He grew, and his body became stronger and his heart a little more distant. By the spring of his eleventh season, the young man's eyes had lost some of their bright innocence.

OF THE CHILDREN IN HIS group, Suqata was known for being … difficult. The line-men would call him Scrapper, Wild One, or The Mad Brown Dog. Sometimes they would use coarser and less creative names, but they all meant the same thing: fighter. Every morning the line-men would come and rouse the young boys from their sleep, lining them up outside of the longhouse just before light. Suqata could remember it very clearly for many years after and it always seemed to be cold in his memories. There they stood barefoot with hands held outstretched, palms up and eyes down. This was the way slaves were taught to stand when in the presence of

authority. Every morning they were met by their line-master, Mr. Snodgrass, and he would yell in his rough, groggy voice, "Good morning, worms."

Mr. Snodgrass was a very round man, with short stubby legs and long hairy arms that hung awkwardly from his frame. His face was covered by a coarse black beard, which regularly held bits of whatever he had last eaten, and his small beetle-brown eyes were usually bloodshot from nights spent in his cups. When he walked down the line of boys, sucking on his teeth, he filled the air with the pungent smell of onions, bad ale, and horse meat. He stumbled slowly along, grinning and thumping the head of his leather cudgel against the palm of his overlarge hand.

"You all know that drill! Sing me a song, dearies!" he bellowed.

He always made the same request. In unison the boys sang out a chorus of "The Baker's Bonny Daughter," Mr. Snodgrass's favorite song, while the vile man listened to make sure every word was perfect. "No more of your gibberish, you ignorant savages. You're going to be civilized now, and talk like civilized people do."

After two years in the camps, everyone knew the words of the song by heart. In truth, they were the only words of the outlanders' language the boys knew. Rarely would they make mistakes, but when they did Snodgrass was quick with his club. Usually it was a hard blow to the stomach or a bash to the shoulder. Mahatowa was knocked unconscious when he forgot the line "and she'll never sail away, away." Even if there were no mistakes, Snodgrass always had Suqata to deal with.

"And will the Scrapper be gracing us with a few words today," he sneered. Suqata never sang, even though he knew all the words backwards and forwards. Some part of it was fear, and some was defiance, but mostly it was that he knew the power of his voice and loathed wasting it for the foul Mr. Snodgrass. Some days, when the line-master had been particularly red-eyed from drinking, howling about how bright the light was or how loud their voices rang in his head, he would ignore Suqata altogether. But on others, when Suqata took his place in line, Snodgrass would bring the club down hard on the boy as the rest continued to sing. This was Suqata's life. This was his day-to-day reality until the autumn of his twelfth year. One gray morning a stranger came to the camps and changed everything.

MEN HAD COME TO THE slave camp before. Hopano said they were farmers, looking for strong backs to take with them downriver. Rarely did they bother with the children. That day, a man stood beside Mr. Snodgrass as the boys were marched out of the slave quarters. He was at least a head taller than the line-master, dressed in a fine dark uniform. He wore a tri-cornered hat and a long, black cloak with a high collar. As they walked the line, his cloak caught the wind and rustled like a flight of dry leaves, and his spurs rang sharply with each advancing step. There was a stern, cold look about his features, and his eyes were like two chips of darkest coal.

"Straighten up, my little worms," Mr. Snodgrass said, walking with a little more pomp in his manner than usual. "We have a guest with us. One of some distinction, I must say. Not that that kind of thing matters to your sort. That being said, I will have none of your lack-wit dragging about today."

The stranger appraised each of the lined-up boys, all of whom kept their eyes to the ground. Suqata stood like the others, but never looked away from the man. When he reached the last of them in line, the man reached out and raised the boy's chin with his gloved hand.

"Not a very impressive lot, Mr. Snodgrass." His speech was curt and to the point. "I don't think any of these will do for my needs. They're too small, too slow, and obviously lacking the intellect to complete the level of tasks I require. Not at all a fair showing, I must say." With that, he sharply released him. "I must admit I was expecting more."

"Oh, come now, Captain. I don't think you've had time to take a good weighing of my boys." The old line-master had lost a bit of his swagger and stumbled obviously over his words. "They've been worked in, the whole lot of 'em. They're strong, obedient, and smarter than most savages to boot."

"Are you wasting my time, Snodgrass? I do hate to be wasteful."

"No sir! Never. I just want to make you sure you're gettin' what you came for. Look, I even taught them how to speak our proper tongue."

Snodgrass nervously motioned to the line to begin. Their voices rose unsure and wavering, but soon everyone found the rhythm—all except for Suqata. It took a moment for it to be noticed since Mr. Snodgrass was preoccupied with those boys who were singing, but when he saw Suqata standing silently amongst the other boys, his face took on a very unflattering shade of purple.

"What's this," he bellowed, "doesn't Scrapper want to sing today?"

Suqata stood quietly. His mouth was set hard, but it was impossible to miss his trembling hands. Unbidden, Hopano's lessons came flooding into his mind. *Your voice has power*, it said, *the power to change the smallest or the largest of things and circumstances. You should never use it unwisely or without purpose.* He couldn't help but think that singing this cruel man's song was an unwise use of power. The tension amongst the other boys grew with each second, and quickly Suqata began to regret his own stubbornness.

"Still not talking, huh? That just won't do." Mr. Snodgrass's knuckles cracked as he balled up his fists. "I think Scrapper needs to learn a thing or two today."

Forgetting the cudgel at his belt, Mr. Snodgrass swung hard at Suqata's face, but his fist never connected. The boy was just too quick. As he side-stepped, Suqata felt the force of the punch move past him, and Mr. Snodgrass's bulk and momentum sent the man careening face first onto the muddy ground. He lay there sputtering out clods of muck as the boys watched in stunned silence—none more shocked then Suqata himself.

"YOU DOG!" Snodgrass bellowed. He sputtered and a very impressive mass of mud fell from his mouth. "You damned brown dog! I'll kill you!"

Suqata stood perfectly still. He knew he had nowhere to run—no home beyond the high wall of the camps to find safe haven. His home had been lost to time and memory. There was no one who could help him. Then, something inside him lit up, roaring to life inside his thin frame. Maybe it was fear, or bravery, or pure desperation. Whatever it was, it drove him to speak.

"I'm not your dog." His words were hoarse, and spoken with a thick and unpracticed tongue, but plainly enough in the outlander's language. The other boys turned to look at him, mouths agape in pure shock.

"I'm no one's dog!" This time Suqata's voice was clear and strong. The sound of it hung in the air like the ghostly ringing of distant bells. At the far end of the line, Mahatowa smiled a delightedly crooked smile at Suqata. They all did. This was a victory of sorts for every boy that had ever faced the line-master's unforgiving hands. His face covered in mud was a vindication, but like so many victories, it was short lived. Suqata felt a hand grab him roughly from behind, forcing him to turn, while the other wrapped tightly around the width of his neck. He was lifted up until only the tips of his toes touched the ground, his breath coming in short, shallow gulps. As he struggled, his nostrils filled with the smell of the man called Graye's leather riding gloves.

"You know our tongue, do you now?" He held Suqata at eye level, never blinking or letting his grip waver in the slightest. "What is your name, boy?"

Suqata did not answer at first, but quickly the man's grip began to tighten. He knew it wasn't a request—not from this man. Graye stood watching every agonizing second with a look of mild disinterest.

"Suqata! My name is Suqata," he finally gasped with his last full breath.

"Suqata." Graye said the name slowly, rolling the sounds about like a strange new flavor in his mouth. His grip began to relax and Suqata could breathe again. When the captain dropped him onto

the ground, he looked down at him with a satisfied sort a smile. "I think you will do," he said plainly, then turned to the line-master. "Where did you acquire such a rare specimen, Snodgrass? I have it on good authority that there are no Chinequewa slaves in the colonies, and yet we have one right here in your lovely establishment."

Snodgrass was shaking with fury, pulling clods of thick mud from his tangled beard, but he answered as civilly as he could manage. "I don't know where the beast comes from, sir, and I don't care what he is. Slaving parties found him wandering out in the forest alone. The hunters thought he was some kind of ghost at first, or at least that's what the fools told me. Should have left the ungrateful whelp out there for the wolves, you ask me. He ain't worth a copper coin."

"Truly. So small a price for such a rare child?" The captain smiled shrewdly.

"Well captain, sir, I'll be expecting a fair price for the lad, considering all the trouble he's put me through."

"That may be, Mr. Snodgrass, but I do believe our business is at an end for today. Please have this boy prepared to leave with me tomorrow morning." He addressed the line-master without looking in his direction.

"Yes, sir. Right away, sir."

"And one more thing, Mr. Snodgrass."

"Yes, captain."

"If you ever display such a lack of control over your charges again, I will have you strung up by your toes until your head turns black. Do we have an understanding?"

"Yes, captain," Mr. Snodgrass answered in a low voice, "we definitely have an understanding."

Suqata could feel Graye's eyes fall back on him. "Get up, boy. I will not have my servant wallowing in the muck," he said. Suqata got up from the ground and stood arm's length away, unsure of what to make of his savior.

"How many words of our language can you speak?"

"Some."

"I see. Well, that is better than none at all."

"What do you want with me?" Suqata asked, fearing the answer more than anything.

Graye's brow furrowed, and in one graceful flourish he moved his cloak aside. At his hip sat an ornate weapon—the most beautiful Suqata had ever seen. The hilt appeared to be woven from thick strands of gold and silver, covered in swirled markings. The captain drew the dangerously curved sword from its scabbard. The blade sent out a perfect ring that sang startlingly in the air.

"Do you know what this is, boy?" he said, leaning forward with the sword held bare across his open hands. He handled it like it was an extension of his being, as much a part of him as his arm. "Whatever you think it is, you are mistaken. This is power. This is the right to move the world towards darkness or light, and it belonged to my father." He looked pensively into his reflection on the blade and smiled. "Sir Alton Graye of the sacred order, the Knights of Ascalion. A righteous man, and though he was pious he knew what it meant to hold this weapon in defense of a cause. He died holding it." He said those words through gritted teeth. "With this sword, I plan on making this land into an Eden, free of ignorance and wickedness. Today I will begin with you."

"I don't understand," Suqata said.

Graye's voice was like iron—cold and immovable.

"You have spirit in you, and a keen mind I can see. But you are still wild. Like this place. I will change that, in time."Graye reached out his hand and held Suqata's shoulder in his vise-like grip. "I will have none of your defiance, young one. From this day forward you are mine. Work hard and be loyal, and you will see that I am not an unkind master. Do not, and I can show you another side. My will can crack mountains. Do you understand? Forget what you were before this moment. Today you have become my servant."

Suqata nodded his head, his eyes beginning to water under the

captain's hold on his shoulder. When he finally released him, Graye let his cloak fall closed before him and stood again at his full height.

"And first off, I would have you finish this song Mr. Snodgrass was so keen to hear."

And Suqata sang.

# CHAPTER 4
# TAKING LEAVE

"WE HAVE TO GET YOU OUT OF HERE, SUQATA. TONIGHT." HOPANO said in a harsh whisper. The old man had been in a state ever since Suqata recounted the events of that morning, and his meeting with the one called Captain Graye. Now, hours later, Hopano moved with an obvious tension, scanning the longhouse with his sightless eyes as if in search of danger.

"Calm down. No one is paying us any heed, like usual." Suqata said. Despite the trouble he had caused, the other slaves had gotten used to their routine of ignoring the strange Chinequewa boy and his master.

"What could have possibly gotten into you to make you do something so reckless?" Hopano wrung his hands nervously. "Now things have been undone. We needed more time!"

"But now we can leave, like you always said, Hopano. This Captain Graye will be expecting me in the morning, and I don't think he would accept a refusal." Suqata could see Graye's cold figure looking down at him and a shiver ran up his spine.

"When the others are asleep, we'll get you over to the mill house," Hopano said frantically. "We can sing the doors open, and find you provisions for the journey. I'm sure the line-men keep some extra boots and clothing there as well. They will be big, but adequate enough."

"Why do you keep talking like I'm going alone?"

"Quiet, boy. Now is not the time for your questions. You are going to have a long way to travel to get clear of this place, and not a lot of time to do it in. I will help get you what you need, but then … "

"Stop! Just stop!" Suqata cried. The boy was livid. "You aren't coming with me, are you?"

Hopano lowered his head under the hot sting of the boy's

accusation, but when he looked up again, all emotion had drained from his face.

"I cannot." Hopano seemed to have diminished a little, like admitting this aloud had taken a measure of his strength. "Now is not the time for me to leave, but your time has come."

Suqata felt his throat tighten as the weight of reality settled on his narrow shoulders. *Alone. He wants me to leave alone.* The thought echoed in his mind. In a few moments' time, the world had grown more immense and frightening than ever. All that Suqata had dreamed of since coming to the camps was to stand in the forest, free of shackles and chains. Now, all of a sudden, he feared that freedom more than he feared Captain Graye. To stand alone in the night amongst the shadows of the wood now seemed as foreign and mysterious as the moon. It was like the vision Hopano had shown him in the muddied pool: standing at the edge of a great precipice with nowhere to turn.

"We can still leave together, Hopano," he whispered, almost pleading. "Just teach me the songs that will make me strong enough. We can still leave together."

"Stop your arguing. It's not about strength. I could sing up a storm so fierce that it tore the trees from their very roots and blasted this place from existence. That is the strength I wield." For a moment the old man reclaimed some of his old fierceness, and his eyes burned with a confidence that made questioning him seem moot. "But this is not about strength."

"What then? What is this about?"

"Destiny, boy. Destiny and change." Hopano said those words as if no further explanation was required. Suqata could only stare back with confusion and fear in his eyes. "Listen, young one, and hear my words. Remember the day we met, and your vision—your path through life will take you many places. You were never meant to remain here, that is certain. This man has plans for you that will take you away from your current path, and I would spare you what trials lie before you if I could, but my past mistakes have shown me

that destiny lies in the choices men make. So, if fate has laid this decision before you, then you must choose the path to take."

Faced with so many questions, to choose leaving alone or staying a slave, Suqata felt a wave of anger overtake him—much larger than his small body could possibly hold.

"You said this is not about strength, but you're wrong!" he cried. Suqata felt the hot tears welling up in the corners of his eyes, but he fought them back. "It has always been about strength. The outlanders have strength, and we don't. They get to decide who comes and who stays, he eats and who doesn't. Who lives and who dies. And here, with everything you've taught me, I'm still not strong enough to leave by myself." He turned away from Hopano and slumped down onto his sleeping mat. "I never really understand what it is you want from me, or where things would lead, but I followed you. I'm tired of waiting! Captain Graye said he could make me strong today. That I understand."

"Strong like the outlanders. Bah! Our people have a strength they will never know. You are Chinequewa. You are bound to destiny's call—just as your ancestors before you. There was a time, when the world was young and wonders existed in every stir of the wind, that a boy like you would be drawn to do great things. You would walk amongst spirits and monsters and not fear, for you were chosen. You would not question it, and yet here you sit afraid of the forest. That is your home! These men seek to take who you are away from you—to empty out your sense of self and replace it with what they want you to be. This must not happen. You must remain Suqata. You must not doubt yourself or the path that is laid before you. If ever there was a time to abandon doubt, now is that time. You are Chinequewa, and your time of sacrifice is at hand."

"Stop it! You've always said that our people are strong, but my family is still dead." Saying the words aloud left Suqata cold inside. "I don't even remember how it happened, but I know that I am alone now. Whoever my family was, or my people, they couldn't have been strong."

"Foolishness!" Hopano snapped. He then stared at the boy with his sightless eyes—eyes that seemed to see things that no man could. "Is that what you truly believe?" he asked in a hushed voice, his words salted with defeat.

"I don't know." Suqata laid his head down and wrapped himself in his ragged blanket. With his back to Hopano, the tears finally trickled down his cheeks. "The only thing I know is that he is taking me with him tomorrow, and I don't think I ever really had a choice."

THE NEXT MORNING, SUQATA WAS prepared to leave. When Mr. Snodgrass took him from the longhouse, early before the rest of slaves were roused for work, Hopano appeared to be sleeping. Even though he never stirred, Suqata knew the old man could hear him leave.

The ground was cold outside, and there was a layer of frost forming on the roofs of the buildings and along the tops of fences throughout the camps. Suqata didn't have anything to bring with him on the journey, save for his two river stones that now lay hidden away by the Hiding Song. The only possessions that most slaves ever owned were the ragged clothes on their backs, which the captain had destroyed and replaced with more suitable attire; a white cotton shirt, a brown vest and coat that were rather itchy, a pair of loose tan breeches, and worn boots.

As soon as the sun crept over the tree line, Suqata found himself sitting beside a gruff-faced man at the front of a wagon laden with supplies. The man was young, but had a thick red mustache that went across his face and along his jawline, making him look older and sterner. He wore a dark blue uniform like the captain wore and a tall, black cap shaped like the smoke stacks coming up from the lumberyard.

"Captain Graye tells me that you understand our tongue, little one," he said, never turning his attention away from the team of horses tethered before him.

"Yes." Suqata answered.

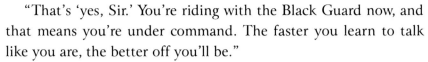

"That's 'yes, Sir.' You're riding with the Black Guard now, and that means you're under command. The faster you learn to talk like you are, the better off you'll be."

"Yes … Sir." Suqata tried again.

"That's more like it, bucko." The gruff man gave him a quick wink and returned his attention to the team.

Soon there were other soldiers taking formation behind the wagon. They all wore similar uniforms to the driver—dark blue with white trim and high black caps, and all with black half-capes draped over their left shoulders and rifles on their right. Grouped together with the sharp points of their bayonets shining in the crisp light of morning, they looked like some great, dark animal covered in bristling quills.

Captain Graye was at the lead of the line astride his tall black horse, which stood perfectly still, its head held high and proud as if it too were standing at attention. When he pulled lightly at the reins, the stallion wheeled around slowly and cantered past the contingent of men. It was the most magnificent creature Suqata had ever seen.

"Sergeant Fletcher," Captain Graye said as he brought his mount to a halt near the supply wagon, and Suqata could feel the gruff man beside him straighten up quickly. "I hope we are ready to be under way?"

"Yes sir. Everything is accounted for, stowed, and secure," Fletcher replied smartly, snapping his forearm across his chest in salute.

"Good man. Black Guard, move out!" Graye called the company into motion, and in unison the soldiers marched forward towards the looming log gate of the camps. Suqata looked around silently, taking in a long shuddering breath as the cart carried him through this place that had been his home and his prison since he was five years old. Here and there he saw familiar faces, but none looked up to acknowledge him. Across the yard, by the door to the mill, he noticed the boy Mahatowa quickly wave before disappearing

inside. Everyone else continued to work undaunted as the Chin-equewa boy moved past them.

The cart clattered towards the gateway on the wide dirt track that wound its way out of the camps and off into the woodland. Suqata turned one last time, searching for the one person he needed most to see before leaving. Just as the boy thought he would not appear, Hopano stepped out from inside the longhouse. Once again, he seemed smaller and weaker, leaning heavily on the heavy doorframe in which he stood. He was staring blankly into the ever widening distance between him and Suqata, while his young student waited desperately. If ever were a time for magic, then now was that time. There were only moments before the gates closed and he was gone forever.

"Do it, Hopano, do it now!" Suqata repeated under his breath, over and over again. But as the wagon and soldiers moved beyond the borders of the camps, Suqata saw Hopano lift his hand and wave. There was a smile on his face—a broad, sad smile, then slowly the twin pine gates swung closed.

THE CAPTAIN SET A BRISK pace for his men, and in three days they had covered miles of road and countryside, stopping only sparingly for meals and rest. The line of soldiers quickly passed through the small farming settlements along what was commonly called the Last Road. The rutted highway was the only maintained path into the woodland. Suqata rode quietly, watching as the world moved past him in a silent march of fall-colored leaves. Things felt different here, away from the cramped confines of the camps and the grey, oily sky that never seemed to change over them. Out on the road everything felt so broad and open. The stands of white spruce seemed to shine silver in the midday sun, and the sweet smell of late season honeysuckle blew past him with each cool breeze.

As they traveled, the Black Guard would occasionally ride out of tree cover and Suqata saw acres of tilled earth stretching out from

the road to the forest edge. The settlements were usually small, and Suqata could tell they were approaching one by the heavy scent of chicory smoke coming from the chimneys. Occasionally, but not often, some farmers and their families would come out onto their porches, or stand at their fences, waving to the marching soldiers in a wary sort of manner. It was as much a salutation as it was them saying, "Here we are. We are not a threat." Their small log and stone cabins were spread apart with miles of road separating them from their nearest neighbor. Such a solitary existence did not promote trust in strangers, even those wearing uniforms.

During the night, Suqata would sleep in the cart and think back on Hopano, missing the deep sound of his voice. *Always listen to the world around you*, he would say, *listen to men, beasts, and nature. It will give you all the knowledge you need*. After a meal of hot stew and biscuits with the soldiers, Suqata would do just that. They were a talkative group around the fire, in stark contrast to their trained silence during the long march. They traded stories and boasts late into the night and always with Sergeant Fletcher there to keep them in line. They were not the monsters Suqata had always seen outlanders to be, and not one of them seemed to mind the addition of their new "little red brother" as one of the men had put it. Even so, Suqata kept quiet and smiled when addressed. He knew the difference between being tolerated and being accepted.

"How are you faring, bucko?" Fletcher asked one night while the men were settling in. The sergeant had made a point of keeping an eye on the young man, and usually bedded down not too far away. At the moment, he was stretched out beside the cart wheel, his cap tipped over his face as he lay dozing.

"Fine, sir," Suqata replied. He couldn't help but like Fletcher. There was something about his eyes that went against his gruff exterior. Maybe it was the small smile lines, or the way he never looked away when speaking to someone, but whatever it was, it put the young Chinequewa at ease around him. "Can I ask you a question, sergeant?"

"Ask away. But make it quick, I can feel my lids closing up on their own accord."

"Why doesn't Captain Graye eat with you and the other men?"

Fletcher looked surprised by the question. "Don't let him catch you questioning the things he does. The captain is a lot less casual about that sort of thing. Truth be told, he's an important man with important things to plan, that's why." He flared his mustache, as he was prone to do when flustered. "A man with responsibilities. He don't have time for knocking about with the likes of us enlisted lumps. No sir. I bet you right now he's over there in his private tent writing a fine letter to somebody important, like General Arnold over in Mooretown, or maybe even the Governor of Vorhaven. You never know."

"Why is Captain Graye so important? Is he a chief?"

"A chief? Well, I guess you could say he's something like that. He's in charge of the whole of Orin's Hollow as its protectorate. The finest we've ever had, too. He's a soldier's soldier, born to command, and descended from a line of nobility. His parents were some of the first settlers from Kael. Religious folk, I believe—some kind of Providential priest that was killed during the Winter Massacre."

"What was the Winter Massacre?" Suqata asked, but regretted it right away. Fletcher's face took on a stony countenance.

"Thought you'd know about that for sure, since you're a … " He paused, considering his words carefully. "It happened over thirty years ago—the year the Chinequewa came down from the mountains. Back then The Hollow wasn't much more than a logging village. In the dead of the night they came, quiet as ghosts on the wind. They killed twenty men in almost the blink of an eye, and then just disappeared into the forest. One of them was Captain Graye's father."

Suqata sat quietly and let Fletcher's words sink in. The captain's father had been killed by his people.

"Why would they do that?" he said.

"Who knows? Raids weren't uncommon in those days. What

was strange was how they did it. They fell on us in force, but only killed twenty and took nothing else. Some said they used evil spirits or witchcraft, but the truth is they were just faster, stronger, and more organized than anyone ever dared imagine. Orin's Hollow almost didn't survive the attack, but here we are years later, the only settlement this far north."

"Orin's Hollow is your village?" Suqata pressed, hoping to change the subject, and despite Fletcher's obvious frustration, he answered.

"If you want to call one of the largest settlements in these colonies a village. I guess you never wondered where all the lumber in the camps came from. Or the grain, for that matter. Orin's Hollow, that's where. It comes down the river from our town, at the edge of the Great Northern Woods and the very foot of Ma-Que Mountains. It's where we are from, and it's where we are headed now."

Suqata tried to picture a place that could be the home to such men—a grand place, shrouded in mist and surrounded by majestic mountains.

"When will we get there?" he asked, but Fletcher had already pulled his blanket over his head.

"Tomorrow. Now to bed with you, lad! Stow those questions of yours," he said, his voice muffled by the thick wool as he drifted off.

# CHAPTER 5
# ORIN'S HOLLOW

THE NEXT MORNING, THE MEN QUICKLY ATE THEIR BREAKFAST OF HOT porridge and were once again marching down the Last Road. After some miles, the character of the surroundings began to change. There were fewer planted fields and fewer farms as they descended into the valley. Before long, Suqata saw none at all.

The forest had grown more dense, and the light was blocked or absorbed by the dark green branches of the king pines. The road was still even and maintained, but the deeper they moved into the woodland the more it seemed the wilderness pressed in from all sides, in some constant struggle with the narrow length of rocky civilization. Beyond that thin border lay the untouched realm of nature, lorded over by beasts and spirits of the ancient world. Occasionally, Suqata would catch glimpses of movement just beyond his sight, most likely deer moving from one pocket of sunlight to another. Perhaps it was something else entirely.

Dusk settled and Suqata strained his eyes to catch the last glimmers of light through trees. Then, as the soldiers rounded a wide bend, Suqata saw Orin's Hollow for the first time. It sat nestled in the deep hollow of the valley, only miles from the foot of the mountain. The town had to be three times the size the camps, but felt even larger, and even from a distance Suqata could see that it was alive with movement—a center of light and humanity in that dark part of the world. The buildings were built close together, some of them two and three levels high, and each with its own character, far different from the aging, grey, wood walls of the camps' longhouses.

The Black Guard marched to a tall gate, and with a wave of Captain Graye's hand, the doors slowly creaked. Once inside, Suqata's ears were filled with the sounds of voices, laughter, and the steady rumble of cart wheels over the cobbled roadway. There were the smells of evening meals cooking, and from each window poured warm, welcoming light. Other soldiers, most without black half-capes on their shoulders, would stop as they patrolled and salute the captain, which salute he would smartly return.

The Black Guard didn't linger in town, however. They marched past the houses, shops, and down the cobble streets towards the river that ran through the middle of Orin's Hollow. Suqata could hear the sound of rushing water in the distance, and along the edge of it ran a dock filled with boats and barges tethered for the night. Spanning the grey-green water was a grand bridge made of dark, wet stone, just wide enough to two carts to cross side-by-side. The thick pillions groaned as the soldiers crossed and continued on past the lumberyard and a large planted field until they came to another gate leading out of the town. It took another mile, but soon they were standing before a grand iron gateway the likes of which Suqata had never seen. It was covered in swirling, vine-like shapes, and at its peak was a woven emblem of a great serpent holding a tree limb in its fanged mouth. Two soldiers stationed there saluted the Black Guard on approach.

"Welcome back, Captain Graye," one said. "Should we signal your return to the manor?"

"No need, private," the captain replied, "it is late, and they should know who we are." The gates were opened, and the men followed the captain inside.

"There it is, Suqata my lad." Sergeant Fletcher pointed through a thin stand of trees. Across a long lawn and down a thickly hedged path stood the biggest house the young Chinequewa had ever seen. It was built all from red brick and stone, at least three stories high, with scores of tall, ornate windows and a fist of chimneys thrusting up from the roof that haloed the house in wispy wreaths of smoke. The entire building felt as if it were surrounding them when the Black Guard marched into the courtyard and faced a grand lime-stone staircase leading up to the columned entryway.

"Is this where the captain lives?" Suqata said, barely managing to sputter out the words.

"Not exactly, no. This is the manor house. Some years ago it was built for Lord Orin Brockholm, who was to be the governor of the province."

"Governor?"

"Oh, big chief, I guess you might call it. He came here from Kael, along with a hundred men and a dozen families looking to settle the Great Northern Wood. The Chinequewa didn't like that too much." Fletcher sharply drew his finger across his neck while contorting his face into a gruesome mask.

Suqata understood the meaning all too well. "He was killed too?" he asked.

"Yep. Now the house is mostly empty. The soldiers' barracks is on the grounds, so we have the advantage of these strong stone walls to keep out any enemies."

The cart came to a halt at the foot of the steps. Captain Graye had already dismounted and was now talking briskly with a tall soldier who had come from inside the manor to greet them.

"Report, major," Graye ordered.

"There have been no real disturbances to speak of, Captain Graye, sir. We have some issues the townsfolk would like to talk with you about. More wolves have been spotted out by Master Addams' farm."

"Winter will be here all too soon. The wolves will keep till morning. Right now I have some more pressing matters to attend to. You and the sergeant can organize getting the supplies unloaded. Fletcher, make sure it is done before the men bed down."

"Yes sir," Fletcher saluted, "and what of the boy, sir?"

"Bring him along. It's time to get him acquainted with how we do things here in The Hollow. But first things first. Get down here, boy, and follow me."

Suqata quickly jumped down from the wagon seat and followed right behind the captain, struggling at times to keep up with him. Graye was obviously a fit man in his prime, and his stride was long and confident. Suqata found his road-weary legs to be no match

for his new master's. Once they were in the middle of the courtyard, Captain Graye turned to Fletcher.

"Go fetch us the practice swords, sergeant. Double-quick."

"Really sir, at this hour?"

"No time like the present."

Fletcher walked away a distance and returned with two thin wooden staves, about four feet long, both with crude basket hilts. He handed both over to Graye and then moved aside. Suqata stood perfectly still and waited, all the while feeling his fear rise within him. Anytime an outlander had brandished any kind of stick before him, the outcome had always been painful.

"Now pay attention, Suqata," the captain said. He twirled the one of the practice swords deftly in one hand, and then the other. "As my servant you will also be what is called my swordbearer. It is a traditional position given to slaves of some skill or cunning, and these slaves serve under a ranking officer. This means that you will not only be my personal valet, but also my, shall we say, 'sparring partner' as well."

Suqata didn't know what the word "sparring" meant, but from the look of disbelief on Fletcher's face, he knew it didn't bode well.

"Sir, you don't truly intend to fight this pup? He doesn't look like he's ever held a weapon in his life."

"As I said before, sergeant, there is no time like the present. This is the beginning of a grand experiment—a test to see if these stubborn, backward people can be taught to serve, and I can think of no better way to begin." He glanced at Suqata with challenge in his eyes. "I once heard a man say that the Chinequewa's spirit is impossible to bend or break. We shall see about that."

Captain Graye tossed one of the practice swords to Suqata, who grabbed it in mid-air, to his master's delight.

"Good. Maybe this won't be a total waste of effort. On guard!"

Suqata held the sword up with both hands clumsily and walked in slow, tightening circles—always in match step with the captain, his eyes locked on the stave in Graye's hand. When Graye struck,

the swing was quick and controlled. Suqata barely saw it in time. He reacted, lifting his sword to defend. The staves met with a resounding crack, vibrating sharply through his hands.

"Good reflexes," Captain Graye said matter-of-factly. Two more attacks, and Suqata met each one, but only barely. Another swing came wide and this time Suqata ducked the attack.

"Consistent, and inventive. Good."

Some part of Suqata knew the captain was holding back, but to what purpose? *What's he waiting for?* he thought. The question was still fresh in his mind when the captain attacked again. This time, the older soldier came with a series of blows unlike before. These were precise, and vicious. Blow after blow rained down on Suqata, the power of each ringing deep into his hands, but he never let the tip of his wooden sword drop. They continued in lockstep, Suqata becoming more comfortable with his weapon with each new advance, the sound of combat echoing off the manor walls like the rat-tat-tat of a snare drum.

"Come on boy, show me something new! I've seen your people run barefoot on the limbs of trees, surely you can do better than this."

Graye made another wide swing and Suqata prepared to duck beneath, but suddenly there was a flash of white, piercing pain. It felt as if his skull had exploded! The practice sword connected hard with the side of Suqata's head, sending him sprawling to the ground in a heap.

"Captain, that is enough!"

Suqata could hear Fletcher's voice, but like it was far off. His vision blurred and all the world seemed to warp with each dull throb that permeated his senses. The blood dripping from beneath his hair and the hot tears pouring from his eyes mixed and trickled warm down the side of his neck, pooling on his shoulder. All the while, Captain Graye stood over him—a dark silhouette in the dim torch-light.

The boy was no stranger to pain. He had felt it in a dozen different ways, but never like this. Every physical ache was coupled

with the stab of shame. The captain's judging eyes cut into him with each reproachful glance, and all Suqata wanted at that moment was to be away from them. To hide himself away from those cold, judging eyes.

"Never use the same trick twice, boy," the captain said. "Your opponent will always see it coming. Get up now, and stop blubbering. What have you learned from this? Well, speak up."

"*Anashi na, da unuk cha.*" Suqata said the words quietly, barely loud enough to hear, but it was enough. Each word rang out with power, but this time, something was different. Suqata felt it hum through his very skin and at the ragged edges of his very being, rising to a crescendo. Then, suddenly, Suqata faded from existence. To the eyes of the captain and Fletcher, he had disappeared into the shadows of the dimly lit courtyard, but to Suqata the world had taken on a bizarre and frightening new light. It was still the same space, but altered, like a bad copy of reality—smeared and distorted. There was no air, and he found himself gasping for breath. When he tried to run, he found it only winded him more quickly. Before there was no breath left in his body, Suqata summoned his strength and sang the Finding Song that Hopano had taught him.

"*Die e unashi!*"

When the song ended, Suqata fell gasping on to the ground, now yards away from where he had started.

"He's over here, captain." Sergeant Fletcher pulled Suqata up from the ground roughly, and spun him around. "That was foolish, trying to run and hide like that, boy," he whispered into young Chinequewa's ear before addressing Graye. "He's a fast one, I'll give him that sir. I never saw him move."

The captain was less impressed. Without warning, Graye struck Suqata with the basket hilt of his practice sword hard in the face. There was a dull crunch, and Suqata felt the hot sting of his lip splitting, and the salty tang of blood flowing freely over his mouth and chin. He collapsed to the ground, and this time he wasn't getting up right away.

"Never again will you run from me, boy," Graye said. His breathing was heavy, but his tone was without inflection or emotion. He then pointed with the tip of his sword to gash across Suqata's mouth. "Let that be a reminder of it."

Suqata only nodded, not having the strength left to answer.

The captain turned and tossed the sergeant the practice sword. "Fletcher, have the boy cleaned up. I want him healthy for tomorrow," he said, and with that, Graye walked silently into the manor without a backward glance.

Sergeant Fletcher picked Suqata up from the ground slowly, pulling a handkerchief from his pocket and placing it gingerly on the boy's bleeding mouth. It soaked through right away with blood. Suqata was unsteady on his feet, so the gruff man helped him along towards the barracks.

"Come on, my lad. Let's have that looked at. Don't want it leaving too nasty a scar, do we?" He spoke in an almost soothing tone, but Suqata didn't answer. He quietly followed along, his hands clenched tightly into fists. Inside those fists sat two perfectly smooth river stones, both white as bone.

*You were right, Hopano. You were right all along.*

# PART 2

# THE SWORDBEARER

# CHAPTER 6
# THE MONSTERS YOU KNOW

S UQATA COULD SEE HIMSELF CLEARLY, STANDING ON THE SAME WIND-
swept cliff side as he always was, staring down into the foggy
valley hundreds of feet below. He wasn't wearing the blue uniform
he usually wore in the dream. Instead, he was wrapped in bands
of dark fabric, wound tightly around his arms, legs, and torso. He
could almost feel the stinging, icy wind whipping his hair against
his exposed neck. He reached for the sky, waiting to feel his body
lift free from the ground and take flight, but he did not. Something
was holding him down. Suqata looked to his feet and instantly felt
fear tear through his chest. All around him, snarling and pulling
at his outstretched limbs, were the yellowed, unforgiving maws of
ravenous wolves. The creatures were as dark as pitch, save for their
eyes, which flashed silver. Together, they pulled Suqata inch by
painful inch down, down, down over the cliff face and into the
open air below.

SUQATA AWOKE WITH A START. He was no longer on the cliff, but his
right hand was still outstretched, reaching towards the sky. His
breath came in panicked, short gasps at first, but in a few moments
he was able to compose himself, remembering where he was and
wiping the beaded sweat from his forehead.

"STUPID, SUQATA. REAL STUPID," HE mumbled aloud. He always felt
embarrassed when he had nightmares, even though no one ever
saw them. It was as if the fears of childhood still clung to him,
taunting that he still was not a man. He sat up and chanced a
look around—making sure no dream shadows had lingered into
his waking world. The room was a small, solitary cell that barely
had enough space for him, let alone witnesses to his overly active
imagination at work. *Next thing you know I'm going to start up crying
like a scared little pup,* he thought.

It wasn't quite dawn, and his room was still dark and filled with morning chill, but Suqata got out of his bed anyway. No use wasting time, especially on a special day like this one. He wiped his hand over the foggy glass of his window, which looked out onto the square courtyard of the barracks, and he noticed the rising smoke from the kitchen chimney across the way. On the ground lay an even layer of untouched snow that had fallen that night and was now forming a clearly frozen crust.

"Where did autumn go?" he said quietly.

Suqata washed up quickly in his basin. The splashes of cold water helped, clearing away the last remnants of the persistent dream. He put on his uniform, following the strict military fashion that had been drilled into him dozens of times since he was a boy. Within minutes he stood at the door of his master's room, shoulders straight and buttons polished to a burnished shine.

He entered without knocking, pulling the double doors to the gallery open and striding methodically across the captain's quarters in a practiced and routine manner. He had done so for many years, and had the motions memorized to the point that he could perform his tasks blindfolded. He prepared the wash-basin, laying out soap and razor in the required manner, then prepared the captain's uniform for wear. He polished the captain's tall leather boots and set them beside the uniform just so. Lastly, he pulled open the weapons closet, first unlocking it with a small key he carried around his neck. Suqata retrieved the captain's musket, which he set aside for later, and a long mahogany box, which he opened. Inside it sat his master's saber. As the captain's swordbearer, Suqata handled the weapon with a certain amount of reverence as he lifted it from the velvet-lined casing. With a length of worn hide, he polished the hilt and pommel, then the silver inlaid scabbard. Lastly, he drew the blade and delicately wiped the length of it, checking here and there for signs of rust and wear.

A tall mirror stood opposite the weapons cabinet, just across from the captain's bedroom door, and Suqata turned to look at

himself holding the sword. He had grown a whole six inches since last winter, and for the first time he could see the beginnings of a beard shadowing his chin. Suqata was taller than most of the other servants in the barracks, but still thinner than he had hoped to be at sixteen. His arms were longish, but well muscled, and he was sure he was finally growing out of his awkward stage where none of his limbs felt quite proportionate.

He flourished the sword, spinning it deftly in the space before him, the blade whistling through the still air as Suqata flowed from one sword stance to another. He moved from repose to lunge, then, sweeping the blade in a broad arch over his shoulder, he returned to a high guard. The captain had always been astonished how quickly he had taken to the sword, just as he had taken to reading and other skills. He inevitably said Suqata was a voracious learner, but always in a way that sounded as though he were surprised such a feat was even possible for a Chinequewa.

Suqata spun the blade one last time, ending in a rigid final pose, the very picture of a skilled swordsman prepared to strike. He once again looked towards the mirror. His dark hair was now slightly tousled and hung over cool blue-grey eyes. Some had said he had a handsome face. Mistress Hodges up at the manor house had once told him, "You know, apart from that dark look you carry around with you, you might be a very fetching man someday." If so, Suqata figured that the crooked scar that ran from the corner of his nose through his lip was the ruin of it.

The wound had been stitched closed almost six years ago, the night he had first faced Captain Graye, but even now it stood out starkly against his features—a reminder of who and what he was.

Quickly Suqata returned the sword to its scabbard and placed it with the captain's things.

He turned and finished preparing the room, and did not look in the direction of the mirror again.

AFTER HE WAS DONE, SUQATA ran across the courtyard, leaving the first footprints in the fresh snow. The manor loomed to his left, the windows dark and shrouded, but ahead of him stood the soldiers' barracks. He walked through the kitchen door and was greeted by the welcoming smells of warm biscuits baking and the pleasant simmer of sausages. The mess hall wouldn't start to fill for almost another half-hour, but the cook and scullery slaves were already hard at work preparing food to feed nearly one hundred fifty soldiers of the Black Guard. Stacks of hotcakes and pots overflowing with porridge would disappear in a matter of seconds once the men got going.

"IF YOU'RE NOT PLANNING ON helping, Su, you might want to move your carcass out of the way," a strained voice said from Suqata's left. Obrie came whipping around one of the large fire pits carrying an over-large and steaming pot of boiled potatoes, his face twisted in mock strain. Suqata stepped quickly out of his way.

"Careful, my friend. You don't want to toast yourself zipping around here so carelessly. I'd hate to find you simmering in one of these kettles."

Obrie grinned, with a devious look in his eye. "I'd probably be pretty good, with the right seasonings. A little sage, some sea salt, and presto! Obrie Surprise. A dish fit for our good Captain Graye. Very little gristle, and jammed full of honest humility."

"Humility, huh? I truly doubt it." Suqata smiled a rare smile. "Did you see the snow outside? Winter has finally made itself known. I know you are excited."

"Of course. You know what this means, right?"

"Enlighten me, sir."

Obrie looked off into the distance wistfully. "Meat pies, my friend. Meat pies," he said, as if the answer had been obvious.

Obrie was a short and dark young man, like most of the Nogra people, with rich mahogany skin and tightly curled black hair. But unlike most Nogra, Obrie had a well-fed look about him. His wide, welcoming grin and dark brown eyes always had an expectant look about them, like he was waiting for visitors. After working his

whole life in the barracks kitchens, his hands and arms were criss-crossed with shiny burn scars, which never seemed to bother him at all, or dissuade him from reaching for hot cooking implements with his bare hands.

"You need the captain's breakfast and a pot of black leaf tea, I take it. Oh, and I haven't forgotten … 'the good stuff this time,' right?" he said, knotting up his brow and holding his hands rigidly behind his back. It was his best "somber Suqata" impression to date, but the round little cook could never hold it for long before bursting into laughter. Everyone knew Obrie's laugh. It was deep, unapologetic, and infectious. Before long, Suqata found himself laughing as well.

"You are correct. And make it quick, would you? He hasn't woken yet and he'll want things perfect today."

"Quick, quick! Everybody wants everything in a hurry. Fine food is an art, and not to be rushed, my red brother." Obrie replied in mock disgust. "You just wait, Su. Things are going to change around here, and then I'll be the one telling everyone else to hurry." He expertly cracked two eggs into a saucepan filled with boiling water, simultaneously wiping off one of the good silver serving trays. "That is to say, when the new governor arrives."

Suqata stopped short.

"So you know? Why am I not surprised, even though that is supposed to be privileged information. What have you heard?"

"Oh you know," Obrie said, winking, "I have my sources. Mistress Hodges up at the manor does get a little chatty after a few cups of my 'good' cider."

Suqata only smiled. "You're a crafty devil, I'll give you that. Well, out with it then. I want to hear what you think is about to happen."

Obrie stopped his constant movement. He looked pointedly around the kitchen, then leaned in with a more serious tone. "She said that a Kaelish lord is coming to take control of the manor, The Hollow—everything! He's a Brockholm, from what I've heard, but not very popular amongst the other highborns. Apparently there

was some kind of scandal. So, here he comes to our cozy little part of the world to claim his inheritance. He also has a daughter with some strange illness, but here's the most amazing part: this lord doesn't believe in slavery. Not one bit. Can you imagine that?"

Suqata felt the muscles in his jaw tighten, and he stood a bit straighter. "Sounds like a lot of idle gossip to me. You should stop listening to the manor servants, and watch what you repeat around here, Obrie," he said darkly.

"Su, don't be that way. Besides, Mistress Hodges told me she is moving me over to the manor kitchens. No more pots of mash for the soldiers, no sir. I'm going to make real food. Refined stuff. And who knows, a couple of years there and things might really turn around. For all of us, if you know what I mean. Just think of it, me working in my own kitchen or maybe even an inn. Serving my own customers at my own place. We'd be free men. You could get that soldier's commission you are always talking about. I can see it now, you all proper-like with rifle and spurs and everything! Suqata of the Black Guard."

Images did begin to stir into Suqata's mind, like so many dandelion seeds caught in the wind. He saw himself, dressed in the Black Guard uniform with a black and gold brocade half-cape draped over his left shoulder and his rifle against his right. The images floated away just as quickly and were replaced with cold reality.

"It sounds an awful lot like a dream to me, Obrie," he said, his demeanor a little darker than it had been.

"Maybe so," Obrie replied as he set the two poached eggs and a heel of brown bread on a plate. "But it's a nice dream."

"I guess so. Good luck with your new job. I know that the men will miss you around here." Suqata took the tray and was turning to leave when his friend tapped his arm expectantly.

"Wait. We aren't done here yet."

"What, did I forget something?" Suqata said, looking at the tray.

"Yes. You forgot to do the trick. It's been three days, and you promised."

"Seriously!" Suqata laughed.

Obrie was literally hopping on the balls of his feet.

"I suppose you're right. I did promise. But come now, you've seen it at least a dozen times already."

Obrie shook his head. "Does that matter? Come on, I haven't figured it out yet. I promise I won't ask again."

"You've said that before," Suqata said, grinning. He huffed in defeat and turned to Obrie. "All right. Close your eyes and I'll count to three." Obrie excitedly did as he was asked.

"No peeking." Suqata began counting, snapping his fingers with each count. "One. Two. Three." He then focused his mind and listened for not even a second before he heard the hum of the Hiding Song hovering on the edge of his perception, as it had been since he was a boy. The familiar melody moved through him until it felt as if his very bones were vibrating in sync. Then, with only a thought, he allowed the song to overtake him, and the world took on its altered look. Suqata held his breath as he disappeared from sight.

After years of practice, he had come to expect the breathless void that came after, even though it still gave him a thrill of fright. Before his breath ran out, Suqata turned and left through the back door. As he did, he pocketed two carrots from the cutting table, then left Obrie to stare about the room in awed silence.

SUQATA RE-ENTERED THE CAPTAIN'S QUARTERS more quietly this time, the tingle of the Song still lingering on his skin.

"I have been waiting, boy," a cool voice said, coming from the still and shadowed corner of the room. "Where have you been?"

Suqata set the tray down on the nearby table, then turned to bow to his master. Captain Horatio Graye was not the young man he had met at the camps anymore. Shocks of white now ran from his temples into his dark red hair, but he was just as commanding a presence as he had ever been. He could still stare down any man that stood before him, and his voice was like the distant rumble

of an autumn storm. More than once, Suqata thought he heard some trace of power in that voice, even though he knew it to be impossible.

"I am sorry, captain. I was in the kitchens having your breakfast prepared. I didn't think you would be up so soon."

"Oh, you know today is not one for dawdling," Graye said. He stood slowly from his chair and walked over to the tray. He tore a corner of bread and used it to delicately break the surface of the egg, spilling the yolk across the plate. "You've been gossiping with that Nogra boy again, hmm? What have you been whispering about, I wonder?"

"Nothing at all, master. We spoke of the preparations for the march today, and of the early snow. Just idle talk and … "

"And?"

"I think he may have heard some of the men talking about the governor's arrival, but nothing of consequence."

Graye lifted one eyebrow and turned his gaze on his young servant. "Oh, let me be the judge of that," he said.

So, Suqata recounted parts of the conversation he had just had with Obrie, making sure to play up the innocence of the whole thing, and was surprised to find the captain quietly laughing when he finished.

"Expecting some big changes then, are we?" he said. His thin mouth formed a smile that was condescending and menacing all at once.

"I don't presume to understand the intent of my betters, master," Suqata replied, hoping that a little humility would take some of the sting out of the captain's mood. "I only guess that the people will be very excited about his lordship's arrival. It's been some time since this part of the colonies has had a real governor."

"A 'real' governor indeed," said Graye dismissively.

Suqata continued with his morning duties, helping the captain into his vest and coat, making sure to keep each crease sharp and even. He gave the boots one last buff before helping with those as well, then secured his belt and buckler. Lastly, Suqata laid the

blade of the saber across his bowed arm, as he was trained to do, and presented it to the captain, who quickly took it. The blade sang slightly as it was drawn along Suqata's sleeve, and Captain Graye held it delicately before him in the space between servant and master.

"I would hope that your friend's naïveté has not given you false ... expectations, lad," Graye said, his voice even and without emotion. "Don't believe for a moment that our new Lord Brockholm has anything in mind but to dominate this place. For all their charm and ceremony, these aristocrats of the Imperium are nothing if not pragmatists. They see this place as a means to increasing their fortunes, and you as a tool to that end. Nothing more. They care nothing for the realities of this wilderness, nor of the blood that is spilt to win it."

Graye stared hard at the blade of his sword before sliding it into its awaiting scabbard. "They have forgot the true calling — the calling my own father followed when he came across the Scalan Sea to this place, but I will remind them. *We* will remind them." He placed his hand on Suqata's shoulder. "I have had a vision, my boy. A grand vision of our destinies — like a voice in my mind calling me to do great things ... for the good of the people. There are changes on the horizon, Suqata. When the time comes, you must trust to my judgment and stand with me. So to that end, you will accompany me today to receive Lord Brockholm."

"Really, sir?" Suqata could barely believe what he was hearing. He hadn't gone much further than Addams' farm outside of The Hollow, not since the day he had arrived there.

"Are you up for the ride?"

"Yes sir, but I thought we were awaiting the governor's arrival here at the manor?"

Graye's hand tightened as anger washed across his face. "No, boy. My vision said go," he said in a low voice. "Go into the wilderness and meet your destiny, and that is what we shall do."

"Yes sir. Thank you, sir, for this opportunity. It is a great honor," Suqata said, grimacing in his master's grip.

At once Graye's grip loosened, and he smiled and said, "Yes, I should say so." He turned back to his desk and crossed his arms behind his back. "I know you must think me cruel sometimes, Suqata. A cold monster. I don't blame you. I thought of my father much the same way. Sometimes men have to be cold monsters to do what is needed. Do you understand?"

"Yes sir," Suqata replied automatically.

"Good. Stay alert today and don't make me regret this boon. Remember, sometimes in the midst of a shifting world, you must side with the monsters you know as opposed to those you do not."

Suqata wasn't quite sure what the captain meant by this, and he felt a sense of unease settle over him. He bowed to his master nevertheless.

"I am yours to command, my captain, as always," he said. The words always left a strange taste in his mouth, but for once Suqata didn't have to try quite as hard to hide it.

# CHAPTER 7

# THE LAST ROAD

T HE CHILL OF PRE-DAWN CONTINUED INTO THE MORNING. AS THE SUN broke through the slate-grey fog, the soldiers awoke to a trill blast of trumpets. Within minutes, the barracks were emptied and the courtyard was alive with the rush of movement. His tasks completed, Suqata left the captain's quarters and headed to the stables on the other side of the manor grounds. He moved without being noticed much, most of men accustomed to seeing Graye's sword-bearer about the grounds fulfilling one task or another. He was an oddity, to be sure—a native boy dressed in uniform was about as usual a sight as a priest in a jester's cap, but most took it in stride.

In the stables, the men were already prepping the horses for the long ride. Carts were loaded with food and supplies, while the rest prepared for the almost eight-day march to the port of Vorhaven on the coast of Scalan Sea. Few knew the purpose of the journey, but it was not uncommon to make this trek, though rarely this late in the season. The Black Guard served as the only law in this mostly unsettled part of colonies, so patrols were part of their mandate.

Captain Graye's horse, Augustus, stood awaiting Suqata in his stall. He was a grand specimen—black as a storm cloud and almost two hands taller than any other stallion in the territory. Much like his master, he was proud and impatient, but the similarities ended there. As soon as he saw his young caretaker walking across the hay-strewn floor, he let out a welcoming snort, to which Suqata smiled as he pulled the freshly cut carrots from his pocket.

"Sorry to keep you waiting, your highness," he said, stroking Augustus' nose affectionately. He offered the carrot, which Augustus munched down with relish. "Not a good day to be late. Looks like things are moving pretty quickly around here."

By the time Suqata had brushed Augustus down and put on his saddle and bit, he could hear the captain's voice approaching over the din of preparations, followed closely by the grumbling voice of the newly promoted Lieutenant Fletcher.

"This was a foolish move. I would have expected better from a highborn," Graye said gravely, his voice holding more than a hint of irritation. "How long have they been riding?"

"At least three days, sir, considering how long it took the hawk to arrive with the message." Fletcher replied. Suqata could see the two men walking towards the stall from between the slats. Fletcher was still holding an official looking message roll in his hand, his brow drawn and knotted—the way he always looked when he gave the captain bad news. Suqata had seen these kinds of communiqués before. They only came from the offices of the governor of Vorhaven.

"That would put them at the edge of Great Northern Woods."

"Yes captain. They are most likely following the river at present," sniffed Fletcher. "Must think they're on some kind of damn fool holiday."

"Indeed. Was any indication given of how many are in his escort?"

"No sir. To be honest, it sounded as if they had no idea we were planning on meeting them at port. Why would that be?"

"Because, Lieutenant, we weren't supposed to know they were coming. Providence save us from the folly of ambitious men."

"I'm not sure I follow, sir?"

Exasperated, the captain snatched the parchment from Fletcher's hand and read over it again, passing it back harshly. After a moment's consideration, Graye raised his hand into the air.

"Attention, men." The captain never needed to raise his voice, and he never repeated himself. Immediately everyone stopped in mid-task, stood straight, and saluted. The sharp clicking of heels even got the horses' attention.

"It seems our plans have changed this morning. Fletcher, have two units continue patrols of the western forest edge, and two units sent to outlying settlements, like usual. I want a small group of eight men prepared to ride with me immediately. We need speed, not numbers today."

"Only eight, sir?"

"Yes, eight. If his excellency is in such a hurry to reach The Hollow, then let's not keep him waiting. Back to work, men!"

Everyone returned to their tasks, while the captain and Fletcher turned their attention towards Augustus' stall, and Suqata.

"You're with me, Lieutenant. I want to be ready to leave within the hour. With any luck we will meet the governor's party before anything ... befalls them."

The roads between the towns and provinces on the coast were the picture of civilization—or as close to it as you would find in the colonies. Heading south, every traveled byway was patrolled by soldiers and colonial guard from outpost to outpost, even into some of the more remote regions like Moorehaven, Silver Lake, and the Golden Plains. No such luck if you were traveling to Orin's Hollow. The Last Road was aptly named, for it was the last established trail into the Northern region, a region mostly unsettled and known for being wild and untamed. Caravans and traders were frequently the victims of thieves, or bands of escaped slaves fighting for survival in the unforgiving wilderness. The Black Guard kept most of these desperate types at bay, but a lone carriage with a small guard would look quite appealing. An image formed in Suqata's mind of those dangerous men, more of them brown skinned than white, beaten by cold and hunger into something barely resembling men at all. It wasn't hard to image his own face, drawn with hunger, staring down the length of a cruel weapon at some quivering lord. *That could have been me—what Hopano would have had me become,* he thought, remembering angrily the decision that was placed before him all those years ago.

"Permission to speak, captain." Fletcher asked. When they walked in the stall, Suqata was double-checking the saddle girth. Graye nodded a distracted approval. "Why only eight men? There are plenty I could pull off other patrols for something like this— something this important." He glanced at the young Chinequewa from the corner of his eye. He knew Suqata would never gossip about his master's discussions, but it was still unusual questioning orders in front of the captain's swordbearer.

"Don't ever play at politics, Fletcher. You are far too blunt a man for it, I dare say." Graye looked up at Fletcher, a mocking smile playing at the corners of his lips. "I hoped you would see what this rather rash move is meant to accomplish. Lord Brockholm knows that the people here see him as—an outsider. Some rich Kaelish noble who knows as little about the North Woods as a fish does about flying."

"That may be true, captain. But I don't see … "

The captain cut him short. "Of course you don't, my friend. You are a soldier. A man of action, which is what Brockholm wants to be seen as. What if he were to brave the Last Road, unaided, and arrive in Orin's Hollow? Suddenly he is not so much the interloper, and he gains their respect. I will not give him the satisfaction, nor will he be greeted with fanfare. He will arrive here like any other milk-fed, rich man: with as little praise and pomp as necessary."

Before he realized he had done so, Suqata was speaking aloud.

"What if the Black Guard is attacked, sir?"

It was a logical question, but Suqata knew he wasn't to speak out of turn. The captain didn't miss the breach in protocol, turning his steely gaze on his servant. The hard set of his mouth twisted ever so slightly, and Suqata quickly bowed his head, awaiting his master's anger like a blow that never came.

"Bright boy," Graye said, a hint of ice in his usual calm, "but you forget that it's late in the season, and the cold is already here, swordbearer. Most of the highwaymen are moving south looking for easier prey around the camps and Moorehaven. We should be safe, but let them come if they wish."

Graye mounted Augustus in one fluid kick from the stirrup and wheeled him around towards the stable entrance, causing both Suqata and Fletcher to clear out of the way to avoid trampling.

"A little danger might be a good welcome for our new Lord Brockholm."

THE MARCH OUT OF ORIN'S Hollow was not what Suqata had expected. There were no drums played or horns blown, and only a few were out to notice the thunderous sound of hooves as the riders rode hard over the bridge, through town, and out the main gates. Beyond the walls of The Hollow, the surrounding woods were dense and still, and the rumble of hoof beats echoed down the natural corridor of skeletal trees. Suqata rode beside the captain on Old Whisper—a thin gray stallion that was getting on in years but which Suqata had tended to since he was a boy. The young swordbearer was only allowed to ride when situations required him to, but of all his duties, the opportunity to ride was one that he relished. The chill wind on his face was invigorating, liberating even, and for a few precious moments he felt like he could almost fly.

The memory of the first time his saw this road was still very clear in Suqata's memory, as well as the thoughts that raced through his mind. *What life awaits me at the end?* Now, nearly six years later, he was riding with a contingent of soldiers in the opposite direction. The absurdity of the reversal wasn't lost on him. As a boy had dreamed of riding as hard as he could for the horizon and never stopping. He would ride until his horse had nothing left to give, and then he would take foot and run. He'd run until Captain Graye, Orin's Hollow, and all of it was nothing but a memory. For one bitter moment Suqata glanced down at his uniform and thought back on Hopano's withered, old face. *What would you think of me now, old man?* he thought solemnly. Hopano was often in his thoughts—more so of late.

The soldiers rode on for hours down the hard-packed trail, and Suqata's body was sore all over when the captain finally called a halt. They had put miles between them and The Hollow, and both the horses and riders needed a rest. They came to stop at a small creek that flowed from beyond the wall of trees and ran near a bend in the road, going on to meet with the river.

"Let's make it quick, men," Captain Graye said to the group, "we

must press on and cover as much ground as possible before nightfall. With any luck, we may meet them before we lose the light."

Suqata dismounted onto unsteady legs and took Augustus' reins from his master.

"Water them quick, and give my boy a little something extra," Graye said, patting Augustus' neck affectionately.

"Yes master." Before Suqata could reply, the captain had turned and walked away to check on the men.At the creek side, Suqata knelt down and ran his hand through the cold current, watching as the light played delicately though the ripples and made wavering shapes on the stones beneath. The horses nickered quietly beside him and leaned in to drink, both nudging their young caretaker playfully as they did.

"Okay you two, no need to shove! There's plenty for everybody." Suqata reached in his pocket and produced the last of the carrots from earlier that he had wrapped in his handkerchief. He ate one quickly before giving one to Augustus and the last to Old Whisper.

"No use in any of us going without, is there?" he said. Almost in response, Lieutenant Fletcher approached from behind the horses.

"Don't let the old man catch you sharing in Augustus' treats like that," he said in his usual gruff manner, but a slight wink put Suqata at ease.

"Oh, I don't think he minds at all. Augustus I mean, not the captain," Suqata said.

"I know what you meant." With a groan, Fletcher knelt down as well and drank some water from a cupped hand, shaking away the excess drops. He then looked sternly across the creek into the darkening woods beyond and his brow furrowed, shadowing his eyes.

"Something wrong, lieutenant?" Suqata said. He felt the other man's tension radiating off of him like heat from an open stove.

"Things feel off today, Su. Don't you feel it?" Fletcher's words were barely a whisper. "This whole thing has a bad air about it. First, the snow's come early this year, I'm sure you noticed, just as cold as a blade in the night. Right to the bone, ya know?"

Suqata nodded. "I noticed. What does that have to do with anything?"

"Nothing directly, but I haven't lived in these woods so long without learning to take notice of change. Nothing in these lands changes by coincidence. You add in the governor's early departure from Vorhaven, and the captain choosing to bring just a handful of us to fetch him and, well, that feels like something brewing to me."

Suqata had known Saul Fletcher since the day they rode together from the camps to Orin's Hollow. Of all the men he had met since that day, outlander and native alike, Fletcher had proven himself to be as even headed and practical as he was fair and true. In fact, it was his practical nature that made him so trusted amongst the Black Guard. So, to see him full of such apprehension made Suqata nervous. In truth, Suqata too had felt something amiss since entering the woods: a certain absence of sound, or deepening of shadow where there should have been light, or maybe it was just the unseasonable cold that set his teeth on edge.

"Keep your wits about you, young Suqata, and those sharp eyes of yours on the watch for danger, you hear me?" Fletcher said as he stood.

Suqata saluted sharply and smiled at the rare compliment. "Sir, yes sir," he replied.

The lieutenant left to rejoin the captain, leaving the young swordbearer to finish preparing the horses to resume the ride. As he checked the saddles, his gaze drifted across the creek to where Fletcher had been looking only moments before. Suqata had seen something move. It was quick. Almost too quick to notice unless you were looking straight at it. As Suqata watched, a crow lifted off from a low branch in a blur of shadowy motion. It shot up through the trees, not disturbing one leaf as it did, and soared soundlessly into the sky. In seconds it was out of sight.

"Strange," he whispered to the horses, "have either of you ever seen a crow take off like that without calling out? Not a sound at all. That's strange for a crow, isn't it?" They both whinnied and

paid him no mind. When Captain Graye called the men to mount up, Suqata tried to put his feelings of unease aside for the moment.

They rode on into the forest, lighting torches as the late autumn light dimmed from bright day to orange, ruddy dusk. The riders slowed, hoping to avoid pitfalls in the uneven path, but even with that precaution Suqata knew that they couldn't be on the move for much longer. That was when he saw something on the road ahead.

"Light up ahead, sir," Private Ashton called back from ahead. Soon they could all see distant torch-light, and the scene that it illuminated. To the side of the Last Road, leaning precariously against a tree, sat a wrecked coach. It was elaborately adorned with gold carvings and black panels that shined dimly under the torches. It could only belong to a noble. A few yards from the wreckage lay the body of a uniformed man—bloodied and still.

"We're too late," Suqata whispered, though no one noticed.

# CHAPTER 8
# THE ATTACK

THE DEAD MAN LAY AT AN ODD ANGLE, WITH HIS ARMS PINNED BENEATH him, but head twisted so that Suqata could clearly see the empty look in his eyes. He must have been holding his stomach when he fell, but it was hard to be sure. The Black Guard stopped just short of the carriage and readied their weapons, scanning the edge of the tree line with muskets and flintlocks pointed. Everyone in their party was preparing for danger, but all Suqata could seem to see was the man on the ground. The wavering light gave an eerie semblance of movement to the body, and he could see long, wet gashes crisscrossing the man's gold and black livery. All around him dark pools glistened across the leaf-covered path.

Suqata had seen dead men before. There had been the bandits Captain Graye had hung last spring for hijacking the grain barge, and then there were the two lumbermen that were pulled from the river the summer before that. But Suqata had never seen anything like this. This man had died fighting something—something ravenous.

"Check it for survivors," Graye said, motioning the men forward. Lt. Fletcher and the fresh-faced private named Ashton were the first to respond, jumping down from their mounts and moving cautiously towards the carriage. The curtains were drawn so both men had their weapons at the ready. When they were a few feet away, a voice called out from inside.

"Don't shoot! We have wounded here!" It was slight and shaky, but clear. Quickly, Fletcher and Ashton pulled open the carriage door while the rest of riders dismounted. From inside came a moan of pain, and out stepped three figures. The first was a guardsman dressed in the same livery as the fallen man. His arm was in a sling and his forehead darkened by a large, purplish bruise. Once out, he and Fletcher extended their hands to help the second man down, who without a doubt was Lord Governor Brockholm.

He was an older man, thin, with a worried sort of face and large eyes that darted about from shadow to shadow. He wore a large white wig that hung down to his chest over his black and gold embroidered coat, and he moved gingerly down from the coach, avoiding putting weight on his right leg. He leaned heavily on the shoulder of the last occupant to leave the carriage. Out stepped a young woman, no older than Suqata, who spoke reassuringly to the governor as they descended.

"Careful, Papa, not so fast," she said, huffing with exertion.

"I'm all right, child. Stop fussing over me," Lord Brockholm replied kindly.

She wore a cloak of black and gold over a cream-colored dress that lost some of its grandeur as it swept out over the dirt trail. She swept the dark hair from her face as she moved out, revealing her expressive eyes and the same thin-set features as her father's.

"Lord Brockholm, sir." Fletcher and Ashton both saluted.

"We can dispense with the formalities, men. Thank Providence you found us." Brockholm spoke kindly enough, but through clenched teeth, his body tensing in pain at each step. "You are men of the Black Guard, I presume, under Captain Graye?"

The captain approached at the mention of his name. "That they are, Your Excellency. I am Captain Horatio Graye of Darvisham, commander of the Black Guard at Orin's Hollow, and your servant, sir." He bowed courteously. "It is a shame to meet under these circumstances. What has befallen you and your men?"

Brockholm's face went pale, and he visibly shivered a little before answering, "We were attacked a few hours ago," he said. "I never saw them, but I heard ... the most horrible sounds. Our guard, Tully, said it was best that we try to escape, but eventually we were run off the road and overturned."

"Run off the road? By whom, Your Excellency?"

"I cannot be sure. I blacked out during the crash. When I came to Tully was at our side."

"And you have no recollection of the attack. None at all?"

The governor closed his eyes. "There were sounds. Distant and sharp. They were, so chilling … "

The young woman softly touched Lord Brockholm's trembling hand.

"Calm yourself, Papa. We're safe now. Captain, is this really necessary?" she said sternly.

"I assure you that it's absolutely neccessary, Miss … "

"Lady Auralyn Brockholm," she replied with a hint of challenge in her voice. Suqata couldn't help thinking that she wasn't at all what he expected of Lord Brockholm's "sickly daughter."

That's when their guardsman, Tully, spoke up. "Pardon my boldness, but we really don't have time for a formal report, captain. We need to organize your riders if we hope to save the others."

"Others? What others are you talking about?" Graye regarded the man squarely.

"The rest of the escort. There were twelve of us total. Five men broke off to draw the creatures away, Tully replied anxiously.

"You're not making any sense, soldier. What creatures!" The captain was losing his very limited patience.

Tully's face took on a haunted air, and he began to tensely wring his hands. "We weren't sure, even as they descended on us in the waning light," he said, glancing off into the darkness. "Janson went down first, that I'm sure of. Screaming. Next thing I knew, it was as if the night itself walked among us—taking us one by one. Lieutenant Monroe told us to leave them and get the governor to safety. We weren't two miles away when something ran the horses off the trail."

"And what happened to him?" Fletcher pointed at the dead man on the roadside.

"Our coachman, Gibbons. He said he would stand watch outside

of the coach. Before you came, we heard him cry out. That was almost an hour ago."

Captain Graye looked over the scene one last time before making his final decision. "Fletcher, you and Ashton stay here with the governor," he said. "See to his wounds and get the carriage righted before we return. Tully, you're with us. You're taking us to where the attack took place. Suqata, give this man your horse."

Suqata did as ordered, handing Old Whisper's reins over to Tully. The man took them like they were a death sentence.

"Keep the torches burning. We shall return." With that, the captain and the Black Guard rode off into the murky night.

After properly covering the fallen driver, Suqata, Lieutenant Fletcher, and Private Ashton got straight to work repairing the carriage. The damage was not bad, considering, and the harnesses needed only minimal mending. Lord Brockholm stood to the side, watching powerlessly. He looked weary and in pain, and Suqata found himself feeling an odd sense of sympathy. *Huh, sympathy for a lord, no less,* he thought. To have traveled all this way only to have his men attacked before he even set foot in Orin's Hollow. His daughter, on the other hand, was quite a different story. There was a superior air to the way she held herself, shoulders back and chin thrust forward as if she was meeting a foe. That kind of defiance was uncommon for girls her age—at least amongst the girls Suqata knew. The ones that worked in the manor or as scullery maids were silly at the best of times, always so worried about secrets and gossip. But here, in the face of this grisly scene, Lady Auralyn Brockholm appeared shaken but not afraid.

The young swordbearer helped diligently, lifting when asked, and pulling when needed, all the while finding that his gaze kept drifting back to the girl. *What does she think this is?* the thought arose sharply in his mind, *standing there all high and mighty while men risk their lives for them.* Just as the annoyance began to show on his face, she turned and her eyes met his for split second. They were

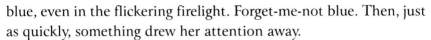

blue, even in the flickering firelight. Forget-me-not blue. Then, just as quickly, something drew her attention away.

Something was moving near the tree line.

"Lieutenant," Suqata whispered. He pointed away towards the woods where Lady Auralyn stared and instantly Fletcher saw the movement as well.

"What is it, Su?" he whispered back. The shadows shifted slightly at their notice, and in the glow of the torchlight Suqata could now make out pairs of large eyes staring back at them through the low brush, gleaming silver-white, and his heart began to race.

"Your Excellency, I think you should return to the carriage." Suqata tried his best to sound calm and composed, while Fletcher slowly pulled his saber from its scabbard and readied his pistol. Lord Brockholm began to protest until he heard the sharp click as Private Ashton pulled back the hammer on his rifle.

"Damn it all!" Ashton said, dropping all semblance of poise. He removed his cap and ran his fingers nervously through his sandy blond hair. It was slick with sweat, which kept running down into his eyes.

Suddenly, they all heard the sound of low, menacing growls coming from just beyond the halo of torchlight.

"Get back in the carriage now!" Fletcher barked. This time the governor didn't argue, and Suqata quickly helped him inside, trading a worried look with Lady Auralyn as she followed. He slammed the door shut and turned just in time to see the beasts pad silently into the light.

DIRE WOLVES. FOUR OF THE biggest beasts Suqata had ever seen or heard of, standing before him like nightmares made solid. Their dark fur bristled at the hunch of their shoulders as they stalked forward, their heads low, their eyes gleaming with each movement. Once they were a few yards away, the leader pulled back its lips, revealing rows of saber-shaped, yellow teeth. It snarled hungrily, sending cold tremors up Suqata's spine. He could feel his heart

beating a thousand times in that moment, threatening to stop completely if the creature made one more move forward.

"They have us surrounded," Ashton whispered, his voice high and panicked. "There's nothing for it now!"

To his left, Suqata could hear Ashton's short, frantic breaths coming quicker and quicker, as his shaking hands rattled the strap buckles of his rifle.

"We're only going to get one chance at this, boys, so hold until I say." Fletcher pulled back the hammer on his flintlock and motioned towards the lead wolf with his head. "That's the beastie to hit. Maybe that'll scare the others off. Suqata, maybe you should get under the coach."

"I'm with you, lieutenant," the swordbearer replied, trying his best to disguise the fear in his voice. He felt powerless. No gun, no sword, not even a decent knife.

"Good lad. Here, take this." As if responding to his thought, Fletcher pulled a hunting knife from his belt. He handed it over, handle first, and Suqata regarded the weapon as if it was on fire. It was unthinkable! The only weapon a swordbearer was to ever touch was his master's, or one given to him by his master. To be caught doing so was a punishable offense.

"Sir, I can't!"

"Oh quiet, boy. This is not the time for silly rules and … "

Without warning, a shot rang out.

Ashton had fired at the large wolf in the lead, but only grazed its shoulder.

"You fool! Too soon!" but Fletcher's cries fell on deaf ears. Ashton pulled his pistol and fired again, this time hitting the beast in the neck, but instead of being startled by the echoing sound of gunfire, the wolves howled even louder, their eyes glowing with ghostly, unholy rage. The leader's mouth dripped shining streams of blood-laden saliva, but it did not fall. Before either Fletcher or Suqata could say a word, Ashton turned and made a run for the tree line.

"Ashton, no!"

One wolf pulled from the pack and, wasting no time, bound effortlessly into the darkness. In one lunge the beast brought Ashton down, sinking its teeth into his calf. It dragged him into the shadows until all Suqata could make out were Ashton's muffled cries.

KACHOW! Another shot rang out, this time from Fletcher's pistol, taking Ashton's would-be-killer down cleanly. It lay in a heap beside the private. Neither moved. Fletcher then reached for Ashton's discarded rifle, but the pack leader wasn't waiting for another shot. It lunged forward with blinding speed, biting down hard on Fletcher's outstretched arm.

"AHH! Run, Suqata!" Fletcher screamed before he was dragged clear of the carriage towards the rest of the waiting pack, which descended on the soldier without mercy. He flailed and slashed with his saber until it was pulled from his hand.

Suqata responded on instinct, reaching out for the hum of the Hiding Song. *The length of a breath, the length of a breath,* he chanted in his head. Ever since his first fight with Captain Graye, he knew the power of the song could only conceal him for the length of one full breath. As he drew in, the world shifted quickly. Swathed in its power, the young Chinequewa ran forward and buried the dagger blade to its hilt into the pack leader. When he exhaled, the world rushed back in around him, and Suqata stood eye to eye with the monster wolf, his hand slick with the creature's warm blood. In an instant he knew this was no ordinary animal. It wasn't driven by hunger, need, or madness. This creature hated him—as surely as men hate.

Suqata pulled away and Fletcher fell free of the wolf's grasp. It stood there, staring intently at him, the knife still embedded in its throat. The rest of the pack, stirred into a frenzy by the coppery tang of blood in the air, all bristled with anticipation, barking and snarling in feral waves. Suqata snatched Fletcher's saber from the ground where it had fallen and held it before him, just as the captain had trained him to. The wolves kept their distance for only a second longer before bounding towards him, as if released from

hellish will. Suqata slashed down hard at the first, and a sharp yelp split the air.

"Come on then!" he yelled as a fire built inside of him, pushing him to fight. Another wolf launched at him, and was met with the basket hilt of the sword. Then came another, and another, launching at him one by one. Suqata kept swinging, deflecting those that came too close, and wounding those that came closer. It didn't take long for him to feel the strength in his arm begin to wane.

"Run, Su," Fletcher whispered. He was bleeding badly, and his eyes were barely open.

"Don't worry, sir. I'll get us out of this," Suqata said breathlessly. He tried to sound reassuring, but knew full well that it was a lie. One more rush would be the end of them. *Think Suqata, think! There has to be something you can do.* Then, unbidden, Suqata heard a familiar voice arise in the recesses of his mind.

*Uiek, kiyi, uiek nu tiyuk, uiek kiyi, uiek manas tuk.*

He heard it as clearly as he had that day outside of the camps, echoing through time and memory. He remembered those shining, menacing eyes at the forest's edge, and the voice that hung ominously on the wind. *The song! It's a spirit bind!* he thought urgently. Hopano had told of such songs—an impossibly ancient tongue he was taught never to utter alone. Suqata mouthed the words, remembering how they felt on his tongue, and how they made his heart pound. Then he chanted them aloud, soft at first, then louder, and then again, louder still.

*Uiek, kiyi, uiek nu tiyuk, uiek kiyi, uiek manas tuk.*

With each line of the song, Suqata's voice became stronger, filling the space around him with the thrum of its power. He was the center of a beating heart, radiating out waves of strength in all directions.

*Uiek, kiyi, uiek nu tiyuk, uiek kiyi, uiek manas tuk.*

At the peak of the chant, a pale blue light formed near Suqata's mouth, like a frozen breath in winter, moving in time with the chant. Within it, small silver shapes took form—archaic symbols that were

foreign and familiar all at once. Suqata's voice rose, sounding like a multitude of voices singing in unison, and the wolves all cried out howls of pain, their bodies racked by unseen forces. They snarled and snapped at the air, but could not get within arm's length of the swordbearer. Angered and defeated, the pack ran one by one back into the concealment of the forest. Suqata did not stop chanting until he felt safe that they were gone. As the song died away, a wave of exhaustion came over him, and Suqata fell to his knees.

"They're gone, Fletcher," he said breathlessly. "I think it's over." But Fletcher did not respond, nor did he move. Suqata reached out and touched his friend's hand cautiously.

Nothing. He was gone.

"I'm sorry, Saul."

In the distance, Suqata heard the sound of hoof beats on the hard-packed road, and soon saw the approaching torches cutting through the gloom.

"The Black Guard are on their way, lieutenant. Captain Graye will be here soon," he whispered, knowing Fletcher couldn't hear. Suqata looked up to the carriage. Peering down was the highborn girl, Auralyn, her eyes wide with disbelief. She had been watching the whole time.

Suqata's breath formed grey clouds in the air before him as he sat very still on the roadway. He was cold, but not from the wind that moved over his shoulders—this cold was inside him as well. Lieutenant Fletcher lay dead in his arms, and Captain Graye stood before him staring down on his swordbearer. Graye was shaking with thinly cloaked fury, and when Suqata looked up he noticed that the captain's hand was wrapped in a bandage, roughly made from torn cloth and stained with fresh blood. Blood. He looked down and noticed it was all over his hands as well. As the haze sharply lifted from his mind, Suqata knew the focus of Graye's

angry stare. In his right hand was Lieutenant Fletcher's still bloodied saber.

"Explain yourself, boy. Quickly!" Graye said, motioning towards the sword. Suqata said nothing. He was still drained from the song, but more than that, his spirit was too weary for him to speak. It was as if a dam had formed inside of him, keeping at bay all of the fear and sadness he felt, but leaving him numb. Instead, he lowered his head and sat in a servant's pose, Fletcher's sword held across his upraised hands.

"What happened here, Suqata? I leave you with two capable men, one of them my second, and return to find them both dead and you, my servant, standing over Fletcher's body. I want answers."

Suqata tried in vain to speak, but could barely bring himself to look his master in the eye. Seconds passed. When no reply came, Captain Graye reached down and jerked Suqata up by his jacket front.

"You will answer me, you misbegotten … "

"Captain Graye! That is quite enough." Before Suqata could force out a word, Lord Brockholm and his daughter re-emerged from the coach. "Release the young man at once. You would treat our protector in such a way?" Gone was the pitiful noble from only a few hours earlier, replaced now with a man who carried the bearing and authority of a governor, even as he limped forward on his twisted ankle.

"I am glad to see you safe, Your Excellency, but this is none of your concern. My slave has forgotten his place and taken up a weapon without my say. I will deal with him as I see fit."

"He took up the weapon in our defense, captain," Auralyn said, "when we were left with no other defenders but he. Would you rather he had stood by while we were all torn to shreds? Would that have been a wiser move on the boy's part?" Her nostrils were flared with each sharp word she spoke.

"Be calm, sweetheart. I'm sure that Captain Graye was merely caught up in the excitement of the moment," Lord Brockholm said. "Isn't that right, captain?"

Graye's mouth was drawn tight, and he flexed his wounded hand repeatedly as he fought to calm himself.

"Of course, Your Excellency," he said, "the strain of tonight's losses have tested us all." He forced a smile. "We met the rest of the wolves on the road but a mile away. They descended like demons from the pit. I'm sorry to report that the others in your escort did not fare as well as you, and now we must add your man Tully and the lieutenant to our losses as well."

"Tully, too? Dear Providence!" Brockholm held his daughter's shoulder, visibly shaken by the news. "We should head for Orin's Hollow with all speed, captain."

"The road is dark, governor. We will camp and make for home at first light."

"Captain, my daughter is not well. I will not have her in this wilderness for a moment longer. It is too great a risk to her health."

"A necessary risk, I'm afraid. These beasts have the advantage by night. I will not have another of my men hunted down like animals on this road," Graye replied.

From beyond the torchlight, one of the Black Guard yelled out. "Captain! It's Private Ashton. He's still alive!"

Graye smiled humorlessly at the governor. "Well. Providence has not abandoned us completely."

# CHAPTER 9
# HONORS LOST

AT DAWN THE SOLDIERS BROKE CAMP AND BEGAN THE LONG RIDE BACK to The Hollow. They rode in silence, half of the men on constant lookout for the wolves' return, the others keeping watch on the carriage, which had been mended as best they could manage. Everyone was too weary to speak. Of the eight Black Guard riders that left town just a day past, only five were returning, while the governor had lost all of his guard. And, to add insult to injury, Private Ashton's injuries had put him into a feverish state.

"Wolf bites sometimes cause a brain fever in men, driving them mad," Suqata heard one of the soldiers say on the road home. "Poor Ashton will have a time of it, sure enough."

Suqata was left to ride beside the coachman and tend to him, but all the while he kept watch on the forest edge, remembering those cold, shimmering eyes staring back at him.

Once they were back in town, people knew right away that something had gone terribly wrong. Word spread like tongues of fire on dry birch twigs. Before the riders had brought the carriage to a halt at the manor steps, almost every ear had heard news of the governor's arrival, and of the attack. Stories of monsters and dead soldiers stirred everyone to unrest, and for the next three days no one talked of anything else. Dire wolves had been just a legend until now. Woodsmen told stories to travelers of beasts touched by ancient powers, making them more than just animals. Myth to some, but Suqata knew a little more about beasts of myth than he cared to.

Patrols were sent out daily, and teams of hunters were paid to search the forests surrounding the town and the Last Road, but barely a trace could be found of the beasts. It was as if they had never been at all.

Suqata tried to stay busy, and keep away from the reports and gossip. He only wished to put the whole thing behind him. In the nights following their return, he wasn't sleeping. Every time rest came, images of gnashing teeth and blood-stained claws would appear in the blackness. His work was beginning to suffer, and the captain's mood of late was not very tolerant of mistakes. Although his injuries were not severe, Graye had taken a fever and had been ill and distant for the first few days. Suqata couldn't help but notice that the captain was speaking less and less to him, and instead finding excuses to send him off on long errands to fill his days. It was after one particularly hard afternoon of helping in the practice yards that Suqata was called to the captain's quarters just after dinner.

"Come in, boy," the captain said from within the dark study. He sat at his desk, papers laid before him in disarray, and a tray of roast pheasant sitting untouched on the corner. As he entered, Suqata felt a strangle tingle come over him, going up his arm like cold rain drops on his skin. Quickly the feeling subsided, and Suqata stood awkwardly at attention.

"Lieutenant Dodds has been telling me how helpful you've been in his transition to Fletcher's post," Graye said, never looking up from his work.

"Thank you sir," Suqata replied. Dodds had been Sergeant Dodds just a few days ago. He was a serious sort of man, and not as well liked amongst the men, but intelligent. He took to his new leadership role easily. "The lieutenant is too kind for mentioning my performance." Somehow Suqata knew right away this wasn't why the captain had sent for him.

The office was in a state of neglect, which he was not used to seeing. If Captain Horatio Graye was anything, it was meticulous.

"Do you require any tending to your wound, master?" Suqata said, reaching out towards Graye's wrapped hand. The bite was healing slowly, but the captain had forbade any physicians to tend to it. Even now, he recoiled from the young man's touch.

"Leave it be," he growled. "It's the least I should suffer, especially

when you think of the men we lost. Maybe it's a blessing—something to remind me of my foolish pride."

The captain poured himself a drink from the bottle on his desk. "Those creatures were not of this world," he said in a hushed voice, "filled with some witchcraft that was beyond our power to defeat—beautiful, savage, and altogether otherworldly." He stopped, realizing he had said more than he intended, then drained the cup. "Besides, I did not call for you to be my nursemaid. I have orders here for you." Graye waved distractedly to a folded letter which sat open on the dinner tray. Suqata's heart fluttered when he saw it.

*This is it! This is finally it,* he thought tensely. *I am finally going to be a member of the Black Guard.* After days of wondering if his actions on the road had ruined his chances, Suqata finally felt some sense of relief. He kept his demeanor even and read the eloquently handwritten letter aloud:

> *To Captain Horatio Graye,*
>
> *The slave, Suqata, is here by requested to the manor house. As a reward for his brave acts in defense of Lord Brockholm, Suqata will assume the role of valet to the Lady Auralyn Brockholm as soon as possible. As such, he will be also appointed guard and protector of her person, until such time as his services are no longer required. He will be required to relinquish his responsibilities as swordbearer immediately. This is no small honor, and we expect your response in the affirmative as soon as possible.*
>
> *Best regards,*
>
> *Lord Ignatius Brockholm, Knight of Ascalion, Third Baron of Darvisham, and Governor of the Northern Territories*

As Suqata finished, his mouth went instantly dry, and he could feel a lump tighten in his throat. His thoughts reeled as each word settled slowly on the surface of his consciousness. They echoed

through his mind in his own voice. *Relinquish his responsibilities as swordbearer.* The very sound of it made his stomach tie into knots.

"There must be some kind of mistake?" he whispered. To this, Captain Graye barked one sharp laugh.

"No mistake, my boy. You are a member of the household now. You had best move along and report to Hodges. She doesn't take well to being kept waiting."

"So soon," Suqata said. He was trying his best to absorb all that had changed in the last few seconds, but events were moving much faster than he could have ever expected. "Surely you can tell them no, master. Who will attend to you as swordbearer?"

"A suitable replacement will be found, never you mind. It is no longer your concern."

"But sir, I've been with you for years. Surely ... "

"No more questioning, Suqata!" Graye said sternly, looking up from his work for the first time. "It is for this very reason you are leaving. You have a problem following orders, don't you?" The captain regarded him disapprovingly, flexing his wounded hand. "But it has always been thus, hasn't it?" When he spoke, the shadows seem to deepen around him. "I thought to mold you, boy, into someone worthwhile, in spite of who and what you are, but there has always been something in you, just under that cool surface, that has rebelled against me. I know it. Something that you won't let go off. That is why you people will never truly be part of this world we are creating here—you won't let go of who you are."

As he looked at Suqata, something in his features seemed to shift. Gone was the haughty composure Suqata knew, replaced with something primal and full of fury. Then, just as quickly as it had come over him, it passed, and the captain waved Suqata towards the door. "Now go. Your time here is done. Your things will be brought to your new quarters. Best to not dawdle."

Suqata could taste the angry, dangerous words he wanted to say, burning like bile in the back of his throat, but instead of saying

them he only replied, "Yes, master," and bowed. With that, he moved to leave the study.

"Suqata," Captain Graye said softly. The young man turned and snapped to attention.

"Yes, captain."

"Be sure to leave your key to the weapons cabinet with Lieutenant Dodds, will you?"

"Yes, master."

Suqata left quietly, closing the double doors behind him. The following latch click had a finality to it, and in that moment realization washed over the young Chinequewa. No matter what he felt for Graye—anger, fear, respect, hatred—he had been his mentor and keeper since he was a child. He had given him purpose. At that moment, standing alone outside of the captain's quarters, all Suqata could feel was loss.

SUQATA HAD BEEN INSIDE OF the manor many times since arriving in Orin's Hollow. Although most of the living quarters had been sealed up after the Winter Massacre, the larger rooms were still used from time to time for town business. As such, Suqata had stood in the grand entryway quite a few times performing his duties for the captain. Now, as he stood awaiting the head of the household, it felt oddly alien and unfamiliar. Stoic faces looked down at him from high portraits, judging him with their unmoving, pompous stares. Everything, from the high polish of the brass door handles, to the delicate vases filled with imported silk flowers from Kael, all seemed to say in no uncertain terms, "Leave, you do not belong here." Suqata was of the mind to oblige. He was so distracted by his unease that he almost missed the small, round woman who walked briskly up to greet him, her clothes typically as somber as her expression.

Mistress Ingred Hodges was the widow of the late Master Timon Hodges, the old master of the household. The position had been mostly honorary for years, since no one lived in the manor, so after his death his wife was passed the title. With Lord Brockholm's arrival, the position had become a great deal more demanding, but she was definitely suited for it. Although she only stood five feet tall, with a round, full face and a slightly upturned nose, there was always something fierce about her large, demanding eyes that set Suqata on edge.

"Well, well, well. Captain Graye's young Chinequewa has come to grace us with his presence. How marvelous," she said. Her speech was clipped, sharp, and covered in an obvious layer of sarcasm. "You are quite late, you know? The captain must have received that letter hours ago."

"My apologies, ma'am," he said courteously, followed with a swordbearer's bow.

"Oh no, none of that. House servants bow here, at the waist and nothing else." Mistress Hodges demonstrated, which would have been comical if Suqata had not been in such a dark mood. "Come along and I'll present you to her ladyship. Don't touch anything."

"Yes, ma'am."

The two moved quickly up one of the curved staircases, down corridors, and past lavishly furnished rooms that looked as if no one had ever set foot in them. They walked past marble busts of austere-looking men that guarded the corridors of the house, until finally they came to the end of the hall and a large white door stood before them.

"Now, boy, you will maintain a disciplined manner with Lady Auralyn at all times. Keep your eyes down and hands crossed, and only speak when she addresses you. Is this understood?"

Mistress Hodges didn't wait for a reply. She knocked once, loudly, then pushed the door open wide and walked straight inside. Suqata followed closely behind, trying to look relaxed even though it felt as if his entire body had tensed up all at once.

The room was immense, with a high ceiling and cream colored walls adorned with paintings of fanciful settings. All throughout

the space, thin candle sconces were alight, filling the room with a delicate golden glow, and sitting amidst it all was Lady Auralyn Brockholm. She sat comfortably on a divan seat, reading a large red-leather tome which she promptly set aside when Suqata entered.

"Oh, you're here already. Wonderful." She rose and walked to meet them, her long, blue dress trailing behind her. Both Mistress Hodges and Suqata bowed when she stopped before them.

"Your ladyship, may I present … "

"I know who he is, mistress. We have met before, and I am the one who sent for him, am I not?"

"Of course, m'lady. Tomorrow we will have the boy in more … suitable attire, but I thought you might want to look him over before you made your final decision."

Suqata felt like a pig on an auction block.

"That won't be necessary, mistress. However, I would like to speak with him alone. Please leave us."

Hodges' eyes widened at the request, and Suqata noticed her blush ever so slightly before she replied, "M'lady, I'm not sure that is wise. What would your father say to me leaving you alone with this heathen? I'm sure that … "

"I'm sure he would see nothing wrong with it at all. As I'm sure you know, my mother was Umbaric, and it is custom there for young ladies to have a male valet."

"That may be, m'lady, but these are the colonies. Young ladies just aren't left unchaperoned."

Auralyn clenched her hands before her and stood very straight, never taking her eyes away from Hodges. "I hope that you are not insinuating anything about my intentions?" she said, cocking her eyebrow just a bit.

"Not at all, m'lady," Hodges stammered.

"Good. Then we will speak no more on the matter. Close the door please as you leave." Auralyn left no room for further discussion, so Mistress Hodges bowed her way awkwardly out of the room and closed the door.

There was a moment of silence while Auralyn seemed to wait until Hodges' footsteps faded away. Suqata scarcely breathed, but once they were alone she turned towards him with a warm smile.

"It is a great pleasure to meet you, Suqata," she said. "Your name is lovely. What does it mean?"

"It means 'Watched by the Crow,'" he said. She waited for him to elaborate. "It is a name given to an unlucky child, or one who is destined for a hard life. At least that is what my teacher told me it meant."

"Oh. Indeed." She smiled courteously. "The captain was kind enough to share a few things about you. I've been reading about the tribes of the colonies ever since we landed in Vorhaven. Your people, the Chinequewa, are fascinating. There is very little written about them, though, and this book was the only one my father was able to procure for me. I haven't been able to put it down since we arrived." She sat down again, regarding Suqata with her large, keen eyes.

"The book says that the other tribes of the continent call you the Silent Ones, and that your people are descendants of the first men to walk on the world. Do you believe that is true?"

"I have never heard that before, m'lady, but I'm sure it is as you say." Suqata replied. He was finding it difficult to follow Mistress Hodges' rules as every time she asked him a question he wanted to look up at her, to say something more.

"How old are you?"

"Sixteen, but I'll be seventeen by Winter's End."

"That makes you older than me by almost a year."

"Yes, m'lady."

"Oh please, stop with the courtesy," she said, rolling her eyes. "You may call me Auralyn, or Lynn if you like. After all, I do owe you my life. The least we can do is talk plainly to one another."

Suqata almost stopped breathing, and looked up at her. No one had ever made that kind of request of him before, especially not a lady, and definitely not a highborn. What was he to say to such a request?

"I cannot," he said, realizing as he spoke that denying her wishes was just as dangerous.

"Of course you can. I have given you my permission."

"It's not permitted," he said, testing these dangerous waters slowly. "Besides, you wouldn't like what I had to say."

Auralyn's smile dimmed a bit. "It doesn't matter. I insist. You must speak to me like I was any old girl in the town: a miller's daughter, or better yet a washer girl. I can hear anything you need to say." She then crossed her hands delicately before her and waited, once again raising one eyebrow slightly higher than the other.

Suqata swallowed hard. *It's not like I have much else to lose*, he thought.

"Why did you do this to me?" he asked. It was all that could come to him, but even then it came with a slight hint of a growl to the words.

"Did this to you? I don't understand. Your master, that captain of yours, was horrid to you. I thought you would be glad, even grateful to be rid of him."

"Grateful?" Suqata could feel the hackles of his neck prickle. "You took everything from me. Everything I have ever had, on a selfish whim. I was a swordbearer, the only native to ever be chosen as one. Do you know what that means? That is who I am, and you took it!" Suqata was breathing harder now, and when he spoke he could hear the distant ring of power in his Voice.

"No. That was your job. It wasn't all of you," Auralyn said as she stood and walked towards Suqata. "Maybe what I did was wrong, yes. It was selfish and pigheaded, and I was wrong to do it without asking you, but you are more than a swordbearer. I saw what you can do."

*Now we come to it.* Suqata had known, in some quiet part of his mind, that this day would come eventually. Hopano had always been so secretive about their abilities, always whispering when he spoke of them. Suqata had realized early on that no one could ever know about the power of his Voice. Now this girl had discovered what he had spent a lifetime hiding from the world.

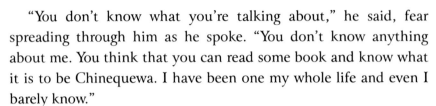

"You don't know what you're talking about," he said, fear spreading through him as he spoke. "You don't know anything about me. You think that you can read some book and know what it is to be Chinequewa. I have been one my whole life and even I barely know."

"You Sang." Auralyn's face was alight with wonder and apprehension all at once. "You Sang those beasts away when iron, powder, and cold steel did nothing. There is power in your voice. I felt it."

Suqata had to say something: to protest; to lie; to say anything to dissuade her from this path. Before he could do so, Lady Auralyn Brockholm spoke first.

*"Min aska to, min aska to, u-gwa lay, u-aye to."* As she spoke, the air rang sweetly like the sound of a single clear bell. It vibrated the undisturbed space until it touched Suqata's skin. The sensation was all too familiar, but at the same time different from any Song he had ever heard or felt. Then the hum gathered suddenly at the peak of Suqata's chest, forming into a thin, white light. The hum and light grew, and in an instant a ghostly shape took form and emerged from within him. It only lasted a moment, but in that moment he knew what the shape had become. A crow spread its wings before him, gliding in a silent sky, and then was gone. Suqata stumbled back, his breath coming fast and ragged, and then looked up at the unassuming young woman before him. She tried to smile, but the corners of her mouth quivered as she did.

"What was that? What did you do to me?" Suqata asked as he grasped his chest where the apparition had formed.

"You're all right, I promise." Auralyn was winded, but giddy as well, and seemed quite pleased with herself. "It's called an Ajanti, or Animal Soul. My mother's people, the Umbar, believe people have two natures, one worldly and one spiritual. I used that song to learn about your spirit self—the shape you just saw. I am the only person to have this power in many years, and the last. That is, the last until I met you."

"So what did you learn about me?" Suqata's heart was beating like a drum, fast and steady. "Do you have the answers that you seek?"

Auralyn closed the space between, walking unsteadily, until she was within arm's distance. "Your Animal Soul is the crow. The crow seeks knowledge. He is curious and eager to learn. That is why I know you will help me. You love a good mystery. Don't you?"

Suqata wanted to argue the point, but just as the words came to him Auralyn's eyes lost focus and she swayed dangerously. Suqata was reaching for her as her legs gave way, and she fell heavily into his awaiting arms.

"Take me to the chair," she said wearily, and Suqata walked her slowly to where she had been sitting when he arrived, her arms wrapped around his shoulders. "Sometimes singing is difficult. It takes a lot out of me to do that. I'm sure something like that would be nothing for you. I just know it." She looked up at him and gave him a strange look, one that Suqata was unaccustomed to.

Admiration.

# CHAPTER 10
# THE MANOR

Mistress Hodges walked briskly through the doors of Auralyn's parlor and promptly swooned, almost dropping the tea tray she had carried from the kitchens. She then stood there, seething in puritanical horror as Lady Auralyn lay in Suqata's arms. He was slowly helping her back to her seat, but the girl's arms were cast around his broad shoulders in what must have been an unseemly way.

"Scandal!" The stout woman quickly discarded the tray. "What in Providence's name is going on here? I am gone for a few minutes, only to return and see you with your hands all over the poor girl!" She shuffled indignantly over to the two. Suqata wanted to raise his hands to fend off any blows she might decide to deliver, but they were full at the moment.

"She's had some kind of fainting spell," he said quickly, "I was trying to help her down."

"Well, get to it then and be quick about it. I will not have the likes of you pawing all over the young woman in such a fashion."

"But … "

"But nothing. It's disgraceful. I know this was a bad idea from the jump, but does anyone listen to me?"

Once settled, Auralyn looked up sternly at the old housekeeper and said in a weak but determined voice, "That will be enough of that, Hodges. Suqata has been very … helpful tonight, and I would appreciate it if you would stop yelling at him."

Auralyn was drained and her skin had gone pale and clammy. She pulled her blanket up to her chest and regained some of her previous poise, again laying her hands delicately over the patterned surface. "I'm sure Mistress Hodges will show you to your new quarters." As she spoke, she avoided eye contact. "Until later then, Mr. Suqata. Good night."

"Good night, m'lady," he replied. He turned to leave, glancing back once as he left. By the time he had reached the door Auralyn was already sleep, and Hodges wasted no time in hurrying him out of her quarters.

The male slaves' quarters in the manor were well hidden. Mistress Hodges held a small flickering candle before them as they made their way through the large kitchens towards the rear of the sprawling estate. In the pantry was a large wooden door that slid aside to reveal a room that consisted of a common table, five chairs, and five small beds all lined up along the walls. Suqata's bed was positioned under a north-facing window near the door, and all of his belongings had been placed in a wooden apple crate that sat beneath it. As he and Hodges entered the room, the three men in the other beds stirred awake and stood. One of them moved forward, and Suqata found himself looking at a familiar face in the candlelight.

"Well, if it isn't long-faced Su!" said a laughing voice. Suqata instantly recognized Obrie's large figure and broad smile coming through the dark, and he couldn't help smiling back.

"Good, you know this one, do you?" said Hodges, already bored and glad to move past introductions. "Suqata is Lady Auralyn's new personal valet, but will be working with you in the kitchens when she has no need of him. Since Obrie works under Master Borgins, then you will report to Obrie, do you understand?"

Suqata nodded and replied, "Yes, ma'am."

"Excellent. Work hard, and no funny business, and we should all get along just lovely." She the grinned an impressively fake grin, one that never seemed to move past the thin corners of her mouth, and bade them a brisk goodnight. As her candle light disappeared from under the door, Obrie waved to the other men who had been sitting in their beds through Suqata's late arrival.

"Tano, Cheneska, this is Suqata. He's a pretty decent fellow, once you get past his slightly gloomy exterior." Obrie then did his best Hodges' impression and said, "I'm sure we all will get along, ahem, just lovely." The other men did not laugh.

"Good evening, brothers," Suqata said. He met their hard gazes and nodded a greeting, which they were slow to return. They were both Tenaskowa, with sharp, angular features and untrusting eyes. Suqata could suddenly remember the stares he received the day he had arrived at the camps.

"Evening, young man," Tano replied, and with that they both returned to sleep, leaving Suqata and Obrie standing together in the dark.

"Don't worry about them, they're just quiet. Damn near thought they were mute when I moved in."

"Well, not everyone is as expressive as you, my friend," Suqata said, sitting down on his hard bed. He was suddenly very tired, but Obrie still hovered, obviously waiting to ask the ton of questions that were fighting to come out. It was the last thing Suqata felt like doing: laying out the whole of that week's events from that night on the Last Road till now, but he knew that Obrie wouldn't be able to sleep until every detail was known. So together they talked into the night. Suqata omitted a great deal, but the rest was enough to keep Obrie's mind occupied. They talked in hushed voices in that room which smelled of old meals and cider casks, and when they were done Suqata removed his swordbearer's uniform and placed it in the crate beneath his bed. So much had happened that day, and the details swirled about in his mind even after his eyes were shut. When sleep finally came, the one image he could not purge was of the strange girl standing before him, singing.

WHEN SUQATA WOKE HIS NEW uniform was waiting for him at the foot of his cot, and he rushed to put it on before his daily duties began. The clothing was a great deal finer than he was accustomed to. The soft black coat was embroidered along the color and cuffs in gold thread, as was the waistcoat, and his new tan breeches tucked into tall black, leather boots that were freshly shined. He looked much the same as the other house valets, save for the red sash he wore around his waist, along with a belt holding an ornate scabbard.

From it, Suqata pulled forth a dull silver dagger, not much larger than a table knife and about as sharp. He turned the blade in his hand, rolling it between his nimble fingers, and all of his training came roaring to the surface of his mind. The knife might as well have been a battle axe. When the valets lined up for morning inspection, Suqata stood at the end of the line, and as Hodges came to examine his new attire, Suqata snapped to attention.

"That looks fine, young man," she said, looking quite pleased with herself. She reached up and straightened his collar. "Looks to be a nice fit. Be sure to keep it clean. It's not a pair of old soldier's rags, mind you."

"Yes, ma'am. May I ask, what am I to do with this?" Suqata held the dagger belt before him as if it were on fire. "I am not permitted."

"It is Lady Auralyn's wish that you should wear it. Her mother was Umbaric—strange people have strange beliefs. Apparently, a young lady's 'protector' always wears one of these. Maybe it's for buttering bread?" She snorted and chuckled for a moment before continuing. "Regardless, as long as you are hers, you will carry that, understood?"

"Yes, ma'am." Suqata strapped it on, but couldn't shake his feeling of unease, as if the captain would descend on him at any moment.

For the remainder of the day, and for the next two following, Suqata barely left the manor house, and since Auralyn was occupied with tutors and the like, he spent the majority of his time with Obrie, bent over a bucket of soapy water. The old Brockholm household had gone vacant for many years, and getting it back to a lord's standards took many hands. It was hard, and mostly tedious, but Suqata appreciated the distraction from his current state, and Obrie's constant chatter was enough to keep it from becoming too monotonous. They worked all through the day and into the evening. Every few hours Suqata would see pairs of Black Guard troop by, the sound of their boots echoing down the hallways as he cleaned. It felt like a taunt, a cruel mockery of his current status.

Suqata kept his eyes down scrubbing even harder, almost rubbing clear the inlaid patterns on the hardwood floors.

TRIPS INTO TOWN WERE INFREQUENT, and usually brief for servants at the manor. Officials and merchants that had business with the governor made the two-mile trek out to see him, and not the other way around, but with the cold season descending quickly, a visit to The Hollow had been planned.

"WE'LL BE GETTING SUPPLIES OFF the ferry up from Danesville and the camps. It's the last one before the river starts to freeze too bad." Obrie said as he and Suqata prepared to leave with the wagon train. "I had to pull a lot of strings to get us this detail; the least you can do is smile a bit." He stood in the doorway of the kitchen with his thick arms crossed before him, and his mouth puckered in frustration. Suqata smiled, as requested, and pulled on his winter cloak.

"Sorry, Obrie. I have a lot on my mind is all. Let's get out there before they leave us. I don't want to spend the day clearing the hearths again."

Outside, the supply wagons were lined up with two servants per wagon, and at the lead of the procession was Lord Brockholm's personal carriage. As they loaded into their places, Suqata could see the governor come down the front steps with Auralyn on his arm. They were dressed for more of a state function than a trip to The Hollow, Lord Brockholm finely adorned in a coat of woven gold and black velvet and Auralyn with a long hooded cloak of the same. For a second, Suqata thought he saw her glance his way, but that instant Captain Graye appeared at the top of the stair.

"Guards, mount up," he called to the waiting soldiers. He strode imperiously down to where a nervous looking young man held Augustus. It had only been a few days, just a collection of hours and simple duties, since Graye had dismissed Suqata from his quarters, but even in that time something between them had changed. Maybe it was the gray light of day, or the fact he was not standing at his beck and call, but something about the captain seemed different. His stride had a certain predatory glide to it, as if he was coiled and ready to spring. Even his eyes, which had always been hard and impossibly distant, had taken on something feral in nature. They seemed to scan the edges of his vision, and when his eyes shifted towards his and Obrie's wagon, Suqata instinctively looked away.

"Well, captain, I would like a proper tour of the river dock and mill yards while we are in the village," Lord Brockholm said brightly, pulling on a pair of leather gloves. "And I know Auralyn has been excited about taking in some of the local color. Perhaps we might stay in town until nightfall, let the men have some time to wander."

"This is not a social visit, m'lord," the captain replied.

"Well. I am making it so. No use working the servants into a lather, as they say. Happy help is productive help. Unless you see any reason to disagree."

Captain Graye did not reply, instead taking Augustus' reins roughly from his new page.

The ride to The Hollow was pleasantly short, a fact Suqata was thankful for. He was loath to admit it, even to himself, but he had feared traveling. Since that day on the Last Road the wide expanse of forest, once so familiar, now held a specter of danger looming behind those walls of upraised branches. Every sway of the king pines caught his attention, fanning to life images of dark nightmares. Creatures with claws and teeth that caught the cool light of day. Suqata felt a slight pang of guilt as the wagons came within sight of the town's outer wall and he felt his body slowly relax. It was only then that he noticed he had been gripping the side of the cart. When he looked at his hands he saw the long, thin lines of the wood grain pressed painfully into his flesh.

ORIN'S HOLLOW WAS A-SCURRY WITH preparation now that winter had shown its face. The last of the barges had been arriving over the past week, pulled upriver by oxen teams tethered to the large and

heavily laden skiffs. They now lined the quay on either side of the river covered in barrels, bins, and frost-covered burlap sacks. The men from the manor were on the ground as soon as the wagons were over the bridge, getting straight to the task at hand, Suqata and Obrie amongst them. It was only early afternoon but already the light was beginning to dim.

Puffing on their clay pipes and glowering, the dock workers watched the slaves from the manor began to lift and carry cargo to the awaiting carts. Suqata could feel their eyes on him. He paid it no mind, focusing his attention on the work, but as the day went on he couldn't seem to shake the growing sense of unease that had come over him.

"Those are some pretty eyes you got there, darky," the barge captain said as Suqata and Obrie moved past, their arms filled with heavy bags of potatoes. "You must be a Chinny. Don't think I've ever seen a real Chinny before." The man smiled a yellow, twisted smile through a thick mess of red beard. He smelled of old wine, and Suqata couldn't help but remember Mr. Snodgrass and his heavy club. Something dangerous was about, so he ignored the man and continued working.

"Look, Suqata. I think he's sweet on you." Obrie said, huffing as he dropped the sack onto the wagon. "I'm sorry, sir, but my friend is shy. Maybe a nice bouquet of flowers would loosen his tongue. Or chocolates! Nothing like chocolates to make a good first impression."

"Oh, we have a smart mouth here." The red-bearded man wasn't smiling anymore. "Keep your tongue about you, fatty, or we'll have to remove it for you."

"I'm sorry that my smart mouth offends you. I promise to speak slower and with smaller words."

Suqata touched Obrie's shoulder flashing him a warming glance. Somehow his sense of danger was reaching a peak with every passing heartbeat.

"Don't, Obrie. Not today," he said under his breath.

"This is nothing I can't handle, my friend." Obrie puffed out his large chest and gave Suqata a wink. "Besides, this dock rat is ancient, snaggle-toothed, and filled with hot wind. What's to worry about?"

But it wasn't the red-beard captain who concerned Suqata. Just over his shoulder, lurking in the afternoon shadow, another man stood waiting. Suqata had only noticed him by chance, skulking behind stacks of cargo and obviously anticipating something, or someone. He had the thin, pale look of a man just recovering from a long illness, all except for his eyes. They were almost gold, and appeared to gleam with cruel intent, his lips quivering as his attention focused. Suqata looked back at the quay just in time to see Lord Brockholm and his daughter, accompanied by Captain Graye, walking down the causeway.

"Look smart you two. Here come your new masters now." The red-bearded man snickered, but Suqata barely heard him. The man in the shadows had shifted, tensing as if to pounce. He sniffed the air and moved quickly out into the light. Suqata could see him more clearly now. He had a mass of dark, matted hair, and his lean, hungry features made him look like a wild animal.

"You sir," Suqata said to the red-bearded captain, never taking his eyes off the stranger, "who is that fellow there? The sickly looking one."

He paused a second but then answered plainly. "Oh, that's Sully. He's up from Earl's Cross, but he hasn't been much help of late, with the fever and all. Wolf bites can do strange things to a fella, ain't that the truth."

Suddenly, Suqata felt an unsettled sensation spread from the pit of his stomach. Something wasn't right, he knew it. As he watched, the man Sully began walking down the crowded dock, pushing other workers aside, his eyes wide and crazed. He was moving towards the governor and Auralyn. Before he knew he was acting, Suqata dropped the bag he carried and made his way down the dock as well. Behind him he could hear Obrie's cries, but the

meaning was lost to the rush of wind in Suqata's ears. The dark stranger was only a few yards ahead, but growing faster with each step. Suqata sped along, leaping over crates, coils of ropes, and men at work on fishing nets, but all the while he knew he would not be able to catch up with him, not before the stranger reached the girl. Then, slid into his belt, Suqata saw the cold glint off of the stranger's knife blade. He knew he had to act, and quickly.

"Captain!" He yelled over the din of working men. "Captain! He has a knife!" The dock workers turned with questioning looks on their faces, but Graye and the Brockholms did not stir, not hearing the warning. Suqata then turned his attention to the stranger. "Sully, STOP!" The power of his voice reverberated off the low river bank like the sound of a gong.

Just as he spoke, the stranger turned. There was menace written in every line of his face.

"Chinequewa!" he growled through gritted teeth, then pulled the long knife from his belt. Everyone was watching him now. All the river men had abandoned their tasks and stood at the ready, some trying to talk their wild-eyed companion down, while Suqata waited amongst them. Sully looked about now, some of the rage gone from his eyes replaced with confusion and frustration. Just as his growl died away, Suqata a heard a distinct and familiar ring: the sound of a sword being drawn. The captain moved forward, and in a flash of his blade and swish of his cloak, Sully was down. It was as precise and ruthless a kill as Suqata had ever seen.

The commotion that followed was incredible as Black Guard moved to secure the Brockholms, and the river-men moved in closer to see their fallen comrade. Suqata was pushed aside in a mass of excited movement. The red-bearded captain from the barge was there now, crouching down beside the body.

"Who was this traitor, sir? One of yours?" Captain Graye said, sword still in hand. His gaze was hard as ever, but there was something else there as well, a fury that burned underneath.

"Yes sir, he was," he stuttered, "but he's no traitor, sir. He's been

mad with fever for days. He was driving the team upriver, not a week ago, and we were attacked by wolves. Huge creatures, sir. We lost half the team, and Sully was lucky to get out of the whole thing with just that bite, but he hasn't been the same since."

Graye sheathed his sword. "Is that so? Reeks of witchcraft to me. I've been protectorate of this town for some twenty years, and never have I seen a man react that way to an animal bite. I myself was bitten only a few days ago. Are you dealing with the dark arts, sir, or was your friend here a traitor as I said?"

The barge captain eyed the saber at Graye's hip and nodded his head. "It's as you say, m'lord. It's as you say."

"Good, now get this fellow off the docks." As the captain returned to the Brockholms he looked off into the crowd once, directly at Suqata.

THAT NIGHT, SUQATA'S DREAMS WERE troubled again. He couldn't get the stranger's face out his mind. Images of that night on the Last Road began to blend with the events of the day, and soon Suqata saw himself facing of a pack of river-men by torchlight, all snarling and snapping at his ankles. A knock at the door stirred him, and the nightmare faded quickly.

"Get it, Suqata," Obrie grumbled from under his blankets. "It's probably Hodges. Needs help with the cider barrels again. If that woman keeps up drinking like this, she is going to turn into an apple. That or a fish."

Obrie's voice trailed off into sleep, and Suqata pulled on his clothes as best he could. He had no candle, so when he opened the door, the visitor's light blinded him for a second. He blinked his eyes and when he opened them again, Lady Auralyn was standing before him.

"You have an odd habit of being right in the middle of things, don't you?" she asked coyly.

"The same could be said of you."

They stood in the candlelight for a moment watching the strange and wild shapes that wavered around them. Then, she spoke again.

"Come to my quarters tomorrow. There are things happening here, in this place, and I feel you are the key to me understanding things. Tomorrow, then?"

"I have chores, and Hodges may not approve."

"Pish-posh. You are my valet, and you will come when I ask." There was a silence after she said this, and a look of embarrassment on her face. "I'm sorry. I didn't mean to be so bratty. Will you please come tomorrow?"

Suqata nodded yes.

PART 3

# THE SONGS OF
# CHANGING

# CHAPTER 11
# SUMMONING

"**Y**OU'RE DAFT, SU! YOUR HEAD'S GONE SOFT.**" OBRIE WAS KNEADING a lump of thick dough on the table with almost painful ferocity. "I want no part of this. Your best bet is to just go. Seriously, how long do you think you can hide from the lady of the house? This place is big, but it's not that big."

"As long as I have to. Longer if needs be."

"You've never been the type to not follow orders, Su. Even little ones. Why start now?" Obrie said while putting the final touches on a tray of rolls. "You're not going to be able to avoid her forever. You are her valet, which means sooner or later you will have to take her letter, or escort her to her carriage, or something like that. Then what will you do?"

"It doesn't matter. I just need a little while to figure out what to do. You wouldn't understand if I told you, but this girl is ... different." Suqata ran his fingers through his hair. "She isn't like anyone I've ever met. She's not what you would think a highborn girl to be, and she doesn't ... well ... do the kind of things you would expect."

Obrie's eyes became as large as saucers as he listened, and a wicked, hinting smile began to tug at the corners of his mouth. It took Suqata a moment to notice.

"Stop that! Stop what you are thinking right now," he hissed. Suqata grabbed a honeyed roll from the tray and held it menacingly. "You know that isn't what I meant. She is still a lady."

"Of course, of course! My mistake. Just put the rolls down." Obrie had his hands up in surrender, but the smile never truly left his face. From the kitchen door, Master Borgins poked in his overly round head and put on his best stern face possible.

"How are the rolls coming, Obrie? We still have to put the finishing touches on that lamb before supper."

"Splendidly, sir. I'll be right along once these go in the oven."

"Excellent, my boy. Keep working. Idle hands are a demon's tools, as my mama used to say," Borgins said as he disappeared, giggling.

Obrie winked at Suqata. "I'm sure his mama told him not to sit in the pantry eating all the cookies either, yet there he is." Suqata stifled a laugh. "Back to your dilemma. You would be wise to not cross our Lady Auralyn. There are some people you don't want to ... upset."

"Meaning?"

"Well, I shouldn't spread rumors. It's very unbecoming of someone in my position, but since you're begging," Obrie said with an air of seriousness. "There are people saying things. Strange things about the Brockholms. Mainly rumors I suppose, but still, strange is strange."

"Why is it we always end up talking about these kind of things, Obrie?"

"I'm not sure, but you did ask. It has something to do with why the Lord Governor is here, in this backwoods part of the colonies instead of Vorhaven or someplace like that. They are saying things about some scandal back in Kael, and his now passed wife. Things about witchcraft."

And there it was again, that word: witch. It was unsettling idea, even to Suqata. Though Orin's Hollow was remote, it had its fair share of merchants traveling there during the warmer months, bringing with them rumors and whisperings of the witch-hunts. Suqata had learned the words of power when he was a child from a real wordweaver, but the stories that were told of these witches were something else entirely. Ritual sacrifice, blood rites, and accounts of children disappearing in the night were all part of canon, as were the punishments exacted on those caught practicing their taboo beliefs.

"So your source thinks that the governor is some kind of warlock?" Suqata laughed. "And that he's traveled all this way across

the Scalan Sea to, what, steal children? Do you have any idea how ridiculous that sounds?"

"I heard it straight from Hodges' mouth. And who said that it's the governor you should be worried about?" Obrie grinned, his teeth showing bright against his dark skin. "From my experience, most mothers pass what they know on to their daughters."

"How awful," said a distinctly female voice from above them on the kitchen stairs. "Well I sincerely hope that this dangerous woman doesn't hear about these scandalous rumors. You might just be her first targets." Auralyn was standing at the top of the short stairway that led to the kitchen door, wearing a blue riding dress, and looking imperiously down at the two young men, one now extremely focused on his sweeping, and the other up to his elbows in dough.

"I'm sorry, Lady Auralyn, we meant no disrespect. We were ... uh, well ... we just ... "

"Slandering my family. It's fine, Obrie ... isn't it. You had best get control of those wagging tongues of yours. My father is less forgiving than I when it comes to such things. Suqata, since you were to be too busy to come by, I thought I would come to fetch you." She stood tapping her riding crop in a slow rhythm against the side of her dress. "I'm going for a little tour of the grounds, and I'm pretty sure your new position requires you to accompany me."

Suqata stopped sweeping and looked to his friend for help. Obrie shook his head and continued working on his rolls.

"It's pretty cold outside, m'lady. Maybe your ride could wait for another time."

"That is for me to decide, is it not?"

"And you're not the least bit worried? After yesterday and considering the patrols haven't found the wolf pack yet, should we really be out?"

Auralyn barely waited for Suqata to finish before turning to leave. "My dear boy, that's why I have you."

Suqata followed Auralyn out the manor through the servant doors in the rear of the main hall, pulling on his gloves and cloak as he followed. It was indeed cold outside. The snow was about a foot deep anywhere not shoveled or trampled by foot traffic, and the sky was the even kind of gray that said more was to come. Neither of them spoke, which was fine with Suqata since he had no idea what say to the girl in the first place. Her personality was so malleable, changing seamlessly from aloof aristocrat to secretive girl in an instant. He was unsure which one was walking briskly before him at that moment.

Once in the stables, Suqata quickly prepared two horses for the ride. Old Whisper was happy to see him, as was Augustus, who whinnied excitedly from the nearby stall only to snort in disapproval as his former caretaker moved by and prepared a strong blond mare for Auralyn instead. When he was done, Suqata held the reins and offered his arm to her.

"Her name is Autumn. Handle her with a strong hand. She can be willful if you let her," he said. He waited to help her into the saddle.

Auralyn regarded the young man with daggers in her eyes, then snatched the reins from him. "I've been riding since I could walk. I think I can handle one of your colonial horses without issue." With one skilled kick, Auralyn vaulted into the saddle. "And do try to keep up. Heyah!" She snapped the reins sharply and the mare bolted off through the open stable doors like a golden colored wind. Suqata had to run to Old Whisper. He mounted quickly, cursing under his breath, and galloped through the doors after her.

The land around the manor was well tended, and like the house was meant to give the impression of culture, all to distract people from the fact that the Northern Woods shared its boundaries. As they rode hard past the snow-covered fields, Suqata couldn't help but be a little amused. *The place these outlanders fear the most, and it's right in their back yard.* The thought was not a new revelation, but

one that was brought to stark clarity as he watched Auralyn speed down the trail before him.

He urged Old Whisper on faster and faster, the cold turning his breath to vapor, until he was right alongside Auralyn. He signaled her to slow down, but she only smiled and waved back at him. He tried calling her name but his voice was lost in the sound of hoof beats, rolling through the air like the sound of storm clouds clashing. Just ahead, Suqata could see that the trail veered right, away from the manor grounds, and was closed off by a tall, wooden gate. He looked back at Auralyn just in time to see the gleam of challenge in her eyes change to fear.

*She's going to try to jump it.* There was no inflection in the thought, but still his mind flashed an image of him carrying the girl, her body broken, back to the manor house, her infuriated father, and ultimately his own death.

Auralyn lowered her head as Autumn gained speed until Old Whisper could barely keep up. The world became a blur and all Suqata could see clearly was the girl and her horse framed by a rush of snowy evergreens streaking past him. Before she was out of his reach, Suqata had to act quickly. His hand shot out and grabbed the reins. The leather was cold and slick with snow, but he gripped tightly and pulled with all his might. It was a jolting and awkward move, but even as Autumn resisted, they slowly all came to a halt, not ten yards from the cattle fence.

"Are you insane, girl?" Suqata blurted out once his heart had come down from his throat. "That fence is at least five feet tall. You can't jump that! What were you thinking?"

Auralyn was breathing hard, and her proper little riding hat sat crooked on her wind-blown hair. "I know what I was doing," she said, smoothing her skirts and pushing back stray curls. Her manner was haughty and proud, but the quaver in her voice was to obvious not to notice. She was just as scared as Suqata. "Well, it seems that you suddenly care for my well-being. What brought about the change?"

Suqata managed a half-hearted laugh. "Maybe it was the mad dash through the snow, or the fact that you almost got us killed!" He jumped down from his horse and took a moment to catch his breath, Auralyn following suit.

"Maybe you're right," she said quietly. She swayed slightly as she landed on shaky legs. "I think that Autumn may have gotten away from me a bit, and I'm sorry. I just wanted to show you that I can handle it. I'm not some fragile little git."

"Killing us on horseback would have definitely proven that."

"That's not what I meant. You don't have to treat me like there is something wrong with me. You have to admit that you've been avoiding me since that day in my parlor. Here it is I trusted you, and I showed you something of myself that I've never shown to another soul, not even my father. Hours later you look at me like I'm some kind of leper."

Suqata felt more confused by the second. *Why would she care what I think of her anyway?* He thought as he tied off the horse to the fence. "It's complicated for me, m'lady ... I mean, Lynn. I have been a slave my whole life, and I've never been able to speak my mind. Now you want me forget that in an instant. On request even."

"I just want you to treat me like a person, and I'll do the same for you. Anyways, I'm not as proper as you seem to think I am. In Kael, I'm a half-breed, you know. My mother was Umbaric, which makes me just a step above a savage to most of them." Auralyn smiled in a strained sort of way when she said this. "My father wanted us to start out fresh here. No more whispered insults or prejudices. Looks like the 'new world' is a lot like the old one if you ask me. I guess people are always afraid of people they consider to be different, but you and I are more alike than you want to admit."

"You have my sympathies," he said with disdain. "Captain Graye always told me that people are not really different. The only thing that separates us is power. Those who have it, and those who don't. In that regard, you and I could never be more different."

"Do you believe that," Auralyn said, cocking her eyebrow slightly, "knowing the things you do?"

Suddenly, everything became clear. "This ride was just to get me out here, wasn't it? To discuss that which need not be discussed. What are you playing at, girl?"

Auralyn looked unsure of herself, but after a moment answered plainly. "I need your help. You have a gift, and I need to learn more about it."

"I knew it. Well, you want to know something about this power: it's more trouble than it's worth. Lesson over."

"You seem quite sure of yourself," she said.

"Trust me. I spent my childhood learning the *sen-wa* and the *sen-tal*, the Songs of Changing and Making. The whole time I was rotting away in a slave camp. Fat lot of good it did me there." Suqata turned to leave.

"It's probably for the best then," Auralyn spoke quietly in an almost taunting manner. "The songs of my people are powerful. They can unlock secrets you couldn't imagine. Maybe even tell you what happened in the woods that night with the wolves."

Suqata stopped. "How is that even possible?"

Auralyn almost looked relieved that he had stayed. "There is one. It's called a *mata-heyu*. A divining song. Very few could ever sing it. With it you can ask the spirits questions about the Waking World. Or, at least that is what my mother told me. You could try that."

"That sounds dangerous," Suqata said, crossing his arms. "My teacher used to tell me stories about spirits. Never trust them, he said, they always have something they want in return."

"Believe me or do not, but you are the only one who can help me."

He hesitated, mostly for effect, before answering. The thought of giving this spoiled girl what she wanted without any resistance was too much to bear, but already Suqata's mind was filling with possibilities. This was the kind of power that Hopano had always held at arm's length from him, always telling him riddles about the danger. What kind of answers could he gain from a Song like this?

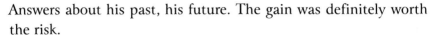
Answers about his past, his future. The gain was definitely worth the risk.

"Tell me the words," he said.

"Excellent," she replied, smiling. Auralyn recited the song slowly for Suqata, making sure to enunciate each syllable, repeating it over and over again until Suqata could hear her voice clearly in his head.

*"Qui calo u naboo nashta, u do cha co'la, ur rosha-nata, calo Anishta, calo Anishta, calo Anishta."*

Even as she spoke, the words sent steady waves through Suqata's body. There was power there, moving beneath the surface of perception, but unlike any he had ever felt, though something was not quite right. It was missing something.

"Do you have it?" she asked as she finished.

Suqata nodded his head, then began to sing. He repeated what Auralyn had spoken, but where she had recited just a series of strange words, Suqata poured out poetry, strung together by rhythm and punctuated by the young man's clear tenor voice. He sang the song twice, focusing on the cadence, and he felt the power rise with each line he spoke, like a fire stoked to life. But nothing happened. After a third time, even Auralyn knew something was wrong.

"What is the matter; why isn't anything happening?" She shivered impatiently and stomped her feet to keep warm.

"Give me a moment." Suqata ran the song through his mind again, this time listening, seeking for some imperfection in the chant.

*Listen. It's like Hopano would say, a Song is like a heartbeat. There is an order to it. A trained mind can find the rhythm in the drops of rain on a roof. Listen.* Then, it came to him. It was the words. They weren't quite right, nor were they in exactly the right order.

Suqata sang out again. *"Qui calo, u nashta, u rosh nata, udo colu cha, calo Anishta, calo Anishta, calo Anishta!"*

Without a second's warning there came a rush of cold, bitter wind, sweeping up from the snowy ground and surrounding Suqata and Auralyn like a hundred frozen hands reaching and clawing at them. The roar of the wind was deafening, and it pulled and

whipped at their cloaks and clothing, even though the trees only a few yards away were untouched by it. Within seconds, the world took on a grey countenance, as if the color had simply been bled from it completely. Suqata shielded his face, guarding against the sharp sting of ice crystals. He reached out to find Auralyn crumpled to her knees.

"Hold on to me," he yelled, pulling her close. The cold was almost unbearable, but just as the wind reached its peak, Suqata thought he saw something take shape within the whirlwind. It wavered, fighting to form itself, and soon Suqata could make out a vaguely human silhouette with long hair moving violently in the wind. It had no features, save for one: its eyes were blood red, and seemed to glow with a hungry fire. It took a step towards them, and just before he could act, Suqata felt Auralyn reach out.

"Mother?" she yelled over the howl of the tempest.

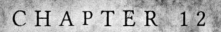

# CHAPTER 12

# WIND AND SHADOW

S UQATA COULD ALMOST FEEL THE CREATURE BREATHING AS THE STEADY contracting and expanding of its shape sent out waves through the swirling air. Its long, willowy limbs moved with a wicked grace that was all at once beautiful and frightening to behold. As it moved closer, its features came into sharper focus until it drifted only a few yards away. Before them hovered the figure of a woman, tall and beautiful, and with the same features as Auralyn. The figure stretched out her arms in a welcoming gesture, but within the swirl of its raven hair Suqata could see its eyes still gleamed red.

"Mother, is that you?" Auralyn asked, standing up slowly and pulling her cloak closed against the wind. "Answer me, spirit. Are you Anishta of Umbar, daughter of Tolnoshtin the Speaker? Answer me plainly." She spoke with authority in her voice even though her body was visibly trembling. The figure did not stir at first, but then appeared to shift forward with unnatural speed until it was now only a few strides away.

"Yes, my love. I am," it said. Its mouth did not move, but rather the words were in their minds, echoing within the recess of consciousness. Suqata was quick to move between them.

"Auralyn, whatever that thing is, it is not human," he said, pulling his silver dagger clear of its sheath. He knew that it wouldn't be much help if the wraith decided to turn violent, but feeling the weight of it in his hand made him feel less defenseless.

Under the sound of the wind, Suqata could then hear a growing whisper. First it was easily lost, but with each passing second it seem to grow more intense and urgent, calling out to them, luring them both closer to the ethereal figure until Auralyn reached towards it again.

"Yes, come to me my light," it hissed, "you have traveled so far." Auralyn was staring wide-eyed, mesmerized by the lilting sound of its voice. "Yes, daughter, closer. I have missed you so much." Just as it moved in close enough to touch, Suqata noticed something. A sweet, sickly smell surrounded the figure. The creature reeked of old death and decay.

"Lynn, back away!" he cried as he slashed down with the silver dagger across its outstretched arm. A scream burst from the creature that felt like hot needles in Suqata's head. It pulled itself away as smoke poured out of the angry wound. When it looked to them again, the beautiful features and raven hair were gone. Now it stared at them through the shadowed, empty sockets of an emaciated skull. The red light of its eyes burned like two hot embers, and the strands of its now grey mane seemed to whip about like the grasping arms of some tentacled beast.

"Meat things have silver!" it howled, its voice sounding like a sharp blast of wind through the trees. "I'll rip you, taste you, kill you." It didn't speak conventionally, instead sending its ghostly words into Suqata's mind, leaving them impossible to block out.

The blade of the silver dagger was still steaming from the first blow, and Suqata held it at the ready for an attack. This time, however, the wraith kept its distance, circling them like a stalking beast waiting to strike.

"What is it?" he whispered to Auralyn, never taking his eyes from the wraith or lowering his weapon. She was speechless, staring wide-eyed at the ghostly figure before them with a mixture of awe and pure terror. "Auralyn!" Suqata said again, louder this time. Finally she pulled her eyes away from it.

"I'm not sure," she mumbled. "I think it may be some sort of spirit, but not animal or human. Not anymore."

"Then what do I do? It's just waiting for an opening."

She hesitated for a moment before answering. "You could sing a banishment song. They are mentioned in the books my mother gave me, but I've never heard one sung before."

"Do you remember the words?"

Auralyn nodded and spoke them to him slowly. *"Qui vanoya u nash wunatio."*

Suqata didn't recognize the song. It was neither *sen-wa* or *sen-tal.* "That's it?" he asked. "Seems like a pretty short chant."

"That's all I can remember. It's all that you should ... "

Suddenly, Suqata felt a burning pain lance through his temples, and the world flashed white. It felt as though white-hot blades had pierced through his very mind, but within the pain he could hear the creature's voice, howling as sharp and merciless as a tempest. He could hear the wraith whispering even as it screamed.

"No power here, Silent One. You have no power against the Varcuya. I will taste your blood, rip your mind to pieces, and leave your bones to rot."

The pain was so intense Suqata could barely open his eyes, and his hold on the dagger was quickly failing. He felt his legs would give out from under him any second. Then he felt Auralyn's hands set firmly on his shoulders, shaking him.

"Now, now! Sing the song now!" she screamed from what seemed like an impossible distance. Suqata steadied himself, feeling the pain of the wraith's attack lift for a mere moment. It was all that he needed.

*"Qui vanoya u nash wunatio, qui vanoya u nash wunatio, qui vanoya u nash wunatio."* Suqata sang with every bit of power he could muster, repeating the words over and over again. The chant seemed to batter the wraith from all sides, pushing it back. Suqata held his hands out, palms forward as he chanted, physically compelling the song as it pummeled against the creature's form. It let out one last primal scream that split the air, but in a flickering moment the wraith and the swirling wind faded, the world returned to normal.

Suqata now stood at the edge of the wood, breathing like had just run a mile flat, the horses rearing and pulling at the fence in fear.

"Lynn, it's over. That thing is gone."

Auralyn did not answer. She lay on the ground only a few feet away, her slow, steady breath visible in the chill air.

SUQATA RODE HIS HORSE BACK to the manor, Autumn in tow and Auralyn positioned on the saddle before him, his arm securely wrapped around her waist with his hands on the reins. When he had lifted her from the ground she was limp and unresponsive, as if she was in some kind of a deep sleep, but as they rode he could hear her breathing become stronger and steadier. Suqata could feel her heart beat stronger against him as they rode, the rhythm almost matching the hard hoof beats against the ground. By the time he had reached the foot of the manor steps, Auralyn's eyes were slowly opening.

"What is the meaning of this?" Mistress Hodges ran bursting through the entryway, flanked on both sides by Black Guard. Obviously someone had seen the young Chinequewa riding back to the manor with Auralyn. Hodges wore a stern look on her lined face. "If you have harmed a hair on her head, sir, I will see your neck stretched, I will," she yelled as Suqata dismounted and lowered Auralyn into his arms.

"It's not what you think at all, mum. She … fell. I'm just bringing her back to be looked after." Before Suqata could say another word, the two guards stood to either side of him and readied their weapons.

"Not that I don't believe you, lad, but this does look suspicious," one of the guardsmen said. The face looking seriously back at him from under the short brim of his cap was that of Lieutenant Dobbs, while the other looked to be Private Ashton, though he had grown quite lean and severe in the days since the attack on the Last Road.

Just then, the doors of the manor house burst open again and out ran Lord Brockholm, attended by a group of finely dressed men. Captain Graye brought up the rear, walking without the urgency of the others.

*As if things couldn't have gotten any worse,* Suqata thought briefly,

realizing the irony of the situation. Twice he had put himself in danger's way to protect this girl from harm, and now twice it seemed he would suffer for it.

"Explain this, young man. Immediately." The governor's voice was restrained, but still held the slightest hint of threat in it. "And spare no detail."

"Well ... " Suqata began, but just as the words were forming he was interrupted by Auralyn gently pushing his hand clear of her waist as she stood with a slight wobble.

"It is as he said, Father. I fell," she said, sounding a little annoyed at all of the attention. "I drove the mare a little too hard and lost control. Young Suqata warned me she could be spirited, but I did not listen. It was quite a feat that I didn't break anything."

"That was foolish, my dear. You know you shouldn't be taking these kinds of risks. Not with your condition."

"Father, I'm fine," Auralyn said, almost cutting the governor off. "Nothing that a hot bath and some mulled wine cannot fix. Mistress Hodges, could you please accompany me to my chambers and have a bath drawn?"

Hodges nodded, even though she still looked suspiciously at her young valet. "Yes, m'lady. Boy, help Lady Auralyn up to her room," she said to Suqata. He turned to obey but was met by her upheld hand.

"That is not necessary. I think you've had to carry me far enough for one day," she said. Auralyn wore one of her proud smiles, annoying and endearing at the same time, but there was a hint of sadness to her voice. Together, she and Hodges ascended the steps followed closely by the governor and his advisors.

Captain Graye stood for moment before leaving, staring down at his former swordbearer with a curious sort of manner. Before he left, Suqata could have sworn he saw a smirk crease the corner of his dark eyes. He motioned once and Dobbs and Ashton stood at ease.

"See. No harm there, Su," Dobbs said and slapped him heartily on the back.

"Yeah. Best watch out next time that she falls somewhere a little more private. You gets me boy," Ashton whispered. He snuck a quick lick of his bottom lip, too, before leaving Suqata at the base of the steps.

THAT NIGHT, AFTER LIGHTS OUT in the servants' quarters, Suqata moved silently down the halls of the house, moving from shadow to inky shadow within the power of the Hiding Song. Each breath brought him down another corridor, his power so deftly used that Suqata barely had to let go of the familiar hum of it. It was exhilarating, and more than a little dangerous, but what shocked him more was not the fact he was defying every house rule he could think of to be out this late, but rather how easily using the Songs came to him now. It wasn't two weeks ago that he could barely bring himself to use his abilities, not even in the strictest of secret, and now here he was slinking through the halls of his new master's house, invisible to the eye.

When he came to Auralyn's chamber door, he noticed a faint light beneath it, glancing across the freshly buffed wood panel floor. Taking a quick breath, Suqata entered the room.

"Who's there?" she asked.

Auralyn lay in her four-post bed, the thin, gauzy curtains drawn. She sat alert with a book laid across her lap and a single candle burning on her night stand. The warm light shone through the curtains with a ghostly quality, making the raven-haired girl appear to be more spirit than flesh. "I won't ask again," she said, this time pulling forth a thin blade from the center of her book. Suqata released his breath and the Hiding Song faded, and with his next full breath of air he sang another brief chant, his voice starting deep and rising quickly.

*"Un dash o."*

As he did, a white-blue light appeared before him, floating as a small orb not three feet from him, casting him in its glow.

"Why is it I feel that you have not always slept with a knife at your side," he said, walking into view with his hands outstretched. "One would think you weren't happy to see me."

A look of genuine relief came over Auralyn's face, and she smiled softly. "You would be wrong on both accounts, Su," she said.

For some reason, hearing her call him that put Suqata at ease right away. It had always been a strange nickname to him. Out-landers had a way of changing the names of people and things that they didn't understand, but at this moment the familiarity of it made him feel that taking the risk to see Auralyn was not as foolhardy as it had felt a moment ago. He moved closer, taking the chair that sat at the foot of the bed.

"Are you feeling better? Hodges wouldn't say anything but that you needed your rest," he said, trying his best to sit in a casual manner. Auralyn returned her dagger to the book binding and moved from under the covers to the center of the bed and sat facing Suqata.

"I'm fine now. I was just shaken up, I suppose."

Suqata couldn't help but notice that she was wearing a soft blue sleeping gown that caught the light, adding to the aura about her. Even though it was very demure, he kept his face pointed towards the floor, appearing to be very interested in the weave of the rug.

"Your light is beautiful, Suqata," she said, noticing his blush even at a distance. He watched her hand follow the glowing ball as it bobbed weightlessly beyond her bed curtains.

"It's a simple Song, really. One of the first that Hopano taught me. It's called a weir light. It's kind of funny that I haven't made one in so long, but all of sudden they come so easily to me. Would you like me to teach you?"

Auralyn's face turned a shade paler and she looked away from the light, almost appearing embarrassed at having brought it up to begin with. "I don't think that would be wise, considering what happened today."

"Not interested in the Songs anymore, are you? I hope you weren't surprised things happened this way. I did tell you they

were trouble. What I can't figure out is why you would ask me to Sing a Song like that, one that was so obviously dangerous." Suqata waited for some kind of response, a rationalization for why Auralyn had put them in harm's way.

"I didn't know what it would do. I was wrong to goad you into singing it, and I'm sorry," she replied.

Suqata had not expected an apology so quickly.

They both sat in silence, fearing to stray too far from the even ground they now found themselves on, but soon Auralyn began to speak in a slow, measured tone.

"When I was a girl, I lost my mother. Not to something conventional, like illness or an accident. She was taken from me, and it was all my fault. I sang her away."

Suqata was frozen, his features betraying the dread that had awakened inside of him. "How is that possible?" he asked, his voice barely over a whisper.

"My mother's name was Anishta, and she was a priestess of Umbar. She was beautiful, and kind, and sad in a way I could never truly understand. Our people have held the secrets of the Songs from the earliest times, and it has been our responsibility to keep them protected. My mother taught me everything she knew: the ancient texts and legends about powers that could change the very fabric of the world. Obviously I was too young to understand the great gift she had given me, or the responsibility of it, so I spurned it every chance I had. I just wanted to be normal, I suppose, like the other girls. To not have this weight on my shoulders. Now I realize how selfish I was. She always said I had a destiny, something I was meant to accomplish, while all I wanted was to be like everyone else."

Suqata listened intently, marveling at how familiar it all sounded.

"One day, I took one of her tomes, and Sang a Song so ancient and forbidden that the words were barely readable on the page. As I did the world changed around me. It was so cold, and I didn't know what to do. My mother Sang the words to undo what I had

done, but it was too late. Before things could be righted, something took her. I never saw what it was. In the end, I was alone."

Auralyn took a long shuddering breath and then looked intently at Suqata. "I tried to bring her back. I Sang until my throat was raw, until … " she paused, looking unsure if she should continue. "I wasn't strong enough, Suqata. I thought that maybe you could succeed where I had failed: open a door, even if only for a moment. Then maybe I could see her. Save her. After all this time, I thought I knew what I was doing, but even after all of my reading and preparation, I still didn't pay attention to the warnings." She then pulled the book she had been reading between them, opening it to a darkly illustrated page. On it was a grim image of the creature they had seen that day, thin and hellishly frightening. Auralyn placed her finger on the line of text beneath the drawing and read it aloud. "'And beware the crossroads between waking and dream, for there dwell the *Varcuya*, the spirit walkers. Avert your eyes and cover thine ears, for they are the very end of men.'" She quickly closed the book again and looked away. "It was right there the whole time and I didn't believe it. It seems silly now, to believe only the parts you want to and discard the rest, but I wanted to see Mother again so badly. It was foolish, I know, but I felt I had to at least try, but I never wanted to put you in danger, never, and for that I am sorry." She pulled her knees in close to her chest and wrapped her arms around them and lowered her head.

"There is a letter on the table with my seal that should explain everything to your Captain Graye. He should take you back to your position as swordbearer, if you wish it."

Before Suqata really knew why, he reached out and wrapped his hand around hers, squeezing gently but firmly. Auralyn looked up and saw for the first time the young man was smiling.

"I knew you were trouble the moment I first saw you, you know that?" he said, trying to stay straight faced. "But to think you had come all this way to learn word weaving was never something I would have imagined. Believe me, I know what it is like to lose

someone and not understand why. If you had asked me to Sing that Song, I probably would have. It's like you said before, I'm generally more curious than cautious. I've tried to be one thing so long that I had almost forgotten that about myself." Suqata looked around at the books strewn across the bed. "Are all these about the Songs of your people?"

Auralyn nodded, not quite sure what the young Chinequewa was building up to.

"Well then, Lady Auralyn, we find ourselves in a strange situation. You need my help, and I will need yours. I have no recollection of my home before I was taken. Maybe in these books, I can find a way to remember what I've lost. So, we will find our answers together. But no more lies, and when we are done you will have no further reason to keep me here, correct?"

"Yes, Suqata. And I promise, no more lies."

They sat for a while longer there, silently considering the danger they were now tempting, while above them glowed the delicate blue-white aura of the weir light.

# CHAPTER 13
# GRAYE AND COLD

TIME PASSES SLOWLY DURING THE WINTER MONTHS, MOVING WITH the steady cadence of a slowed heartbeat. It is as if the seconds and hours had frozen along with the rest of the world. The trickle of visitors to The Hollow had slowed to barely nothing, and the once bustling marketplace is now replaced with empty stalls and the shadows of townsfolk moving about their business, shoulders hunkered down against the frigid wind. The river docks are all but empty, save for the odd ferry bringing woodsmen downriver from logging camps to the east.

As the daylight hours grow short, the windows of every house become alight with the warm glow of hearths and candles, and the chimneys send out the inviting smells of baking bread, honeyed cakes, and pots filled with thick stews bubbling on the fire wafting into the late afternoon air. You could feel a sense of excitement growing. Musicians could be heard playing in the taverns, and the sounds of their music blend into the air that is now seasoned with wonderful smells and the distant sounds of laughter. Soon, colored lanterns of blue, red, and green are hung from the corners of the houses and buildings, and every heart in Orin's Hollow knows that the time they have been waiting for is almost upon them. The Night of the Sundering is on its way.

At the manor, the hum of anticipation moved about the rooms and corridors like a living thing. The servant girls' excited whispering had reached a point that Mistress Hodges had begun to march throughout the house breaking up small chatting sessions amongst the house staff. Obrie was the worst of all, brokering gossip like a market day fish monger. Adding to the fervor was the news that Lord Brockholm was planning a gala party at the manor for festival: a first for the people of town. Auralyn had taken ill again and had been confined to her rooms for the week leading to

Sundering. This left her and Suqata with only rumors and each other to pass the time.

"I don't see what all the fuss is about," she said, blowing a stray strand of hair away from her eyes, "it's just another party. A chance for the well-to-do to come and strut about my father like so many overstuffed peacocks."

"What's a peacock?" Suqata asked, looking up from the large book that lay across his lap. It was just after midday, and he and Auralyn had spent most of the morning together poring over old manuscripts and yellowed texts.

"Never mind that. The point is that it's just going to be another stuffy old party for stuffy old people."

"And spiced cider. Don't forget that. Obrie would never forgive me if I didn't mention it," Suqata said very seriously.

"See what I mean? Just another party."

Suqata sighed. "Spoken like a true little Kaelish princess, if you ask me. Makes me wonder if you outlanders even know what Sundering is all about in the first place."

Auralyn's face alighted with the challenge. She reached over and pulled forth the large red tome that was her constant reference, flipped expertly through the pages, wetting her finger with every other flip, until she came to the entry she desired.

"Sundering, as recorded by Sir Anthony Crocker the explorer, is the customary winter celebration of northern colonial tribes. The practice of singing, feasting, and the ceremonial visiting of neighbors has been widely adopted by settlers, and is always performed on the winter solstice, the Sundering of the calendar year." With a smile and a flourish, she closed the book.

"Impressive, m'lady. We are now quite certain that you have the fine ability to read. Very nice, by the way."

Auralyn responded by chucking one of the smaller, nearby books at Suqata. "Look who's become cheeky? Our dear friend Suqata the Long Face," she laughed.

"I only meant that traditions are more than what can be

140

written down in a book. They have meaning, and substance. I can remember when I was a child, Hopano and I would sit up and watch the dancing in the slave quarters, and the embers flying free from the open fires, floating up to the sky like hundreds of tiny fireflies. And, as is custom, we would all walk from fire to fire and say to each other, *namu nashta*. It means, 'we are together,' and that no one had anything to fear that night. Those were the only times I remember feeling part of something bigger than just Hopano and me. It was like being part of the tribe. We were protected."

"From what?" Auralyn asked, quietly watching her young friend speak. Suqata noticed her do this sometimes, especially when he spoke of his youth in the camps. Her gaze held a mixture of wonder and sadness that left him a little uneasy.

"Spirits. Ghosts. Who knows? Hopano was never one for giving up answers about those kinds of things." He returned his attention to the book before him, but he could still feel her watching him for what seemed like a long time, quietly contemplating his secrets. When there was a knock at the door and Mistress Hodges let herself in, Suqata was a little glad for the interruption.

"Brought you something hot, m'lady. Should do that cold of yours some good." She set the tray down on the book-strewn table, pushing aside the one she had left earlier. She placed her small hand on Auralyn's head and made the same tsk-ing sound she had that very morning. "That fever is taking its merry time coming down. I don't think you're taking very well to the climate, I dare say. You haven't been well since you fell from your horse." The last statement was added especially for Suqata, who noticed Mistress Hodges' disapproving glances, which he decided to ignore.

"Well, maybe if you weren't always checking so, like a mother hen." Auralyn politely removed the older woman's hand and returned to her seat awaiting her to pour.

"Perhaps, mum. Suqata, his lordship has requested you to come to his study immediately. He has need to speak to you."

At this, Suqata and Auralyn looked at each other pointedly. An

audience with Lord Brockholm was a rare occurrence on most days, but even rarer of late. With patrols out still searching for the wolf pack, and the added work of the festival and party, Lord Brockholm had been very busy for the last few weeks.

"Did he say why?" Auralyn asked, sipping demurely at her tea.

"No mum, just that he wanted him there right away."

Suqata set down the books he had been reading and stood to leave, straightening his coat. Auralyn watched him leave, a slight smile disguising the worry in her eyes. Had her father learned about what they were up to: reading through her mother's old books trying to learn more about the Songs? By the time he was at the door, there came a faint sound of humming and slightly spoken words, like the clink of fine crystal. As it rose then ended just as quickly, Auralyn spoke.

*"Ara nawat quvé. Que may a tawai tu'ki manoa,"* she said in Tanaskowa, as clearly as if she had spoken the language from birth. Suqata had been teaching her the languages of tribes, and she had proven to be quick study. He smiled and nodded.

*"Kwi 'nato.* You're getting quite good, m'lady."

Auralyn in turn nodded in acceptance of his praise. The whole while Mistress Hodges watched on in silence with a confused sort of pull to the corners of her mouth.

Lord Brockholm's study was located in the middle of the manor, just above the grand entry hall. The double doors of the entryway seemed to get a lot of use, with servants and merchants and ranking Black Guard always coming and going, but Suqata had yet to set foot inside. When he approached them, he was greeted by a sharply dressed steward. Knowing the young Chinequewa on sight, he turned and announced his name into the study.

"Suqata, valet to the Lady Auralyn," he said, and returned to his post.

"Come in, lad," the governor said, beckoning him in with a polite wave. Suqata did as requested. The room was immense, almost the same size as the great hall below it, with a high vaulted ceiling,

towering shelves filled with volume upon volume of books, and tall windows looking out onto the gardens and barracks beyond. Everything was very orderly, except for the desk that sat in the center of the space. It was covered in papers, open notebooks, and maps of the region. In truth, it looked a great deal like Auralyn's table in her quarters, always covered with the remnants of yesterday's work. Lord Brockholm was not alone when Suqata came in. Seated before his desk was another man Suqata recognized right away as the town priest, Pious Higgins, a small, older man with a crown of fly-away white hair that apparently never wanted to stay in one place.

As he approached the governor motioned him forward and drained the last contents of his teacup. Suqata couldn't help but think to himself what an odd sort of man the governor had turned out to be. He was bookish and thoughtful in a land where most men respected strength over intelligence, but Suqata could help but respect him in spite of all that.

"Thank you for coming so quickly, young man," the governor said in good cheer. "I'm sure you know of our venerable priest, Pious Higgins. He's up from The Hollow to talk about some very important ... town business."

"Yes sir. Good day to you, my lord," Suqata said, bowing as he was trained.

"Well met, young sir," the priest replied, with a great smile creasing his already wrinkled face. He cut his eyes to the governor for a moment before saying, "You are Captain Graye's young swordbearer, are you not? I have seen you about in his company."

Before Suqata could answer, Lord Brockholm spoke up. "Such a bright lad! It didn't take long for us to see he would be a great asset here in the manor, so he is now valet to the Lady Auralyn. Speaking of my daughter, how is she today?"

"Much better, sir," Suqata answered quickly. When he saw the concern written on the governor's worry-drawn face he added, "or, at least that is what she would have me tell you, sir."

Lord Brockholm laughed in a weary sort of way. "Too right you are, lad. Auralyn is very much like her mother in that respect. She's never been one to draw a lot of fuss. I will go see her myself after we are done here, but business must come first. I have a message I need you to deliver to Captain Graye as soon as possible."

"Yes, sir."

Lord Brockholm removed a small, folded letter from the desk drawer and handed it to Suqata. It had a thick wax seal affixed to it, stamped with Brockholm's crest: a hand holding a flaming torch.

"This is to be seen by the captain and no other, do you understand?"

"Yes, your lordship." Suqata bowed again to the governor and Pious Higgins, then turned to leave, but as he did the governor stood from his seat.

"One last thing, my boy," he said. He walked to Suqata and stood before him, wringing his hands. "You were the captain's servant for quite some time, am I correct?"

"Ever since I was a boy, m'lord. Seven seasons." Suqata's scar flared with a phantom ache at the thought of it.

"Would you call him a ... violent man?" Lord Brockholm asked casually.

"It's not my place to say, m'lord."

"Indulge us, please."

Suqata froze and tried to think through his response. Captain Graye was a soldier and had to deal with the chance of violence everyday, but for some reason he felt this was not what Lord Brockholm was asking. Pious Higgins sat quietly in his chair, pretending not to be concerned. The whole thing made Suqata feel uncomfortable, the unexpected candor from highborns, so he decided to tread lightly.

"I'm not sure what you mean, m'lord," he replied.

"No disrespect to your old master, of course, young man. I would just like to get a better understanding of the man. He is a strict follower of the old order, is he not?"

"Yes, m'lord. His father was a Knight of Ascalion, blooded in the Umbarian Wars. He's told me so many times."

Lord Brockholm's brow knotted. "I knew Sir Alton, years ago. He and my father were both part of that ancient order. They are … stern men, and very zealous about their convictions."

"The knights have guided the empire for generations, Lord Brockholm," the priest interjected. "Surely warriors are permitted to be stern men, as you put it?"

"Not in the world we are trying to create, sir," Brockholm replied, his jaw set. "Not when peace is so tenuous. Graye would have us go on witch-hunts to ferret out demons instead of dealing with the problems at hand. That will only bring more fear. This is the reason the knights have fallen out of favor. It's time for a new way."

The Pious did not seem convinced. "I'm not sure your father would have supported that," he said dismissively.

"Probably not, but that is why bloody men meet bloody ends."

Before they could speak again, Suqata tried to break the tension by answering the original question as honestly as he could.

"He is a hard man, m'lord," he said, "but no more than what his command requires. But sometimes, living in the wilds can make hard men grow cold inside."

"Indeed, it does. Well said." Lord Brockholm regarded Suqata for a moment, then placed his hand on his shoulder. "I do have one more task for you, my boy, and only now do I believe I can entrust it to you. The captain has been under some added … stress as of late. His behavior has been in question. I would like you to observe him as you deliver this message, since you know him better than any of his men. Report back to me this evening and tell me what you see. Can you do this for me?"

Suqata answered the only way he could. "Yes sir."

As Suqata hurried across the courtyard towards the barracks, he heard the all too close sound of screams, followed by the crack of a

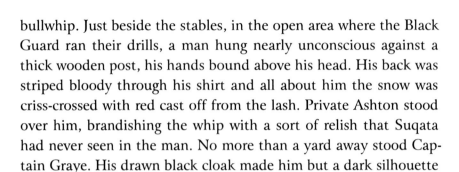

bullwhip. Just beside the stables, in the open area where the Black Guard ran their drills, a man hung nearly unconscious against a thick wooden post, his hands bound above his head. His back was striped bloody through his shirt and all about him the snow was criss-crossed with red cast off from the lash. Private Ashton stood over him, brandishing the whip with a sort of relish that Suqata had never seen in the man. No more than a yard away stood Captain Graye. His drawn black cloak made him but a dark silhouette against the snowy field beyond.

"Again," he yelled, his voice echoing in the emptiness.

Ashton smiled and brought the whip down again with a sharp crack. The man bellowed and then fell silent again. He hung there, limp and quivering, obviously too drained to make any other effort in his defense. When he looked up to watch as Suqata approached, his eyes were full of pleading and pain. Before Graye could call for the private to strike again, Suqata called out.

"Captain, sir. I have a message for you." He strode quickly into the field. Ashton seemed displeased with the interruption, but Captain Graye watched Suqata's approach with a cool and disinterested manner.

"My dark son has returned," he said with an eerie grin. "Come to see your old master after so many weeks. And with gifts no less."

"Hope he brought enough for everyone," Ashton whispered, which earned him a cold stare from his superior.

Suqata bowed before Graye, fighting the almost overwhelming urge to do so as a swordbearer would. He handed over the sealed message and Graye held it as if it were the least important of things, just a handful of nuisance waiting to cast aside.

"How are things faring in the manor, boy? You have been sorely missed at the barracks."

"They are fine, captain." Suqata replied.

"And the Lady Auralyn? How does she fare? I heard she is not well of late?"

"She grows stronger by the day." *Which is not a lie*, Suqata thought.

"Good. She is quite a fair little thing, isn't she? Someone should keep a closer eye on her. We would hate for anything to befall her. You must pay her my best regards, won't you?"

Strangely, this line of questioning made Suqata feel ill at ease, so he kept his answers brief.

"I will do as you wish, sir," he said. The whole thing felt odd, to worry over such pleasantries as some man lay bleeding not six yards away. Suqata's eyes fell on the stranger for only a second, but Graye was quick to notice.

"Oh yes. I know it's horrible, but someone must take measures with these folk. Have you ever seen a witch before, Suqata?"

The question caught the young Chinequewa off guard. "No sir. Never. But, you knew that of course."

"Of course. Yes of course. This man, a slave in Maester Addams' stable, was caught casting spells over his master's stock. Some of the animals have now gone missing, so he was brought to me for justice. But there is only one way to deal with these kind of creatures, and it just so happens that our Private Ashton has a talent with the lash." The corners of Graye's mouth seemed to twitch, fighting back a satisfied smirk. In that moment, Suqata wondered if he had ever really known the man at all. After half his life of bowing and bending to Captain Horatio Graye's will, he had seen him be hard and unyielding firsthand, almost to the level of cruelty. But never, not once, had he seen him take pleasure in someone's pain. The very thought of it made Suqata want to stand clear of him.

"I was told the message was urgent, sir, and from the hand of Lord Brockholm himself." Suqata said nodding towards the envelope. He watched as Graye broke the seal and read. Even without knowing the contents of the letter, he could tell it didn't bode well. As he read, the captain's face took on a hard countenance as his eyes moved over each word until at last he crumpled the letter in his black-gloved hands.

"Curse him for a damn fool," he growled, casting the now balled-up parchment to the ground. His hot gaze then fell on

Suqata. "You knew about this, didn't you?" His dark form almost pulsated with rage.

"I knew nothing of the contents of your message, master," Suqata said. He slipped back into his old, familiar role without hesitation. How many times had he faced this man's anger? Strange, but after so many years, Captain Graye's voice still had a way of sending shivers up the young man's spine. The fear had been beaten into him over the years, but now it was flavored with the bitter taste of shame.

"Stop, Private Ashton. We have orders to release this wretch." He almost spat the words out.

The look on Ashton's face was one of pure disappointment, like that of a sallow-faced child robbed of his favorite toy.

"Stop? But captain ... "

"That was not a request, private!" This time, when Graye spoke, there was an obvious snarl to his words, like the slow rumble of distant thunder. "Release him, now!" Ashton lowered his head like a whipped dog. He pulled his knife from his belt and cut the rope that secured the prisoner to the post, and the man fell to the ground in a heap.

"Men like Brockholm will never understand, boy. But we do, don't we?" Graye said, and looked off towards the forest. "We know there are forces in this world that would destroy us. Forces beyond the world of men. My father knew this as well, and your people destroyed him for it. The Knights of Ascalion came to rid this new land of its demons and evil gods—to win it for Providence and right, but on one dark night the Chinequewa came and gave it back to them. Now, the tide is rising again, and I am the only man who can keep it at bay."

For an instant, there was an eerie cold that swept over Suqata's shoulders, and when the captain turned to address him again, a glint of silver appeared to shine cruelly in his eyes.

"You go back to the manor house, boy," the captain said, regaining his composure, "and tell our dear governor that this man is still alive, but against my wishes. Soon he will understand he has

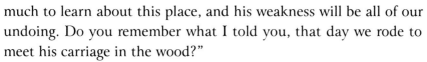

much to learn about this place, and his weakness will be all of our undoing. Do you remember what I told you, that day we rode to meet his carriage in the wood?"

Suqata shook his head.

"I said that the time will come when you will have to side with the monsters you know, or those you do not. Remember that, Suqata."

"Yes, captain. I do remember."

Suqata turned to walk back the way he came, listening as the beaten man lay muttering in snow, "It was a protection. A protection against the wolves. I was trying to protect the horses from the wolves."

GOVERNOR BROCKHOLM'S DOORS WERE CLOSED once Suqata was back in the manor, so he relayed the message of the prisoner's release to his valet, editing Captain Graye's less respectful words. Even now, after everything that had happened, Suqata still felt the need to keep Graye's secrets. The whole experience had left him feeling unsettled. Why would the Black Guard be hunting witches? And why no concern for the wolves that had attacked them? It was as if the world Suqata had known outside of the manor's walls had changed, and not for the better. In his heart, Suqata could feel something coming. Something bad.

When he returned to Auralyn's chamber, he was in for another surprise. Standing before him was the young woman he had left just a few hours ago, but almost unrecognizable. She now wore a village girl's dress: pretty and well made, but nothing compared to the finery she usually wore. Her hair was down, the fall of her thick curls framing her face. Although she was still a little pale from her fever, her growing smile belied anything but excitement.

"You're going to have to wear a cloak over that uniform," she said with a wink.

"Why exactly is that?" Suqata replied.

"We are going into town, and I don't want to be gawked at the whole time." She continued getting ready, ignoring the bewildered look on Suqata's face as she moved about the room.

"Auralyn? What is this all about? Just this morning you were telling me how silly these festivals are and now we are rushing off to The Hollow, for what? Change your mind about the honeyed-cider?"

Auralyn stopped for a moment and looked at Suqata. "I was asking Mistress Hodges about it, and she told me that tonight would be special. There is someone coming to town tonight: someone we need to meet."

"And who would that be?"

"Someone like you, Suqata. A Chinequewa."

# CHAPTER 14
# THE TALE OF WOLF & CROW

AURALYN WOULD HEAR NO PROTEST AS SHE FINISHED PREPARING TO leave, and all of Suqata's questions were deflected with a coy smile and wave of her hand.

"Could you straighten that up before we go? You're a dear," she said as she flitted about the room, beaming and alive with excitement. Even the pallor of her cheeks had faded, replaced with a warm rosy color. Within minutes, Suqata was escorting her down the front steps of the manor and into an awaiting carriage.

"Hodges isn't going to like this," Suqata grumbled, glancing over his shoulder at the house doors. He was just waiting for them to fly open and the short housekeeper burst out, red faced and fuming.

"She's busy with preparations for the party. She won't even miss us," Auralyn replied. "Besides, we'll be back in a few hours."

The driver doffed his cap to them as they climbed into the cab, and then promptly cracked his whip, stirring the team into motion. They rumbled down the manor road, past the snow-laden trees, and out towards the outer gates.

"So, are you going to tell me what this is all about, or are you going to lead me around by the nose for the rest of the evening?" Suqata's voice had an edge of impatience to it, a fact that Auralyn was quick to notice.

"Don't be angry, Su. I couldn't tell you in the house. There are so many gossips about these days and Father would have known we were leaving before we even reached the steps. Not to mention you would have probably told Obrie."

"I would not have," he replied. Auralyn only smiled and nodded in her patronizing way.

"I don't like secrets," Suqata said, crossing his arms.

"That's not true. You do like secrets. You just don't like it when you aren't the one keeping them." To this Suqata had no response.

They rode on in silence, both turned to their own window and sulking until finally Auralyn relented. "Since it's bothering you so much, I will tell you. We are going to see a storyteller." She said the words as if their very mention was enough to explain her secrecy, and as she spoke her eyes brightened. She waited on pins and needles for Suqata to join in, which he did not.

"Why all the fuss?" he said, "Storytellers always come to The Hollow for Sundering. Sometimes more than one. Last year Obrie said there was a balladeer at Pious Higgins' house that stayed a fortnight. He rode all the way in from Chancery, and he could juggle and do sleight-of-hand. This is your big surprise?"

Auralyn was a little crestfallen at the news. "Well this one is different. This one is said to be a Chinequewa, born in the northern tribes. Can you believe it! All my books say that storytellers were the history keepers for your people. Every major event was remembered as a tale that was told and told again around the fire. Maybe this man knows something we don't, about the Songs or the wraith creature we saw: something that's not in the books."

"Or perhaps he is an impostor, using the mystery and legends of the Chinequewa to line his pockets. Bigger crowds equal more silver. He's in for a surprise here, though. Orin's Hollow is not too fond of my people."

Auralyn refused to give up. "You are always so negative; here it is we may have a lead to some real answers, and you are disregarding it offhand. This man may know something about what happened to your people and your family." She crossed her arms in a huff and looked away, moving stray curls from her eyes. "Anyways, how often does a blind storyteller come to Orin's Hollow?"

Suqata felt his breath stop. *It can't be,* he thought to himself. *Hopano? But he would be ancient by now. It couldn't be him, could it?* He did not speak for the rest of the ride into town, but it was obvious to Auralyn that her friend was too intrigued to complain now.

IT WAS NOT EVEN SUPPERTIME when they arrived in Orin's Hollow, but

the sun had already hid itself away beyond a dark tapestry of stars. The streets were bustling, though, as groups of families and friends ducked in and out of houses and stores, all of them lit with colored lanterns. From open windows you could see the warm, golden glow of bee's wax candles that sent the subtle fragrance of honey wafting out into the chill night air. The carriage came to a stop in the town square, near the large inn at its center. Outside of the two-story building hung a large wooden sign that swayed in the breeze and bore the words Ye Olde Black Keg. Painted at the bottom of the sign was a weathered image of a drunken man crawling out of the inn's namesake.

The driver wasn't very pleased to hear it would take some hours for Lady Auralyn to see the town and return, but she left the man with some coin and suggested a drink was in order while he waited. His smile and eager acceptance took some of the worry out of the parting.

"You certainly know how to get people to do what you want," Suqata said as they entered the tavern. There was a slight pause in her step, a hesitation in her usually unshakeable confidence, but she quickly smiled to cover it.

"It's a bit of a talent I suppose," she replied.

FOR THE NEXT HOUR THEY travelled throughout the town. Everywhere—from bakery to drink hall to cozy family homes—was filled to overflowing with light and cheer. There were tall draughts of summer ciders and ales passed around as you crossed each threshold, filling the air with the sweet smell of strong apples and cinnamon. Tables were completely covered with cakes and pastries of all kinds, and children ran pell-mell between the legs of their chattering parents. Everywhere they went, the Auralyn and her silent companion were always greeted with good will and the words, *"Namu nashta!"*

Suqata kept to himself for the most part, keeping watch over Auralyn as she danced and mingled with the townsfolk. She was a natural at it, of course, always kind and personable and instantly

likable. It was as if every demure laugh was special, crafted especially for its recipient.

"Being beautiful doesn't hurt either, I'd wager," Suqata said under his breath as Auralyn chatted excitedly with a group of Miller Johnson's daughters. Just then, Auralyn turned his way and smiled and his stomach reacted like he had missed a step coming down a flight of stairs, and he quickly regretted even thinking such a thing. The night went on this way for two hours, as they asked about where they would find the storyteller, but it wasn't until they were in the home of Pious Higgins, the local church leader, that they found their answer.

"I hear he's out past the river, near the millworks," Pious Higgins said, swaying slightly with a tall flagon of cider in his hand. There were a great number of people inside of the priory, feasting at tables and such, but Higgins met everyone at the door, as was tradition. "Native chap came around saying he would tell stories for half the price of the one we had last year. Too bad, you ask me—this one doesn't even juggle. Interesting sort, though, and can he tell a tale that whips you into a state! No one would put him up in their homes, though, so he's out on the other side of the bridge. But that's no place for a young lass like you, miss. The mill folk can be a rough crowd."

"Well, that's why I have my protector here," Auralyn said, linking her arm around Suqata's. He wasn't used to being this close to her, nor feeling the warmth of her hand against his forearm. Within seconds his red-brown cheeks had become even redder. When he saw this, Pious Higgins began to laugh in a deep, rolling baritone.

"Don't look now, miss, but I think your protector is blushing," he bellowed, sloshing a little of his cider on the floor. Suqata was not one to stand around when he felt insulted, so he quickly turned with Auralyn for the door, the sound of Higgins' voice still fresh in his ears. As they did, they ran straight into a familiar and unexpected face.

"Obrie!" Suqata said, his throat tightening with surprise. "What are you doing here?"

Obrie seemed surprised as well, but more pleasantly so than his friend. "Look who's asking questions? Where have you been? I've been looking for you all day." Obrie wore his usual broad smile, but his eyes held a hint of worry, darting this way and that as if he were scanning the room for danger. "You've been a hard man to get a word with, Su, with all the time you've been spending with … " Obrie's eyes became wide and his mouth sat open in an awkward "o" shape as he noticed the young woman on Suqata's arm.

"*Namu nashta*, Obrie," Auralyn said brightly—maybe a little more brightly than necessary. "Are you enjoying the festivities?"

There was an awkward pause before Obrie stammered, "Uhh, yes m'lady. Very much."

"Suqata said you would never forgive us if we did not try this year's cider."

Obrie chanced a smile. "Well, it is the best we've made in some seasons."

There was a moment of uncomfortable silence amongst them, each searching for some kind of distraction from their chance meeting, but when one did not present itself, Suqata stepped in.

"We should be moving on, Obrie. The coach driver wanted us back before it gets too late, right Lynn … I mean m'lady?"

"Of course. I'll wait for you outside," she replied, and walked quickly out into the night. Once she was gone, Obrie couldn't help but stare at his friend, aghast.

"What is going on, Su? She's not supposed to be out of the manor. I know, I heard it from the governor's own maid. This isn't good!"

"I know, but it's complicated and I don't have time to explain." Suqata moved to leave but found Obrie's hand secured urgently around his wrist.

"You do not know what you are getting yourself into. That is why I've been looking for you. Something is wrong at the manor, things you need to know about."

"And you can tell me when this is all over with. Seriously, Obrie, I have to go." Without another word, Suqata walked out into the cold night, leaving Obrie standing in Pious Higgins' doorway. He didn't like keeping things from his oldest friend, but this may have been beyond his ability to explain. He glanced back and noticed something he had not seen in quite some time. Obrie wasn't smiling.

By THE TIME THEY REACHED the millworks, the crowds were beginning to thin out, most having been there for some hours. The bonfires, however, were still aflame and the people who remained had moved in closer to the man who stood before them. Suqata and Auralyn chose a spot away from the others on a stack of fresh cut pine, which was close enough by Suqata's reckoning. Ever since running into Obrie, he couldn't seem to shake the odd feeling that something was wrong, but then again, he had a lot of those feelings of late. Even as he sat there with Auralyn, so close to hearing from this stranger they had chanced so much to see, Suqata couldn't help but wish he had stayed a moment longer to hear what Obrie had to say. Not knowing brought all of his senses into a state of alert, and every dark corner now held the chance of danger or discovery.

When the crowd settled, the storyteller lifted his hand for silence. He was a small man, and in the folds of his hooded cloak Suqata could see long white hair framing a shadowed face. His skin was the color and texture of old leather, and his hands were as knobby as twisted oak branches. The old man lowered his arm and stood perfectly still—so still that his slight humming was the only sign of life.

Auralyn leaned in close to Suqata, whispering into his ear, "Is he really a Chinequewa?" Just as she spoke, the old man moved forward and sat within the emanating light of the fire. Over one of his eyes was an elaborately carved, wooden eye patch that was held in place by a leather strap. His other eye, a cool green, scanned the

crowd with the intensity of a hawk. In an instant, Suqata felt a wave of disappointment come over him.

"No. He's not," he answered Auralyn plainly. "His eyes aren't like mine. Close enough to fool the crowd, but not true Chinequewa."

This was not Hopano, though Suqata realized he secretly had hoped it would be.

When the storyteller spoke, a quiet rumble seemed to fill the mill yard without much effort. A power lingered in it, untrained in the *sen-wa*, but powerful none the less.

"Gather round, children, and hear my tales," he said in a resonant tone. "The tales passed down to me by my father and his father, a man of the Chinequewa tribe far to the north. Although I've never walked these lands before, I know them in my spirit, for in my veins flows the blood of the Silent Ones."

The people in the audience exchanged whispers, and some angry glances, before the storyteller spoke again.

"What story would you have me tell?" he asked, waiting for a response. Someone near the back shouted, *The Tale of the Golden Salmon.* He shook his head and grumbled, "No."

"How about *The Snow Princess*?" a young girl said from up front.

He smiled to her and shook his head. "I've told that one twice today, dear one, and you asked for it both times." A titter of laughter went through the audience, breaking the tension, and he asked again. "What story would you have me tell, for the hour grows late."

"Tell us one about the Spirit World," Auralyn said, drawing the attention of the crowd. The storyteller considered the request, then he situated himself so that his legs were crossed before him, and his hands lay palm down on his knees.

"That is not one story, dear one, but many woven together like the colored threads of a cloak. I can tell you one of these stories. Because it is the solstice, I will tell you of The Sundering—The Tale of Wolf and Crow."

Everyone instantly became still. All chatter ended, and even

the small babe in the front row nestled closely to its mother's chest until all was silent.

"This world was not always as it is now," he began.

ONCE, A HUNDRED THOUSAND LIFETIMES *ago, and more seasons than we will ever know, man walked the forests of the world with ancient spirits of nature called the mahko, and magic ran in the land like blood through veins. During this time, man had raised great kingdoms from the dirt, and was an awesome power amongst all the creatures that lived. It was through their ability to hear and sing the* sen-wa—*The Great Songs of Changing sung by The One Voice at the beginning of all things. With this power, the kingdoms of man grew in strength. Soon, their power rivaled that of the* mahko. *They were the first to walk in the world, and were ancient and powerful, but few when compared to men. So, there was a great war between the powers of man and spirit, and many were destroyed. This angered The One Voice, and to make an end of it he decided to sing out into the void and split our world asunder, separating men and spirits forever. But before this was accomplished, two* mahko *changed the course of destiny forever. These were Garro Knocta the Wolf, and Cora Vaco the Crow. It came to pass in the cold of winter, a night much like tonight, that the two spirits met each other upon a high hill overlooking a great valley. Of all the* mahko, *Wolf and Crow lamented most what was coming, for they loved the Waking World the most, each in his own way. Cora Vaco the Crow loved the secrets and inventions of man, and would spend his days flying amongst them collecting any piece of knowledge he could find—sometimes even the secrets kept by the dead. Of all the* mahko, *he possessed the greatest understanding of the Songs of Changing and Ending, although he had no power to sing them. This was forbidden, since the* mahko *came from the* sen-tal, *the Songs of Making. Cora-Vaco did not care. He was impetuous. Garro Knocta's love for the Waking World was quite different. What he desired most was the hunt. For centuries he and his children had run the long paths of the wilderness, taking what they wished. Now, all that was about to end. When these two met, they greeted each other with some caution, for though they were brother spirits, Wolf and Crow were not friends. Crow was in a particularly good mood that night, which never seem to bode well for Wolf.*

*"Why so happy, brother?" Garro Knocta said with a rumbling growl. "Don't you know that by the time the sun rises, you and I will be cut off from this place forever?" Cora Vaco smiled broadly and gave his brother a wink. "Yes it is true, my brother," he said, "and sad for most, but I will not be leaving with you tonight."*

*"How can that be?" Garro Knocta said, angered that once again Cora Vaco knew something he did not.*

*"I have learned the secret art that has been forbidden from us since man first stood on land. I have learned how to take the power of man to walk as they do in The Waking World." Wolf laughed as loud as he could, trying to shame his brother, but Crow's smile never wavered and once again Wolf was angered.*

*"There is nothing you can do, Crow, that I cannot do as well. Am I not stronger and fiercer then you will ever be?" he barked.*

*"Well, I propose a wager. Before this night is over, we will meet back on this spot with man. Then we shall see which of us is the most clever." So it was agreed, and the two spirits left into the inky black of night and hours later they both returned. This time Wolf came with his children, but both he and Crow also had a man with them as well.*

*"Come then, brother," Garro Knocta cried, "witness me take this man's power, and then my children and I will hunt in The Waking World until the end of all things." Crow never spoke. He only watched with disinterest. After a moment of focus, Wolf let out a bone-chilling howl up to the moon. The sound was filled with spirit magic that shook the trees to their roots and covered the branches with a thick coating of frost. Just as quickly as it had started, the howl came to an end. Then, faster than a winter wind, Wolf bounded onto the man and devoured him whole.*

*"Yes, I can feel it," Wolf cried. "This creature is now a part of me and has filled me with his power. Surely I have won our wager. Admit defeat!" Crow still would not speak. He only stood silently beside the man who had accompanied him. Once again, Wolf felt his anger rise.*

*"Say I have won!" Wolf bellowed, and again Crow did not say a word.*

*Then, in a blur, Garro Knocta was upon his brother, his teeth flashing in the waning moonlight. He ate Crow all up, leaving only a pile of feathers.*

*"See fool, I am always the victor." Garro Knocta was very full now, so he turned to the man who had come with Crow and said, "Go, you fleshy thing. I am too full to deal with the likes of you. Soon the worlds will split, and you must be gone from here."*

*"Thank you greatly, brother," the man said in Cora Vaco's voice. His eyes flashed of silver light when he smiled and gave Wolf a wink. With that, he skipped quickly into the Waking World, leaving Wolf and his children behind.And so Cora Vaco the Crow stayed in our world as a man, and watches us even to this day, while Garro Knocta the Wolf and his children were punished to live in a world between that of the* mahko *and that of man, still cold from his chilling howl.*

WHEN THE STORY CAME TO an end the crowd stirred to life, as if now free from some spell cast by the storyteller's voice. They all applauded, tossing copper coins on the storyteller's waiting cloak—all, except for Auralyn, whose face held a look of frustration.

"But there must be more," she said aloud, once again drawing the attention of the crowd. "More about the world the *mahko* live in, or this world between and creatures that live there. Can a person still cross between the two? Surely there is more to tell."

The storyteller watched her with strange mixture of pity and fear before answering. "Yes, there are stories of ghosts and such," he said. "Stories so chilling they would fill your mind with nightmares. Those are not for tonight, and definitely no stories about crossing the border between our worlds. That kind of thing is the realm of devilry and witchcraft . They traffic in that kind of knowledge."

Auralyn was undaunted. "Please tell me. I need to know," she said. "I'll give you all I have with me, with more to follow." From her pocket she removed her money pouch and threw five large gold coins onto the storyteller's cloak. Everyone looked at them in awe, some having never seen that much gold in one place, while others looked about nervously. Eventually the old man scooped up the

coins in his withered hands and walked slowly to Auralyn. He then took her hands in his and glared at her sternly.

"My child, I have not the answers you seek, nor would I give them if I had. You are searching for forbidden knowledge, and though knowledge casts light into the darkest of places, some shadows are best left unstirred." Then, without another word, he turned to leave. When Auralyn looked down, she saw that he had left her the five large gold coins, heavy in her open palm.

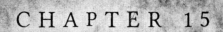

# CHAPTER 15
# POWER CHANGES EVERYTHING

SUQATA AND AURALYN WAITED TOGETHER IN THE MILLWORKS CLEARING until all of the bonfires were extinguished, leaving blackened pits where once was warmth and life. Columns of ash and steam twisted free from the smoldering wood, floating skyward like ghosts pulling free of the earth. With the crowds gone and fires out, the millworks took on a different character. Ropes and tools hung from the wood columns that held the roof aloft, swinging ominously in the long shadows.

"We should go, Lynn. I don't want to linger here," Suqata said. He had never liked the mill. The smell of machine oil and sa dust reminded him too much of the camps, but his true reason for leaving was more than just that. He had an unshakeable feeling that he and Auralyn were being watched. Ever since their run-in with Obrie, Suqata had felt a strange sense of anticipation hanging in the cold night air, just waiting to drop. It was that feeling the urged him to leave. Auralyn followed without argument, and together they walked slowly towards the road back in the direction of town. Torches had been lit all along the path to the bridge and beyond, although it was almost unnecessary under the silvery-blue light of the full moon.

"You can say it, if you want," she whispered, barely loud enough for Suqata to hear. When he glanced her way she quickly pulled up the hood of her cloak hiding her face, supposedly against the wind. The moonlight seemed to hover around her at that moment, embracing her silhouette. "I would, if the tables were turned."

"I don't know what you're talking about, m'lady," he replied, then quickly regretted his formal tone. He wished the closeness that had grown between them in the past weeks didn't always feel so delicate, as if one wrong word could smash it to pieces.

"You can say, 'I told you so.' I'm sure it must be just eating you

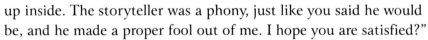 

up inside. The storyteller was a phony, just like you said he would be, and he made a proper fool out of me. I hope you are satisfied?"

"No. Not at all. I too was hoping for more," he replied honestly, wishing he could have come up with something more encouraging.

"Well, I'm sorry for wasting your time," she said.

Suqata couldn't help but notice the weariness in her voice. Auralyn looked so fragile all of a sudden, as if some part of her usually obstinate spirit was being leached away, and with it her strength. Even the character of her stride as they walked together had changed. So, he tried again to be uplifting.

"It wasn't a waste of time," he said. "You followed your instincts, and even though he wasn't what he claimed to be, the storyteller was special. I've never met another of my people besides Hopano, even a half blood. I could almost feel some connection the moment he started to speak. So the whole thing wasn't a total loss."

Auralyn looked up from the shadows of her hood and smiled weakly. "I guess I shouldn't carry on so. You missed an opportunity tonight as well, and for that I am sorry. We've been poring over books for weeks, and still we aren't any closer to answers about anything. I can see why you walked away from this mess and magic. It never seems to lead anywhere."

"You rely too much on those musty old books, Lynn," Suqata said. "There was knowledge in that story that can help us, I'm sure of it. And as for the walking away part—I was wrong. I believe we are on to something. For centuries our people had never laid eyes on each other, but here it is that this one thing seems to bind us. The Songs are a link between us, and that is a discovery in and of itself."

Auralyn did not look convinced. "I'm glad you can find something to be positive about in all of this. I feel like I've caused you nothing but grief since the first moment we met. How do you know this isn't all in vain?"

Suqata stopped walking and turned to her. A light snow was beginning to fall, muffling the sounds of the world till all he could hear was his own voice and Auralyn's breath.

"Because, for the first time in my life I feel like things can change," he said. "It is almost funny, with everything I've been taught and have learned about the *sen-wa*, I truly believed until now that nothing ever changes at all, nothing important anyways. The powerful are always thus, and the weak are always under their boot; answers are always just out of reach; and the people we care about, who mean something to us, always go away. These were constants in my life, until I met you. That day on the road, I made a decision to fight, to protect you, and suddenly everything was different."

"Yes, you lost your position," she whispered, "Not a change for the better."

"Who is to say it wasn't? I think that all this time, I've been afraid of things changing. I've wanted to hold on to things the way they are, no matter how bad. That way I couldn't lose them again. But things change, and we can't control it. That is what the Songs have always been about—embracing the change. I just couldn't see it. But now I do, and I'm not afraid anymore. In your own way, you helped me see that." Suqata then held out his hands before her, palms up, and Sang a Song he hadn't uttered in a long time. *"Die e u nashi."* The words were few, and their effect immediate. In Suqata's hands appeared two perfectly smooth stones, both pearl white and flecked with shimmering color that seem to swirl across the surface and into the heart of them.

"They are beautiful," Auralyn said, watching the moonlight play across their surfaces, "what are they?"

"Just river stones. I don't remember where I found them, but I've always known somehow that they came from my home. For me, they served as a kind of proof that it existed, and that I came from somewhere." Suqata reached out and took Auralyn's hand in his own, placing one of the stones within the warmth of her palm and then curling her delicate fingers over it. "I guess I don't need two," he said, still holding her hand and smiling down at her. They stood like that for a long moment, in the silence of the snowfall.

When Auralyn finally met his gaze, her eyes seemed to shine like the river stones, filled with confusion and delight.

"Thank you," she whispered, and before Suqata could reply, Auralyn quickly leaned in and kissed him.

All at once Suqata's senses were alight. His first thought was to pull away, but that was instantly overpowered by the need to stay—to be near her. He closed his eyes and breathed her sweet scent in, and felt the warmth of her lips against his. It was as if time had stopped for them, and in that shimmering moment they had shared a thousand unsaid words. Then, just as quickly as it had begun, it was over, and as Suqata opened his eyes he felt like he was seeing Auralyn for the first time, smiling shyly back at him.

It was only then that he noticed the power around her.

Standing so near her, he heard a faint sound in the stillness, like the mournful cry of a distant chapel bell. It was coming from deep within Auralyn, heavy and resonant, and right away he recognized the sound of it. It was a spirit song: the same one they had sung the day of their ride when the wraith had appeared, but more complex than any he had ever heard or seen. When he looked at her, his face had drained of color, and in that instant her mood changed.

"There is a song that clings to you. I can hear it," Suqata said, his voice hushed and distant. "The same way the Hiding Song clings to me, but far more dangerous." He couldn't help but look aghast. "A *sen-tal* is part of you now. Why would you do such a thing? How?"

"Suqata, wait. Let me explain," she began, as tears were already forming in her eyes, but before she could say another word, fear washed over her face. Something was moving in the shadows of a nearby shed. Suqata turned just in time to see the forms within the darkness take shape, and the sound of low growling announced their coming.

"You are a bigger fool than I thought, boy," said a voice within the darkness. "This didn't need to be bloody, but your little discovery seems to have made it necessary."

From the darkness within a covered shed Suqata could now see the white flash of predatory eyes staring back at him, and from

amidst them came the figures of two men, one holding the other by the throat. When the moonlight fell on him, Private Ashton grinned menacingly and tightened his grip as he dragged Obrie out, trembling beside him.

"I guess I should thank you for that. I do so love it when things get bloody." Ashton was wearing his dark blue uniform, which was torn and filthy. "Your friend here has been very helpful in locating you two." He shook Obrie for emphasis. "Things are coming together quite nicely, wouldn't you say. Now come along, my sweet, we must not keep Father waiting." Obrie tried to speak, but Ashton only shook him harder.

"Please let him go, guardsman." Auralyn said, "We'll come along quietly. There is no need for violence." Her voice was level and matter-of-fact as she tried desperately to hide the fear she felt at that moment. It was a fear that Suqata shared. "The governor will be very happy that you found us safe."

"Oh no, my sweet, I'm afraid you won't be able to talk yourself out of this. Violence is unavoidable tonight. You will come with me, and your young friend here will get the chance to meet my brothers." As they were announced, two hulking shapes slid out of darkness and stood snarling before them. They had once been men, by the look of the clothes most likely millworkers or dock workers, but now they were something else entirely. They were two, heaving silhouettes, their yellow eyes shining menacingly into the night. Suqata's muscles tensed so tightly he could hardly move, but he quickly willed himself forward to stand between Auralyn and the beast-men.

"Come, little girl," Ashton said and beckoned her with one hand. His eyes were now wide and shining just like the beasts at his side. "Don't keep us waiting. Patience is not one of Father's virtues."

"You don't know my father," Auralyn whispered, to which Ashton seemed to take some joy.

"Oh, my dear. Who said I was talking of *your* father?" He smiled yet again, this time the stark moonlight glinted off of long white fangs and off the tips of his dark, curved claws. In an instant all

traces of humanity were torn away, replaced with the wild hunger, and Suqata recognized it instantly.

The wolves had once again come to destroy him.

Suddenly, Ashton lunged forward, casting Obrie to the snowy ground.

Suqata reacted quickly, pulling free the silver dagger from his belt, slashing at the creature's outstretched hands. The blade cut smoothly across the exposed flesh of its palms, burning and hissing where it touched. When he fell to the ground, howling in pain, smoke eked from Ashton's wounds like hot breath in the night air.

"He has silver! Kill him!"

Before the creatures could truly react, Suqata heard Obrie's voice over the sound of growls. "Get out of here, Su!" he bellowed.

Suqata grabbed Auralyn's wrist tight and sped off down the torch-lit path. It sickened him to know that he was leaving his friend, but he knew that Obrie's best bet was for him to lure the wolves away. He knew that all their lives now hung in the balance.

The bridge to town was just in sight, surrounded by the wavering glow of torches, but much too far away to reach before the beasts would be clawing at their heels. Suqata could already feel them hovering behind, keeping a safe distance but always just a breath away from ending them. It would take no effort for the beasts to lunge in for the kill, and all that kept them at bay was the thin length of silver in his hand. When Auralyn cried out, "Suqata! The Spirit Bind!" clarity quickly cut through the panicked chaos in his mind.

*Uiek, kiyi, uiek nu tiyuk, uiek kiyi, uiek manas tuk.* The words rang clear with power and intent, driving the two beast-men back howling. They ran with abandon, both of them breathing in hard gulps of night air as they made their way quickly up the path. Auralyn was beginning to lag, almost falling twice as her feet found drifts of deeper snow.

"Come on, Lynn! We are almost there," Suqata yelled, pulling her up again. "Beyond the bridge is a guards' post. We'll be safe then." But the words fell on deaf ears. She was fading with each

step. By the time they had reached the foot of the bridge, Suqata had to carry her.

The cobbled stones felt welcome under his booted feet, and he thought to cry out to warn the guards he was coming. Just then he felt pain tear across his arm, and Suqata fell hard to the ground. Auralyn lay a few yards away, jolted alert from the fall, and Ashton stood over him, his clawed hand now glistening faintly in the flickering light. The attack had flung the silver blade just out of Suqata's reach.

"You are a lot more trouble than you're worth, boy," Ashton growled. "When father said you were a wordweaver, I think I expected more." Suqata sang out again, as strong and clear as he was able, but the creature before him barely blinked.

"Pointless, boy. I am stronger than my brother. I've learned the benefits of wearing man's flesh. There is nothing you can do to … "

Ashton stopped and turned his gaze towards Auralyn. She was whispering something—something that rang with a power that grew with each word uttered.

"Impossible" was all the creature managed to say. The distraction had been just enough to give Suqata time to act. His fingers found the pommel of the silver dagger, and with a skill that belied his wound, he spun the blade and drove it home, snapping it off at the hilt. Ashton's eyes were wide with pain and surprise as smoke billowed from dagger embedded in his chest. As he fell forward, he spoke plainly with his last breath. "Kill them, my brothers. Kill them now."

Suqata heard the sound of the beast-men's booted feet thundering across the ground, descending on their prey, the air filled now with their snarls and howls of hunger, but just as they reached them, Auralyn's song reached its peak.

*Shi eash e yota, cama di e, camash qua eshta, cata matea.*

In an instant it was all gone. The wolves; the bridge; the very world had melted away with the last ring of the song, and all Suqata could see were Auralyn's azure eyes looking back at him, saying a thousand words and none at all. Then, even they were gone.

PART 4

# WHERE SPIRITS WALK

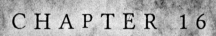

# CHAPTER 16
# THE DARK WOODS

DEATH IS A TRANSITION, FROM THE PHYSICAL TO THE PURELY SPIRItual. Gone are the sensations we knew in life, or perhaps just elevated to a higher understanding.

This, however, was not death.

The world had in an instant become a swirl of grey water and numbing cold. Suqata thrashed his arms against the river's urgent pull, the current coiling around his body like a mass of liquid snakes, constricting and strangling the air from his lungs. He reached up frantically for the surface, but found only more cold water. When Suqata opened his eyes there was only a blur of shadows and movement, but through the rush he could see the uneven glimmer of distant light. With every passing second it seemed further and further away. His muscles screamed with the strain of fighting the water's impossible strength, all the while feeling his own strength wane and his body fail. Where was the shore? How long had he been under? His lungs were burning now and his legs began to cramp from the constant kicking. All at once, Suqata felt his hand break the surface, and he shot up from the icy chaos of the river. Cool air raced in to fill his eager lungs, reviving his mind and his senses.

Suqata was alive.

The current took him a good distance farther down the ever-widening river, but he was content to just float and be carried for the time being. When the shore was close enough, he swam towards the shallows until he could feel piles of smooth stones beneath his feet. Every step out of the water was an effort, with his clothes soaked through and weighing him down, but soon he collapsed onto the sloping riverbank in a sodden heap. Shivering and exhausted, he closed his eyes.

When he came to, Suqata was terribly cold. He didn't know how long he had lain there, but his cloak had begun to turn stiff as the river water in it froze. It made a crackling sound when he stirred to move. He placed his hands onto the ground and tried to slowly push himself up, but felt a sharp pain lance through his arm. When he looked down to examine it, he found his sleeve had been shredded and underneath the tears, three ragged cuts ran the length of his right forearm. The wound was fresh, but had been washed clean by the river. Quickly, memories began to race back into his addled mind: the bridge, the wolves, the image of Auralyn running into the night, and the last sound of Obrie's screams. Everything came back to him in a rush of pain and confusion that made him double over. After the images stopped, and his head ceased to throb, Suqata sat back against the bank.

"Obrie," he whispered, fighting back tears. His friend was gone, Auralyn was in terrible danger, and here he was powerless to do anything about it. "What is this place?" he said aloud. His voice didn't carry. Cradling his wounded arm, Suqata stood up uneasily and took in his surroundings. He was standing at the bottom of a steep bank covered in tree roots and river stones at its foot. Wearily he climbed the bank, grabbing the roots to steady himself until he reached the top and could get a better look around. The bridge and manor house were nowhere to be seen, and gone were any signs of the road back to Orin's Hollow. In fact, there were no signs any man had ever set foot in this place. There were only woods, grey and fog laden, but lit as if cool evening light lay just beyond the mist. The curtain of murk was so thick that he could not see the tops of the birch trees that stood about him like silent sentinels. They reached up to the sky and disappeared. The forest floor was covered in snow, but here and there Suqata could make out patches of exposed ground strewn with orange and red leaves, as if this place were in the last days of autumn. The most unsettling thing, however, was the absence of sound; no birds sang, and Suqata could not hear the sound of wind through the trees. Even the river was a distant rush when it should have been a torrent. It was as if time had frozen here, still and powerless to change.

Quickly Suqata's thoughts shifted to survival. He pulled the tattered shreds of his coat sleeve away and tied them securely around his deep cuts. The bandage was crude, and he winced as he pulled it tight, but at least the bleeding had stopped. Then he shed his frozen cloak, which sloshed unceremoniously onto the ground.

Just then, Suqata could hear the sound of splashing coming from the water's edge, followed by guttural cries and coughing as three dark forms took shape and burst to the surface of the river. Suqata hid himself behind a low stand of brush and watched quietly. Had the beasts been washed here as well? What stepped onto the shore was far from anything Suqata could have possibly expected.

Three creatures now stood dripping in the shallows. To say they were the same wolves would never capture the awful majesty of what they had become, nor would it reflect the pure, unadulterated fear that the young Chinequewa felt after setting eyes on them. The creatures now stood totally erect, in some cruel mockery of men but with the stooped poise of hunters. Their sinewy arms were thin but obviously strong, and their large hands ended in viciously curved claws. Above their shoulders they were anything but man-like. The neck and heads were those of the overlarge wolves that had chased down Suqata, Auralyn, and Obrie: two of them brown in color, and one a smoky grey. The grey had a fresh burn around the front of its snout.

"I almost had her," it growled, "I could have almost tasted her blood on my tongue, brothers. If it weren't for that worthless meat-suit! Men's legs are even worse than useless in a hunt."

"It doesn't matter, Smoke," said one of the brown. "Father will be angry that we lost the girl, and more so that you lost the man-body that he gave you. He will rip you, rip you, and rip you."

"Quiet, Ripper! Soon we will all have to tell Father that we lost the girl and our bodies. ALL OF US!"

The other two lowered their heads, looking genuinely worried, and Suqata shuddered to imagine a creature that put fear into monsters such as these. One thing was certain, Suqata had to put as

much distance as possible between himself and these wolves before this father of theirs made himself known. He moved cautiously, barely even letting out a breath, until he was a few feet away from the edge of the embankment. The creatures were just beyond his sight, and as he turned to make good his escape Suqata's ragged sleeve caught onto a low branch, snapping it. The sound might as well have been a whip crack.

"What was that?" one of the wolves barked. Suqata could hear the deep rumble of growls, followed by sharp snarls and cries. "I smell something, big brother." There was a long intake of breath as one of them sniffed the air. "It's close. Hot and tangy-sweet. It's blood! Man blood!"

In an instant, they were on the hunt, sniffing at every surface on the riverbank, searching for their prey, but Suqata swore not to give them the satisfaction of an easy kill. Before they could properly find his trail, Suqata was off into the woods running as fast as his weary legs would carry him into the mist.

THE SILVERY TRUNKS OF THE birch trees blurred past Suqata as he ran, his lungs burning with each deep breath of cold air. He pushed himself on, past the throbbing numbness in his legs and deep shuddering chill that ran through his entire body. *How close are they?* he thought to himself, but he dared not look back. Instead, he let the images of their saber-sharp fangs, gnashing and biting at his neck, spur him on faster and faster through the woods. He had no idea where he was going, and had even lost his bearing from the river. The fog became denser the farther he ran, and ragged tree limbs and brambles pulled at his clothes like gnarled fingers reaching out to hold him. Then, a mournful sound rang out through the silence. It was howling, as cold and hungry as winter itself. The wolves were very close, and gaining fast.

Running was clearing Suqata's mind, helping him to focus past the fear. In this clarity, he had a realization. *These creatures want me to run myself out. They want me to tire so that I can't fight.* The thought of being chased down like some scared rabbit was almost too much to bear. He refused to die that way.

"Come and get me, dogs!" he yelled with all his might, filling the thick air with the power of his voice. *"Uiek, kiyi, uiek nu tiyuk, uiek kiyi, uiek manas tuk."* Even at a distance, he could hear the pack cry out in response to his Song, and a chorus of howls answered his challenge. Just ahead, Suqata could make out a clearing through the fog. He slowed as he came to its edge, looking about frantically until he found what he needed. A thick branch lay at the base of a tree within reach. He grabbed and broke it to about arm's length with a resounding snap. He spun about in the mist, holding the club before him as if it were his old master's sword.

"My name is Suqata, you mindless mutts, and I don't die easily," he yelled. Brave words come easily when you have nothing else to cling to, and at that moment bravado was all Suqata had. "Come out where I can see you."

Like death's shadow, the creatures came skulking through the brush, pushing through the curtain of fog. The three wolves appeared, bent low to ground with fangs bared, ears laid back, two of them barely containing themselves while the grey leader moved with confidence out into the clearing.

"How is it that you are in this place, man-thing?" the grey leader said, licking his lips. "I've never seen one of your kind cross our borders before. Curious that you would be able to do so."

Suqata held his club before him and smiled a wry sort of grin. "I'm not a simple man-thing, am I? *Uiek, kiyi, uiek nu tiyuk, uiek kiyi, uiek manas tuk!*" The sound of the Song sent tremors through the creatures, but they did not retreat. Instead, the grey snarled louder through the pain.

"You are weak, man-thing," he snarled, "and your *sen-wa* is weak. Soon you will not be able to hold us off, and then we will tear you into wet bits."

"Enough talky-talky, Smoke. Let's eat him now!" One of the brown wolf-men said, hopping from paw to paw.

"Yes, yes. And the bones, too! Let's suck the marrow from his bones!" the other agreed.

Their leader, Smoke, turned and barked at his companions for silence. "Quiet, Ripper! You too, Biter!" They quickly obeyed. Then he advanced again, moving sideways along the clearing's edge. "Make this easy on yourself, boy. We will have you, and if you make us wait we will make your death a long and painful thing. But, lay down now and I promise to end it quick." He continued to circle, the other two taking up position at his flank, the entire time testing to see if Suqata would drop his guard. The whole scene looked akin to a vicious dance, each of the players set in lock-step with the others. With each turn, the wolves Ripper and Biter darted in with a snap of their jaws. Suqata would block the attacks deftly with his club, but as each second wore on, the heavy stick only grew heavier in his weary hands. As the tip of it dipped lower, the wolves' eyes grew bright with a chilling silver glow.

"Aren't you going to save me for your father?" Suqata growled back at the wolves, trying to mask the pain in his voice. *That's it, distract them. Get them talking*, he thought to himself. "Is your father too scared to come and face one small man-thing with a stick, huh? You're not wolves at all, are you? Just dumb dogs."

"Shut your mouth, human! You know nothing. The wolf-father could have had you in his great jaws at any time," Biter snarled.

"Then where is he now? Hiding in the woods. *Uiek, kiyi, uiek nu tiyuk, uiek kiyi, uiek manas tuk!* Come out, dumb-dog father. Let me have a look at you."

"You will die, boy!" In a rush, Smoke leapt through the air, abandoning all signs of reason. Only rage was left in his eyes—just as Suqata had hoped for. Men were worse fighters when driven by fear or rage. He only prayed that the same could be said for these beasts. Before Smoke's claws could touch him, Suqata called on the last of his strength, took a deep breath, and disappeared.

Smoke landed awkwardly where he had stood, his claws digging into the frosty ground. When Suqata released the Hiding Song, he appeared two feet in front of the wolf and brought the club down hard on its snout with a loud crack. Smoke went sprawling to the ground with a sharp yelp.

"Not as easy to kill as you thought," Suqata whispered. He felt a sense of accomplishment looking at the downed creature. The victory was, however, short lived. Quickly Ripper and Biter were at their leader's side, a whirl of claws and teeth lashing out from every direction. He brought up the club and blocked two high blows, and another, but then Ripper secured his jaws around the knobby length of Suqata's weapon. As he struggled to free it from his grip, Suqata felt Biter's claws tear across his thigh. The air filled with the coppery smell of his blood, driving both wolves into a frenzy.

"Where is your sassing tongue now, man-thing?" Biter howled, rushing in again for another attack. He found Suqata's club instead. One deft swing of the weapon cracked hard against the wolf's head, and he spun away yelping. Suqata knew his strength was gone, and all it would take would be an organized rush by all three wolves to finish him off.

Almost in response to his thoughts, Smoke rose from the ground and shook off the lingering effects of the blow that felled him. Ripper and Biter took up their places at his side, moving in unison like one lethal creature. All Suqata could do was ready his grip on the club before the beasts launched themselves for one last killing strike.

Just then, a dark shape moved quickly between them, swooping down like a shadow pulled free from the earth. It sped by like a gust of black wind, whirling the loose patches of leaves up from the ground in its path, and as it dipped and flew about them, Suqata was able to discern the shape of massive wings within the shape's wake.

"This is not your concern, Old One," Smoke howled at the shadow, "leave this boy to us. Father will not be pleased if ... AARGH!" Before he could finish, a line of red struck across the grey fur on his chest,

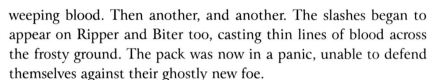

weeping blood. Then another, and another. The slashes began to appear on Ripper and Biter too, casting thin lines of blood across the frosty ground. The pack was now in a panic, unable to defend themselves against their ghostly new foe.

"Run, we'll come back for the boy later!" Smoke cried, and with that the three wolf-men bounded away into the trees. It took only seconds for their shapes to be lost in the mist.

Suqata was now alone in the clearing with his mysterious savior, and yet he felt no safer than when he had faced the wolves. The dark shape sat on a tree branch before him, its wing-like arms hanging relaxed at its sides while it looked down on the young Chinequewa. Its eyes were stark pools of white light, and its head swept down to a sharp point like a crow's beak. Suqata's grip tightened on the club as it moved closer. It didn't feel real the way it glided over the ground, the inky blackness of its silhouette stark against the surrounding woods, and quickly Suqata's mind was flooded with the memory of the spirit he and Auralyn had summoned that day in the field.

"Who are you?" Suqata said. He knew he didn't have the strength for another fight, but he kept the club up and at the ready even as he felt his vision begin to blur.

"I am the Keeper of Ways, boy, and the Claw in the Night. The Storykeeper, and the Soul Speaker. I am your salvation." When it spoke, the silent forest shook with the power of its voice.

"Now sleep. Your fight is over, for the time being." With that, Suqata felt a calm wash over him, and his limbs became heavy. The last thing that he saw before the darkness took him was the strange being's eyes, white as the center of a flame.

# CHAPTER 17
# POM-POKO KUNO

WHEN SUQATA AWOKE, HE LAY ON A THIN HIDE BED, COVERED IN A mass of downy rabbit skins. He wasn't quick to move, waiting first to see if it had all been some strange dream that had followed him into wakefulness. He was used to dreams, so he lay there, staring up at the roughly cut timber and massive tree roots that made up the ceiling. He began to feel his entire body ached with every small move he made, and was finally sure it was not a dream—he hurt too much for it to be. Suqata didn't remember blacking out exactly, just the feeling of his limbs going heavy and then the unsettling sensation of floating. He turned his head, and when his eyes finally focused, he was staring across a cluttered room at a tall and glowing hearth.

"What is this place?" he asked, his voice barely a whisper. As if bidden from memory, images came rushing into his mind and Suqata remembered. The winged shadow had saved his life, and must have brought him here. The thought was unnerving, and he suddenly felt the need to flee, but as he sat up in the bed he immediately regretted it. The room began to swirl in slow, lazy circles and his vision filled with small sparkling points of light that danced mockingly before him. Suqata reached out and braced himself against the nearby wall and waited until the dizziness passed. He sat up slowly and examined the room, letting his senses adjust to his surroundings.

It was large, especially for a crudely made cabin with hard-packed dirt floors, but made cramped by the host of odd objects that sat and hung within it. There were no divisions or separate rooms in the space, so it looked like a storage hut or barn with everything laid out for all to see. All around him were an assortment of tools, clothing, toys, weapons, and relics sitting in corners or hanging from hooks throughout the house. The bed in which he sat was made up against a wall near a barred door and just beneath a small, dirty oculus. Suqata moved awkwardly up to the window seal and wiped away a layer of dirt from the glass with his sleeve. He peered out, but all he could see were the dim silhouettes of wind-blown trees. It was dark as dusk, but he had no way of telling which way the sun was setting, or where the light was coming from at all.

*I could be miles from the river now, or it could be just out back. Who knows?* he thought to himself. *Maybe I should ask that shadow thing to give me a lift back to where I come from.*

He laughed weakly at the thought of making such a simple request of a dark entity. *Sarcasm, the last bastion of the truly hopeless.*

Suqata lowered his feet to the ground. His wet clothes and boots had been removed, so the earth was cool beneath his bare toes as he tried to stand. The dizziness came back for only a split second, but he pushed past it and steadied himself. He checked the wounds on his arm and legs and found them wrapped in lengths of gauze and smelling strongly of mint and carob roots.

*At least I know my host doesn't want to kill me. Not yet anyway.* It wasn't as comforting a thought as he had hoped, and only raised more questions in his mind. Why had that thing saved him? But more importantly, what kind of creature could instill such fear in beasts as ferocious as those wolves: Smoke, Ripper, and Biter?

Suqata wrapped himself in his blanket and walked slowly towards the fire at the other end of the room, being careful not to step on the oddly piled stack of snowshoes, fishing baskets, and heaps of coiled rope that lay in his path. Here and there, he saw bizarrely fashioned clothes and jewelry lying in corners or hanging from the ceiling beams, as if the people who once inhabited them had simply vanished into thin air, leaving only their cast-away husks. Once he reached the hearth, Suqata's senses were immediately assaulted by the bubbling contents of a black cauldron that hung over the fire. His eyes watered and his nostrils burned from the wafting fumes.

"Smells like pitch and dog hair," he choked. He was just about

to remove the pot lid when the door across the room burst open with a jarring clunk and in walked a figure.

"Don't touch that, boy," a hoarse voice cried out, "it's almost done!"

It was a man, his figure casting a ragged shadow into the cabin before rushing inside, flanked by powerful gusts of wind. He was not a monster like the other creatures Suqata had encountered since pulling himself from the river, but to say that this man was normal would not have done him justice. He moved quickly, closing the space between them with an unnatural grace, but once within the light of the hearth he stopped. He cocked his head sideways and looked to Suqata, his dark features unreadable through his mass of steely-grey hair, and sharply gestured him away. Suqata hurriedly removed his hand from the pot lid.

"I wasn't going to do anything to it," he said. "Besides, it smells awful."

The stranger's glare never wavered, even as his head twitched slightly in a nervous sort of way. He reached out from within the folds of his cloak and took a spoon from an iron hook near the hearth, never taking his eyes from Suqata, and began to stir the murky contents of the pot in slow circles.

"The smell means it's almost done," he said aloud, but more for himself than for Suqata's benefit. "It just needs a little more heat." He moved to a shadowed corner and returned with fresh wood for the fire. He laid the pieces in and stirred the embers until they glowed a contented red. The renewed light gave Suqata his first clear look at the stranger's face. He did not seem old, but his features were gaunt and his mouth had a hard and angled set about it. His hair was done in long braided strands, filled with beads and animal bones tied with colored pieces of string, and he wore a long, tattered cloak of dark fabric topped with black feathers that shone almost purple in the fire light. It was his eyes, however, that caught Suqata's attention. They were blue-grey like the surface of a frozen lake.

"You are Chinequewa?" Suqata said. It sounded more like an accusation than a question, but the nuance was lost on the man as he continued to stir his concoction.

"Yes, I am, among other things," he replied. After a moment's pause, he lifted the spoon from the pot and tasted the brew, then sighed contently. "I do believe this is done." He took a wooden bowl from the top of hearth, dipped it into the pot, and then handed it to Suqata. "Drink all of it."

Suqata could feel his stomach lurch at the sight of the dark and murky sludge. It had now taken on an orange, sickly hue, specked here and there with little bits of flotsam and such.

"What is it?" he murmured, holding it close for examination.

"It will help you heal from your wounds. The creatures you faced are known to leave sickness when they draw blood. If you let the wounds fester, you may take a fever and go mad. Better you drink this now than have me have to kill you later."

Right away, Suqata knew the last part was not a joke. He lifted the bowl to his mouth and was instantly confronted by a smell that was one part burned leaves and one part hard liquor. He watched the shimmering, oily sheen on the surface until every drop was drunk. There was a sharp, burning sensation in his nose like eating fresh horseradish, and he could feel the warmth of the concoction spread from his stomach throughout his body. It was like drinking liquid fire.

"Now you might want to sit down," his host said. He was already pulling a bearskin away from a large chair. Once it was uncovered, Suqata could see the elaborate swirling carvings that ran from foot to head. The man then pointed at a stool beside the hearth, saying again, "Sit."

"I'll stand, thank you," Suqata said, straightening his shoulders, though the puckered look on his face caused his proud stature to lose some of its effect.

"Suit yourself." The stranger sat down, undid the bird skull clasp of his cloak, and threw it across the back of chair. He then crossed his legs and began to quizzically twirl the end of his silver-streaked beard. "Now, what am I to do with you, boy? You are quite a long way from where you should be."

"How's this for starters; you will return my things to me and let

me go on my way," Suqata replied. The strange brew was working quickly, and already he could feel the dull ache in his limbs start fading with each passing moment.

"I don't think that would be wise, young one. I dare say it would be the last foolish decision of your short life."

"Still, it is my decision to make. I must get back to town tonight." Suqata was flushed with excitement. So much so, he missed the slight sense of grogginess that began to creep in just behind his eyes.

"So what is your plan? Are you going to run blindly through the never-ending labyrinth of trees and shadows, only to be met by the wet jaws of the wolves—or maybe even something worse. Garro Knocta's children are not the only dangers out there in the mist."

"Things like that winged shadow I saw?"

The stranger laughed. "That creature is the least of your worries. There are things out there that hunt when the wind blows cold and whistles through the branches. They wander and lust for nothing more than warm blood. Yours, Suqata 'Watched by the Crow,' if it's available."

Suqata heard the man's voice as if from a great distance, and he was having a hard time keeping his eyes open. "How do you know me?" he said, feeling the room start to sway like water in a jug. "Have we met before? It doesn't matter anyway. I'm not afraid," he said, slurring his words in defiance, "I am not totally ignorant of the unseen world. I know things, too."

"Yes, I can see that," the stranger seemed to scrutinize Suqata for a moment, taking his measure. "But I know more. Quite a great deal more, in fact. One thing I know is that … "

But it was too late. As Suqata drifted off into sleep, he slumped forward, falling face first into a pile of bundled fish nets.

The man shook his head. "You should have taken a seat when it was offered," he said.

WHEN SUQATA WOKE THE SECOND time, it was in a panic. Once again

he lay on the hide bed in the corner of the stranger's home. The window had been cracked to let in some of the cold night air, but even so Suqata was covered with sweat from head to toe.

"Awake, are we? Good. I was beginning to fear I had mixed the potion to strong." The man sat not three feet from Suqata in his tall backed chair, a roll of yellowed parchment covered in bizarre symbols spread across his lap.

"What happened to me?"

"You didn't take a seat. Looks like your fever has broken. Drink this, it will help." The man offered him a cup, which Suqata looked warily at before accepting.

"What is it this time?"

"Just water, boy. The potion I gave you tends to leave the mouth dry as willow bark."

Suqata drained the cup in seconds. Despite the throbbing feeling in his head, he did feel much better. The aches were gone and when he looked down to examine the wounds on his arms and legs he was astounded to see that they had already begun to scar over. There was no blood, and only the faintest traces of bruising. It was as if the wounds were weeks old if a day.

"How long was I out?" Suqata asked, a slight panic adding pitch to his voice.

"Stop your fretting. It's only been a few hours. Time moves differently here. What seems like a full day can be mere seconds in the place you come from. The potion makes use of that. I'd tell you more, but I doubt you would understand."

The man then pointed at a small stool beside the bed. "Those are for you. Your other clothes were torn and bloodied, so I brought you these. They're old, but sturdy."

Suqata took the strange garments and dressed. Though they did smell of age, the fabric was strong like the old man had said and felt cool against his skin. There was a pair of soft leather breeches and a long, turquoise blue tunic that hung all the way to his knees and was bound at the waist with a dark blue sash and a banded leather

belt. He ran his fingers over the beaded shapes and swirls along the trim of the garments and felt a strange sense of familiarity.

"They fit you well. Now you look like a true Chinequewa," he said.

"Thank you, I guess," Suqata said, feeling a bit awkward. "I appreciate the clothes and you tending my wounds, stranger, but it seems unfair that you know my name, yet I don't know what to call you or where I am."

The old man looked up from his scroll and raised a bushy eyebrow. "I am called by many names, but you will call me Pom-poko-kuno, or just Old Pom. As to the question of where—I am afraid you are lost."

"Lost?" The word resonated in Suqata's thoughts, to the point that he could feel his heart flutter.

"Yes. Far beyond the Waking World and everything you have ever known—a place as ancient as the tales of men." He rolled his parchment, then looked into the fire. "Once, long ago, men and spirits of the ancient world walked here. But then came the great war. So much was destroyed, and the powers of change, creation, and destruction were loosed upon the land like a tidal wave. So, the One Voice saw fit to separate men and spirits from one another. If not for the foolishness of two beings, the separation would have been complete. But it was not. So, this place was formed—the Henis-a-paka. The World Between."

Suqata felt his mouth go dry. "So the story is true," he whispered.

"More or less. All you truly need to know is this: there is no way back to where you come from."

His words seemed to hang in the air for a moment, mocking Suqata. *No way back*. It repeated in his ears until he wanted to cover them to block out the sound.

"That can't be. If there is a way here, then there must be a way back," Suqata said.

"There is not, though I must say that I have never seen a human cross the boundaries before now."

"So what are you supposed to be, old timer?" Suqata asked, to which Pom grinned a wicked sort of smile.

"Oh, I'm so much more, my dear boy. You have something special about you as well. Which only makes me wonder, why are you in such a hurry to return to the Waking World?" Old Pom said, cocking his head. "Men are full of cruelty and malice, of which I am sure you know." He pointed at Suqata's scar. "The old teachings are dead, and people creep about in their daily lives completely unaware of the magic that exists around them."

"For there not to be a way out of this place, you act like you've seen my world firsthand," Suqata said, taking another drink of water.

"I've seen enough." Old Pom took the cup from his hand, and in one fluid arc, he threw its contents. Instantly, the water froze in mid-air, shimmering like a mirror suspended in space. In the distance Suqata heard the distinct sound of music, and across the surface of the water appeared images of children sleeping in slave holds, and of soldiers raiding villages, their eyes alight with the thrill of carnage. Suqata saw ancient forests fall to the blades of the outlanders, and lastly the cool blue eyes of a boy not much older than five or six trekking across a windswept, snowy plain with iron shackles around his hands and feet. When the images were gone, the liquid mirror fell to the floor, splashing cool droplets over Suqata's feet.

"So, I ask you again, boy; what is it that makes you so eager to return?"

Suqata couldn't answer. In truth, he was having a hard time thinking of a convincing argument.

"Certainly it is not your so-called friends. Auralyn and Obrie, I believe you said?" Pom continued.

"How do you know those names?"

"You called them out last night as you lay dreaming. Especially the first: Auralyn. Is she the tether that binds you to that life? I should have suspected. You are young, and affairs of the heart usually overrule reason. It is something I have not experienced in a great many years."

"You shouldn't talk about things you don't understand," Suqata said through gritted teeth.

"What is to understand?" Old Pom said, turning back to his work. "I know weakness when I see it."

Suqata felt his anger rise inside him like a fire stoked to life.

"*Silence!*" He spoke aloud, the word ringing with so much raw power that it stung his ears like the shattering of a hundred panes of glass. For a moment, the old man sat quiet. Then, a smile once again cracked his lips and crinkled the corners of his bright eyes.

"Yes. That is what I have been looking for," he chuckled. He sounded quite pleased with himself. "I could sense there was great power in you, boy, from the moment I laid eyes on you. Now I have seen and heard it for myself. The *sen-wa* vibrates in your very bones, Suqata. There is a great deal I could teach you, if you were willing."

"There is nothing I can learn from you, or this dead place."

"Give it time, my boy. Once you've been here for a while, you'll find that you don't really have a choice."

For a long moment Suqata looked at the man called Pom-poko-kuno—this stranger from the misty wood who had saved him. *He could possibly hold the answers to all my questions*, he thought to himself. Still the image of his friends' faces kept appearing in his mind—especially Auralyn. The memory of that brief kiss was now tinged with fear and pain. All he could seem to remember was the look in her eyes on the bridge, and the melancholy sound of her Song.

Suddenly, something became clear.

"She did this. Her Song brought me here."

# CHAPTER 18
# THE SPIRIT CALLS

THERE WAS REALLY NO WAY OF KEEPING TRACK OF HOW LONG SUQATA had been gone from The Hollow, secreted away in those misty woods. Just as Pom had said, there was no day or night in the Henis-a-paka to speak of, only the endless grey of twilight, so Suqata had taken to watching the day-to-day movements of his new benefactor. The old man had a very strict schedule, and he kept to it with the kind of manic obsession that only those who are truly alone ever know. In a way, it became Suqata's record of time.

Every day was begun with chopping wood, and a pot of the most horrendous porridge imaginable, followed by hours of musing over his assorted treasures. Midday brought herb tea and hard crusts of bread, followed by a few hours of scroll reading. Suqata was warned not to touch anything, but every now and then, while Old Pom was occupied counting through his boxes of carved tusks or ancient spears, he would steal glances at the rolls of yellowed paper. Pom's collection was incredible, and took up a large shelves and little wooden alcoves made with the massive roots of the cabin walls. Although he couldn't read the markings, they held a mystery and beauty to them. The swirling lines and shapes were like an art unto themselves that moved across the pages, rising and falling with an almost musical quality. It had only taken one viewing to realize that similar symbols were drawn throughout the cabin on posts and across the lintel of the doorway. Even the clothes that Old Pom had given him bore the same distinctive markings, as though they were all linked.

Evening brought a roaring fire and a large pot of stew that was almost always burned. Suqata had watched Obrie cook enough meals from barely anything for him to know his way around a kitchen, but no matter how many times he offered, Old Pom refused the help.

"I have a way I like things," he would grumble.

To be totally honest, Suqata didn't mind. Out of the time he had been there, he hadn't seen one rabbit or deer in those woods. Judging by the creatures he had seen scurrying through the layers of old leaves and brush, Suqata wasn't in a hurry to discover the contents of Pom's stew. Instead, they would sit together and eat as Suqata tried desperately to fill the silence. He was used to the lack of conversation, since Captain Graye was never much one for idle chatter, but the unstirred silence of the cabin was beginning to wear on him. At first he thought to ask about the scrolls and the unusual writing, or how the old man knew so much about the *sen-wa*, but Pom would continue eating and pretend that the young man hadn't said a word. So, Suqata would talk about other things, and never of anything of particularly great importance. He would talk about his life in Orin's Hollow, about Auralyn, Obrie, and sometimes even the captain. Pom would nod and say, "Oh really," or "You don't say," and even crack a small smile every now and again. When the meals were done, Suqata watched quietly as Pom prepared himself for his nightly departure.

"Bar the door after I leave," he would always say, pulling on his feathered cloak. He would then strap on a braided leather belt from which hung two long and curiously made daggers. They were shaped from some sort of animal bone or tooth, but unlike any Suqata had ever seen before. The blades looked to be as sharp as any metal knife, maybe even sharper, and the curved edges of them glinted with silvery shards embedded in the bone when they caught the light from the fire.

"Strange knives," Suqata commented as Pom prepared to leave.

"You will never again see their like," the old man said. "They're made from the antlers of the carbato. Those magnificent creatures are gone now, lost to time and legend."

"Why not carry a sword? I saw one or two in here, amongst your 'treasures.' "

"I have no need for steel," he replied. "Wouldn't do me any

196

good against what's out there. Inside these daggers is the essence of silver—the only thing, apart from the Songs, that can harm a spirit."

"So, you are expecting a fight. If so, why go out at all? What's so important out there?" Suqata said and waited for his host's response. He knew the old hermit was keeping things from him, and took every chance he could to poke at the well-crafted wall of mystery Pom had erected between them.

Pom only grinned and slung a large leather sack over his broad, bony shoulder.

"Pray you never have to know," he replied. "Now stay put. This place is protected." And then he was gone, out the door and into the gloom. Suqata tried to await his return, occupying himself by going through the mountains of weapons and artifacts that lay strewn about the cabin, looking for something to aid in his escape from that dismal place. Each time, sleep would eventually overtake him, and he'd wake hours later to the sound of Old Pom again chopping firewood.

After what could have been a few days, but felt longer, Suqata put aside his search began to explore his surroundings (against Pom's warnings.) The large cabin was built into a hill in the middle of a grassy clearing, topped by a massive tree and surrounded on all sides by the endless forest. It was the only green spot in the entire wood. Some days, when the wind had died a bit, he would wander even though there really wasn't too far to go.

Suqata found himself one day sitting near the woodpile behind the cabin, driven out by the smell of burning bread, gazing off into the forest and marveling at the stillness. It surprised him how beautiful that place was, now that he wasn't running for his life. There was a kind of wonder to the silver birches, going on forever into the mist, perfectly spaced and symmetrical—the distant sound of unseen treetops swaying in the cold breezes. Suqata sat for hours listening to that sound. It seemed to whisper to him, erasing his fear and bad memories, leaving only peace. Gone were the images of wolves, with their shining eyes, and Ashton's look of hunger and need, drifting unhindered from his mind. It was only when he came to the memory of Auralyn and the bridge that he paused. Her eyes, azure and filled with fear, brought Suqata back to himself.

"Try not to listen so hard to the forest, boy. It may say something you don't want to hear." The bass voice behind him woke Suqata from his musing, like rousing from a deep and numbing sleep. He turned to find Old Pom sitting beside him on a large stump. Across his lap lay a long reed flute, every inch of it adorned in the strange swirling writing. As Suqata's sense returned slowly, he was able to discern what Pom had been talking about. Just under the whistle of the wind was another sound.

Voices.

They were as light as the rustle of leaves, singing a strange and haunting melody just beyond the border between the forest and the clearing. Suqata was amazed he hadn't noticed it before.

"I hear them now," he said, "singing in the distance. Strange. My teacher would have been disappointed with me for missing that."

"Why so, boy?" the old man asked.

"Hopano could hear a storm on the horizon and tell you where it had begun. Even tell you how long it would last. He taught me to listen and hear the world. Missing voices on the wind—I'm sure he would have considered that a great failure."

"Don't fret. I doubt even he could have heard these voices." Pom then lifted the flute to his lips and played softly, his knobby fingers dancing playfully across the cut holes. The music was light, lilting its way delicately through air, and as he played the voices became more distinct. Just beyond the clearing, Suqata could now make out small points of light, moving and dancing in time with the music. As they did, they began to glow bright blue, and within each halo of brightness he could see a small fluttering form. Before the lights could get any closer, Old Pom stopped playing and laid the flute back in his lap.

"They are called *mino-ski*," he said. "They are spirits, but not great spirits like the *mahko*. In the Waking World they live in the

deep forests nurturing the ancient trees, but here, where life is frozen and unchanging, they are lost and without purpose. Terrible bother most of the time, but they don't taste half bad."

Suqata looked to Pom, his face bearing a combination of confusion and disgust, though the whole thing seemed amusing to Pom.

"I'd be a little more careful if you are planning on wandering about," he said. "The *mino-ski* will call to you, and try to lure you out if they can. You are warned."

"They look harmless. What could they do to me?"

"Oh, not much. Just feed you to those damned trees is all."

Suqata glanced once again into the woods, and at the delicate, shimmering lights, and felt a shiver go up his spine. "Is there anything in this place that isn't planning on killing me?" he said.

Pom laughed as he stood to leave. "Well, I'm not. Not today at least." He turned and walked back to the cabin with his flute held jauntily across his shoulder.

After a moment, Suqata followed him inside. In the distance he could still hear the voices of the *mino-ski* singing.

"Come to us, young one," they said. "There is peace here, in the cold earth. Rest. Trouble no more."

"I have to get out of this place," Suqata said to himself, "while I still can."

THE WIND HAD GROWN STRONGER as the hours passed. By the time Old Pom was ready to leave after their meal, the roar of it threatened to pull boards off the cabin roof.

"KEEP THE DOOR SHUT," POM said, throwing on his cloak and pulling up the feathered cowl.

"Yes, yes, you keep reminding me," Suqata replied. "Every day it's the same thing. If I were prone to offense, I might believe you think me to be deaf or an idiot. I'm not quite sure which is worse." He was sitting by the fire, stirring the embers with his back to the old man. "I know there is a protection around the clearing. How and why it is there are the points you fail to cover. In the end, I guess it doesn't really matter. Just be on your way, Pom. I'll be right here when you get back. There's nowhere else to go."

Pom, however, did not leave. He stood there, perfectly still, watching the boy scratch dispassionately about in the ash of the hearth with a stick. Instead, he walked over and lifted a small object from atop his shelf of scrolls, then sat in his tall-backed chair opposite Suqata.

"Look here boy, and pay close attention," he said. In his hand sat a small carved totem, no bigger than his palm. It was made of bone scrimshaw, but the edges had been worn down, leaving it stripped of any distinguishing features to speak of, save for what appeared to be small grinning face. He held it up to the light and sang a short chant in the totem's direction.

*"Ama tasunamuka, ama tam esque latana."* As he spoke, his words turned to silver light, as if he were breathing out the very glow of the winter moon, and the statue began to glow with the same light. In seconds, Pom stopped, took Suqata's hands, and placed the totem into them roughly.

"That was a spirit ward. It is stronger than the one you sang against the wolf-kin, and I have bound it to this little lump of nothing, and to a chain of protection around this house. That is how I keep this place and the things in it safe. As long as it is here, you cannot be harmed. If you are patient then I will teach you how this was accomplished when I return." And with that, Pom turned and left, while Suqata marveled at the glowing statue in the firelight.

"What a wonder," he said, feeling the totem hum lightly in his palm. As he sat there, an astonished smile came over his face. After days of searching, literally up to his elbows in the old man's treasures, Pom-poko-kuno had just given him the very thing he needed. Suqata decided that moment—tonight, he was going to leave tonight.

It only took moments for Suqata to prepare to leave. The days of rummaging through Pom's treasures had brought about some

useful finds: a set of leather gauntlets that wrapped tightly around Suqata's arms; a dark hooded cloak; and amongst the weapons, a slightly rusted saber, made in the old fashion just like the one Captain Graye carried—the blade's silver edge still keen and sharp.

"Keep your bone daggers, old man. This will work fine for me."

Suqata kept the worn totem in his belt, hoping its steady hum would be enough to protect him from whatever waited beyond the clearing. When all was ready, Suqata walked to the door and unbarred it, but for a moment he hesitated. An unexpected pang of doubt came over him, pinning his feet to the ground. He glanced back at the wall of yellowed scrolls, lined and stacked neatly amongst the chaos of the cabin, and then at the tall-backed chair. Suqata could almost see Old Pom sitting there beside the fire, bent over the rolls of parchment in deep concentration. In the time he had been there, the silent hermit had begun to warm to Suqata, and he to him. Now, here he stood only steps away from sneaking off into the night.

"He will understand," Suqata said to the empty room, as if someone or something there could hear him. Pom would have to understand. Suqata couldn't leave his friends, the only people in his life that cared about him, to face the dangers in the Hollow alone. He was meant to help them, and he wasn't planning on running away from his destiny ever again. Suqata reached over his shoulder and checked to see if the sword pulled clear in the scabbard, then, throwing up his hood, he walked out into the gloom of the Henis-a-paka.

THERE WAS DEW ON THE grass as he left, and a chill blast of wind pulled at the length of Suqata's cloak. He wasted no time, quickly running to the edge of the clearing. There was just enough light to see by without summoning any, so he allowed his eyes to adjust to the darkness. A few steps past where the tree line began, Suqata finally saw what Pom had spoken of so many times. Just under the brush sat a large stone set deep in the ground and covered with the

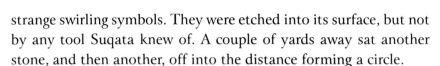 

strange swirling symbols. They were etched into its surface, but not by any tool Suqata knew of. A couple of yards away sat another stone, and then another, off into the distance forming a circle.

"Pom's protection." Suqata whispered. Even then, he could hear the hum of them calling out the statue tucked safely in the loops of his belt. It had been there all along, warding off the creatures in the dark, and now as Suqata stood at their border, he once again felt the ache of doubt creep into his thoughts. But there was no turning back, not now. With one great stride, he crossed the barrier and made his way into the woods.

Suqata traveled for some time, until the hum of the protected clearing had long since faded. He kept his hood up as he darted from tree to tree, sometimes running over the perma-frost turf, other times moving unseen with the aid of the Hiding Song. For the length of a breath, Suqata barely stirred the leaves on the ground. On and on he went, until he came to rest at the foot of a peculiar tree—one that stood apart from the others. In a sea of spruce, all growing straight and tall like a temple of silver-white pillars, this one split at about a man's height into two trees. It was as good a place as any to do what he had come to do. Suqata glanced over his shoulder and out into the grey before crouching down to the ground.

"Well, Lynn, I hope this works," he whispered, then he began to sing.

*"Shi eash eyota, cama die e, camash qua eshta, cama matea."*

He sang Auralyn's Song the way she had on the bridge, slow and mournfully into the stillness, and the very sound of it made his own heart ache. But nothing happened. He continued, and the sound of power rang in each word he uttered, but still there was nothing.

What could be wrong, he thought, his mind racing. He had taken a great risk coming here, leaving the protection of Pom's home, all on the assumption that Auralyn's Song was the key to crossing into this world. Now he stood almost defenseless in the dark, calling out to all of the Henis-a-paka to hear. He didn't have

to call out for long. Just then, Suqata could see points of light appear out of gloom all around him. They gathered quickly, now hovering in dense clusters. It was the *mino-ski*. Suqata thought to stop singing, but he couldn't give up just yet. The song had to work, it just had to. So, he continued. He pulled the saber from its sheath and the statue from his belt, brandishing both against the swelling numbers of sparkling creatures that pressed in around him.

"Come young one, there is peace here," they said collectively, "peace in the earth." Suqata could feel a faintness wash over him, but he fought to keep his eyes wide and alert. It was then that one of them darted past his face, and he felt a searing hot pain. Suqata touched the wound and felt the slippery heat of blood on his fingertips.

"Not so nice now, are we," he said. Suqata slashed at the cluster, cutting a handful of the creatures in two, but even as he did more came to take their place. Two more darted his way, and he caught one in flight, missing the other. It slashed across his side. It was only then that he noticed that the hum of the statue was losing its power, the cool light at its center pulsating like a waning heartbeat. He kept it aloft, slashing at the bright *mino-ski* as they swept in to harm him. To his credit as a swordsman, the young man let few of the creatures past the whirl of his blade, but soon his back was against the split tree, his arms and legs criss-crossed with lines of red. When the spirit ward had diminished to nothing, Suqata held his weapon tightly and prepared for the stirring mass of light to come in for a final rush.

Then suddenly, the lights dispersed, scattering off into the woods just as quickly as they had gathered, and Suqata was again alone at the foot of the tree. Before he had a moment to feel any relief, he noticed that although the *mino-ski* were gone, the light around the tree remained. Not in individual points, but an overall sense of illumination that shifted and moved like waves on the water coalescing into a single shape—that of a woman formed of ghostly wisps of radiance.

"Varcuya," Suqata hissed. He took a defensive stance with his saber, and prepared to Sing out a banishment. Every muscle in his body was now taut and prepared for battle, but just as he began to speak, the ethereal being spoke first.

"Stay your hand, Watched by Crow, swordbearer and wolf slayer. I mean you no harm," she said, lifting her hand before her. "I have sought you out."

"Why, demon—what could you possibly want with me?" Suqata asked, his blue-grey eyes set in defiance.

"I have come to ask for your help," she replied.

# CHAPTER 19

# CORA VACO
# THE CROW

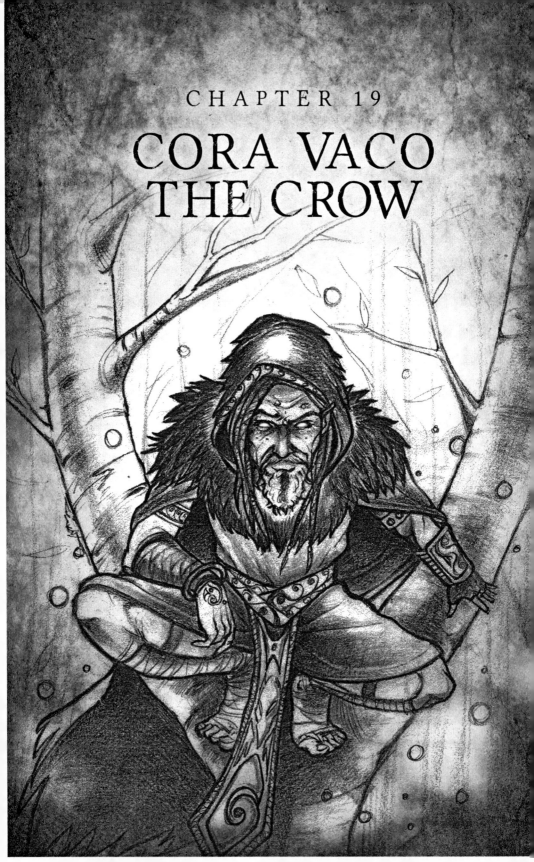

FEAR IS A STRANGE THING. ONE MOMENT IT BURNS WITHIN, ROARING like a furnace, driving you to fight and live. Then, in a heartbeat it washes over you like a winter storm, freezing your resolve until you are still and cold. So it was for Suqata as he stood face to face with the ghostly figure. He watched as it floated before him, trying unsuccessfully to keep the sword in his hand from shaking.

"Keep your distance, creature!" he yelled, holding the totem up in his clenched fist. He hoped that some of the warding song still sounded deep within it, but somehow knew that its power to protect him was now completely gone. The light near the tree had dimmed a little, and the figure had become more solid. She now stood upon the ground, and Suqata could hear the sound of dead leaves and snow crunching beneath her bare feet as she slowly walked towards him. She was quite beautiful, with long dark hair that moved as if she were suspended in water. Her elegantly long features and almond-shaped eyes were strangely familiar, and all along her outstretched arms were glowing symbols. Once again, they were the same symbols as Suqata had seen in Pom's scrolls.

"I am not your enemy. You needn't fear," she said, "You have come a long way, searching all along for truth. For that alone we are kindred spirits."

"All the same, I would feel much better if you would just stop moving." Suqata swung his saber into an offensive poise, its blade now at the perfect angle to strike the ghostly woman's throat if she proved dangerous. *This rusted thing would probably just make her mad,* he quickly thought to himself. "How do you know me?"

The woman smiled. "You know my daughter, so through her I know you, Suqata." Her voice was gentle, with a strange accent Suqata had never heard before. "Just now you sang a song that has been bound to her since she was a child. I know it well."

Right then, Suqata knew who the woman was.

"Lady Anishta," he whispered. The resemblance was so obvious that he felt foolish he hadn't seen it before. She was just as lovely as Auralyn had said—a melancholy kind of beauty. Gradually, Suqata lowered the tip of his sword but kept the totem held tightly in his grip.

"You are in grave danger, Suqata," she said. "We have but a short time to speak before I must go, so listen, I beg you." Lady Anishta stopped walking about three yards away and placed her hands together before her. "There are enemies on their way to your home, Orin's Hollow, and powers so dark that they threaten the lives of not just the people you care about, but the whole of the colonies as well."

"And you want to help me?" Suqata said with an unmistakable hint of distrust.

"Yes. There are people there that I care about as well," she replied.

"Well I know what is coming. I've seen the wolves for myself, and what they can do." The memories of yellowed fangs and shining eyes arose in Suqata's mind, and his grip tightened against the saber hilt.

"Then you know only part of the danger. The wolves are a threat greater than anything the colonists ever thought possible, but they are just the beginning: pawns even, in a larger battle of life and death that began many generations before your home even existed. Do you know what tonight is, Suqata?"

Suqata shook his head. "I do not."

"Tonight Orin's Hollow will celebrate Sundering," she said, and Suqata felt his heart shudder in his chest.

"That can't be. I have been in this place for over a week. I know, I counted. It was a day until the celebration when we were attacked!"

"And yet it is the truth. Time flows through the Henis-a-paka differently than the Waking World: like a wind, sometimes strong and fast, and other times perfectly still. It is because of this place, and its history, that your world is now at a crossroads.

"Many centuries ago, this was the site of a great war between man and *mahko*, the great spirits. When it was over, two spirits and one man changed our worlds forever."

As she spoke, Suqata remembered the storyteller's tale. It felt like a lifetime ago that he had heard it. "The Story of Wolf and Crow," he said. "That really happened?"

Lady Anishta nodded gravely. "Yes, but not exactly as your world remembers it. Stories are like people. Over time they change and grow until they only resemble who and what they once were."

She moved closer, and Suqata could feel her presence on his skin, like static raising the hairs on his arm.

"That ancient war was over power, as most wars are," she said, "Power that man and the *mahko* would not share—the songs. Although it was forbidden for men to learn the Songs of Making, the very source of the *mahko*'s being, they had discovered its secrets. The same is true of the *mahko*. They had no power to use the Songs of Changing, but had found a way to bend it to their own ends. To tip the balance, both men and *mahko* sought to master the power of the *sen-uk*—The Songs of Ending. This was the greatest of blasphemy, for that power was beyond the control of man or spirit. For years, the stalemate persisted, until a single act was committed that changed everything. This act was when Cora Vaco the Crow possessed the body of a human during the night of the Sundering, and nothing would ever be the same."

"So one spirit did all of this. How is that even possible?" Suqata asked. His palms were beginning to sweat, and he knew he was very much in over his head.

"We can never truly know. All that is certain is that when it was over, the kingdoms of man lay scattered across the land, laid to ruin in the aftermath of the Sundering. Some left the old places, fearing them cursed, and struck out to begin anew, leaving their past behind them. Two tribes, however, decided that knowledge of the past and the old powers must be preserved. And so, they divided their ancient learning: one tribe journeying over a vast ocean, the other staying and vowing to protect the sacred places, and keep men safe from the dangers there. They were the Umbar, my people, and the Chinequewa, your people."

Suqata stood speechless, and Lady Anishta paused for a moment to give him time to absorb her words. It was unmistakable by the look on his face that the he was trying to digest the revelations as best he could. Suqata stared out into the forest for a time, but then his gaze drifted back to her.

"We were right. Auralyn and I thought there was a connection, but this?" He swallowed hard, almost overcome. "All my life, people have told me I was cursed, the child of killers, but none of that was true. My people were protectors?" he whispered, as if in that realization lay the key to his very existence. He had spent a lifetime of whispered curses and guarded looks, wondering who he was, and why his people were so mistrusted, fearing the answers would only bring his damnation.

"Yes. They have always been, even before the Sundering in the time of the great kingdoms of men. They held their oath sacred, and for generation after generation they guarded the secrets of their heritage, but after thousands of years a group of men began to threaten everything the Chinequewa and the Umbar had protected. These men had many secret names. Amongst the Kael their order became known as the Knights of Ascalion, but the Umbar knew them by another, more ominous name. The Varcuya. In our tongue it means Spirit Walkers—a power-hungry sect that started a bloody war against my homeland, all so that they could collect the ancient knowledge of the Songs. Some amongst the Umbar thought they wanted to use them as weapons against their enemies, but their ambitions went far beyond that. They wanted the power of the *sen-uk*—they wanted to become gods. So, using a corrupted form of the *sen-wa* and *sen-tal*, their leaders changed themselves into abominations, neither living or dead. The priests of Umbar, my ancestors, were not able to stop their transformation, but were able to imprison them here, in the Henis-a-paka far away from the Waking World. Now, after three hundred years, they have found a way to return."

"How? Pom said there's no way out of the Henis-a-paka. Even Auralyn's song doesn't work."

"He was not completely truthful with you. There is no way for a mortal to escape the place, but there are ways to return for creatures who are of both worlds. The wolf-kin have done so before, since they are born of spirit and flesh, but only when the barriers are the thinnest. This is why the Varcuya have manipulated a powerful *mahko* to aid them in this task—Garro Knocta, the Night Wolf. Together with his children, they have been given the knowledge to do what Cora Vaco once did long ago—to take the living form of men, wearing their skins. To what end, I am not sure. All that is certain is that without your power, Orin's Hollow will not survive. So, the task falls to you, Suqata."

When she finished, Suqata could only hear the sound of heart, pounding in his chest.

"What can I do?" he said angrily, "I barely survived the last time I met the wolves, and you said what is coming is even worse! I have no idea how to leave this place, and even if I could, maybe Pom was right. What do I owe those people?" Suqata lowered the warding totem, letting it roll from his fingers and onto the ground. "They made me a slave my whole life and killed or drove my people away, the very ones who were protecting them. And now it's up to me?"

Suqata stood with his back against the tree and closed his eyes. He felt a wave of exhaustion come over him, like he had been holding up a great weight and finally his strength had failed him. His thoughts were all a jumble, with images of Auralyn and Obrie's faces coming up through the storm of memories, but through the haze of doubt and confusion he heard Lady Anishta's voice, soft and direct, whisper into his ear.

"I had no great love for the Kaels in life, Suqata. For hundreds of years they fought my people, driven by the will of the Knights of Ascalion. I hated them so much that there was no place for forgiveness in my heart. Then one day, I met my husband—a quiet, scholarly man who looked at me and saw the beauty of my culture.

In him I found a kindred spirit, and I knew then that he was not my enemy. I loved him, even though he was a Kael. The question you must ask yourself, Suqata, is not whether they are worthy of saving, but rather if you have it in yourself to save them regardless. You are the last of the Chinequewa. If you do not, who will?"

As she spoke, Lady Anishta brushed his hair aside tenderly. "Think of Auralyn. You can save her, Suqata," she said. "After all this time, I can still hear her heart, and in it she calls you 'hero.' Be that now."

When Suqata's eyes opened again, his indecision and fear were gone. Only determination remained.

"Tell me how to return to the Waking World," he said, the slightest ring of power clinging to each word.

"That I do not know," Lady Anishta replied, looking off into the mist-shrouded forest. She heard a familiar sound in the distance. "Someone is coming who has the answers you seek."

Together they waited and listened to the stillness until Suqata could hear it as well. It was the sound of great wings beating the wind. Then, out of the grey came a huge winged shadow, bigger than a man and shrouded in inky night as thick as pitch smoke. It glided around them, ducking in and out of the fog with fluid grace, and came to rest at the crook of the split tree, wrapping itself in its immense wings. Its eyes flashed silver in Anishta's light.

"Hello, Cora Vaco," she said, and bowed. Suqata watched in awed silence, the saber hanging uselessly in his grip. As if stirred by a great gust, the shape of the winged shadow drifted away leaving only its core behind. A man now crouched in the tree, his head a mass of steely grey hair, and a long feather-topped cloak draped across his shoulders.

"Hello, Anishta. I see you've found our boy," Pom-poko-kuno said with a crooked smile and a peculiar tilt to his head.

"CLOSE YOUR MOUTH, BOY, BEFORE something flies in it," Cora Vaco said. He stared down at them from his perch, his eyes a dull silver,

and looking quite the part of a mysterious dark spirit. Even his cloak, to which Suqata had barely given two glances before now, looked like the massive wings of a crow. Under his unwavering gaze, Suqata involuntarily looked down at the discarded totem, now half buried in leaves. The glance did not go unnoticed, and quickly the old man's smile faded.

"What is going on here? Not out for a pleasant stroll, I imagine." He jumped down from the tree and landed with barely a sound on the dry leaves. He retrieved the statue and said, "Do you have any idea what you have done, boy?"

"You didn't really leave me a choice, did you, Pom, or Cora Vaco, or whatever your name is?"

In a blink of an eye, Pom darted forward. He was barely inches from Suqata's face when he stopped, holding the smooth statue up for him to see. "This only has power as long as it stays within the circle," he growled through gritted teeth, his voice ringing with amazing power. "Outside of the clearing it is useless. All of my treasures are now vulnerable."

Suqata stood his ground. "Like I said, you didn't give me much of a choice. You have lied to me at every turn, since that day you saved me from the wolves. You said I was lost here, and that there was no way out of the Henis-a-paka." Suqata did not raise his voice, but the words held a conviction behind them that was undeniable. "Would you have me hide here from the world like you and forget my friends are in danger? I think you knew I was going to take that the moment you revealed it to me."

There was a moment of quiet tension as they faced each other, there in the dark of the woods. The Chinequewa and the ancient forest spirit. Slowly, Pom's eyes changed back to their usual blue-grey and he stood there with a look of confused frustration.

"What do you have to prove here, boy?" he said, his voice now calm and tempered. "You owe that world nothing. Yes, I may have lied to you, but only to give you a chance to see a deeper truth. The

world of men has no place for you anymore, not with the knowledge you hold."

"And so you would leave it to be destroyed," Anishta said. "You would allow the Varcuya to step back amongst men without raising a finger? All for your selfish wishes."

Pom's eyes flashed silver again. "That's enough of your interference, woman," he said, "or have you forgotten who it was that saved you from the Spirit Walkers?"

Anishta looked down at her arms and saw the elaborate scrolling shapes that glowed a dull silver white. "No," she whispered. "I have not forgotten, but I think you have, Cora Vaco. You have forgotten that you once loved the Waking World, and the people who lived there." She turned to Suqata and softly touched his arm. Her touch was gentle, but cold to his skin. "You have forgotten how brave and resourceful they can be, especially when the odds are against them. If for no other reason than the memory of what they can be, you must help Suqata return."

Cora Vaco stubbornly shook his head as he paced over the frozen ground. Suqata and Anishta watched him go back and forth, apparently in a deep conversation with himself, complete with forceful hand gestures and exasperated huffs. Finally he stopped and turned to young man.

"You were starting to eat too much anyway," he said, frowning.

"Is that a yes then?"

"Well, do I have to spell it out for you? There are places where the way is thin between here and the Waking World, and I know them all, but it is a dangerous trek. The journey alone may kill you, but at least I can let you die with a clear conscience."

"Thanks Pom, I guess," Suqata said with a half-smile the old man did not return.

"Then your way is set," Anishta said, "Go now, for I fear danger will be close behind. But do not fear. There is something great within you, Suqata, if you are brave enough to trust it." As she spoke, the light within her gossamer shape began to fade.

"Wait. How do I stop the wolves once I get back to The Hollow? I don't even know what they are planning." Suqata called to her. He reached out to touch her, finding her hand had become as thin as morning mist.

"That you will have to discover on your own. Goodbye, Suqata. Tell Auralyn I love her. Tell her to be at peace. And may the One Voice protect you, for your time of sacrifice is drawing near." And in an instant, she was gone, swept away with wind.

"What did she mean by that?" he asked in a hushed voice. The gloom began to settle around them, quickly filling the spaces the light had only moments ago touched. Beyond the trees Suqata heard the sound of wolves breaking through the silence.

"Who knows? Come on, boy, we need to get a move on," Pom said, not wasting a second to see if Suqata was going to follow or not. "Try to keep up. They'll be on us soon enough."

Suqata didn't have to be told twice.

# CHAPTER 20

# HUNTERS AND THE HUNTED

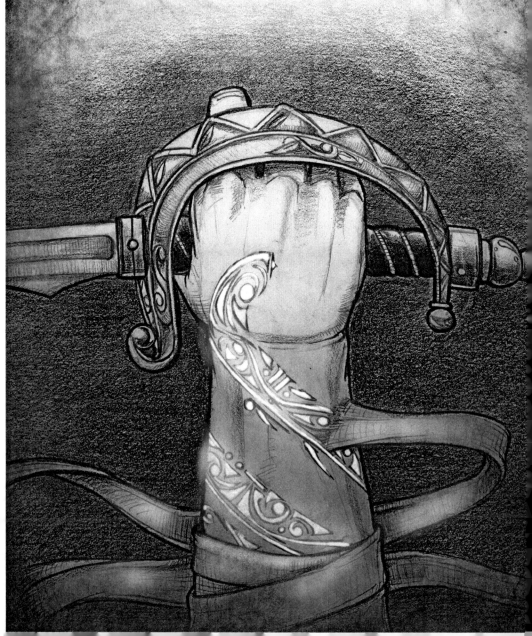

T HEY RAN FOR HOURS, UNTIL THE ENDLESS ROWS OF SPRUCE BECAME dotted with large boulders. The terrain became steeper, and Suqata soon found he was straining to keep up. His lungs heaved in his chest, and the muscles in his legs burned, but he never slowed, not for a second. Even at his current exhausting pace, Suqata would still find himself running alone in the woods as Pom disappeared to scout ahead. The old man was like the wind, shooting off in a blur of motion only to appear again moments later, sometimes a hundred yards off in the fog. Soon, Suqata was climbing over craggy outcroppings, scrambling to gain hand-holds on tree roots to pull himself along. The forest had become the foot of a mountain in a matter of hours and it was all he could do just to keep Pom in sight.

The boulders, covered in thick layers of moss and lichen, were slick to the touch, and between the boulders sat half-frozen pools of water, unstirred by man, beast, or spirit. As Suqata clawed his way forward, his feet would slip and more than once he ended up submerged in the murky pools up to his knees.

"The boots. Leave them," Pom said from his perch on a towering stone. "You'll have more luck barefoot." Suqata was too tired to argue. He pulled off his water-logged boots and cast them aside. His feet were wrapped in tough hide straps, so although he didn't want to admit it, the old man was right and Suqata did not slip again.

"How much further?" Suqata said. "We've been on the move for hours. Surely they can't still be on us."

Pom turned away and sniffed the air, first left then right, then with an exasperated look, he waved Suqata on.

"There is a small cave nearby. We can take a rest there." He then bounded away, leaping from stone to stone. The old man swept through the air like a leaf on the wind. Suqata followed, moving slowly up the incline until he could just make out Pom-poko-kuno beckoning him from a shadowed space between two boulders. By the time he could make out the opening of the cave, Pom was already sitting comfortably inside. The opening was narrow, but the inside was deep enough for both of them to be completely concealed, and sitting before the old man was a large, dark stone. Once Suqata was close enough, he could feel heat radiating from it like it was freshly pulled from a fire.

"I figured you would appreciate a little warmth, so this should do the trick," he said, already toasting his own aged hands over the stone. Suqata warily sat down across from him, and pulled his wet cloak in tight around himself. Every part of his body was sore, right down to the balls of his feet, but even that couldn't dim his ravenous curiosity. This was the first time he had a chance to get a better look at Pom since discovering his true nature.

Suqata watched the old man intently as he flexed his knobby fingers near the heat quietly whispering words of the *sen-wa* over the stone. Nothing seemed to have changed in him. Suqata was now more acutely aware of certain behaviors: turns of the old man's head or small nervous flicks of his ragged cloak, all of which were a very "crow-like," and hard to overlook. Before long, Pom noticed.

"Waiting for me to change into some kind of monster, are you?" Pom grumbled. "I just may if you keep up this gawking."

Suqata continued to stare with curiosity in his eyes. He had the excited look of a child preparing to poke at something with a stick.

"What are you looking at, boy!" Pom barked when his limited patience was spent.

"I'm not quite sure yet," Suqata answered plainly. "A day ago you were just a man. A strange man, yes, but just a man. Now you are so much more, and yet at this moment you don't seem any different."

"Oh, but I am different. In ways you can't possibly imagine. I wear a thousand battle scars from meddling in the affairs of immortals—the kind that never go away. And then there are those you can't see." He pointed at Suqata's head and then at his chest where

his heart lay. "The deep scars. Those are the ones that don't heal quite so neat."

Suqata looked at his own arms, at the now healed wounds from his run-in with the wolves.

The puckered flesh ran criss-cross over his skin, and he couldn't help but think of Obrie and the shiny burns covering his arms. When Suqata would ask why he had never learned to be more careful, his friend would always say, "It's not in some people's nature to look first before acting." He imagined his friend would find that saying amusing at that moment.

They sat in the quiet of the cave for a while longer, until both their clothes were dry and Suqata's muscles were not as achy. The whole time, his mind was working and calculating. When Pom eventually began to stir, moving forward to chant over the stone again, Suqata reached out and touched his arm.

"Let me do it," he said. He squatted down by the massive rock and held his hands over its dimpled surface. Then, without hesitation or mistake, Suqata chanted the short Song. His voice never wavered or lost its intent, and quickly heat began to radiate from the stone again.

Pom nodded in approval. "Good," he said, "You learned that by ear, after only hearing it once, did you? I must say, you do have a gift, Suqata, there is no denying that."

The young man smiled at the praise, especially considering whom it was coming from.

"Hopano used to say I had a mind like a bear trap," he said, sitting down once again and looking pensively at the surface of the stone. "Once something finds its way in, there was no getting it out. I guess it was a blessing and a curse. I can remember just about anything I hear or read, and the Songs he taught me still ring in my head in his voice, but once I decided that they weren't enough—that they weren't real, then suddenly none of that mattered. I just couldn't believe in them anymore, and my power went

away." Suqata looked up from the stone and his eyes met Pom's. "I believe now. I believe I can use the Songs to make a difference."

"What are you going on about? I'm not sure I like were this mood is heading, boy."

"It's not a mood. I'm ready, Pom. You can teach me the Songs that you have bound to your body, the ones that will make me stronger—better."

Before Suqata could finish, Pom was already shaking his head. "No, you fool. You have no idea what you are asking me for. This is not one Song, but dozens all intricately woven together into one grand lay that would test the strength of any wordweaver twice your years. Long ago, the Chinequewa would bind these songs to their greatest hunters, a group called the *Redi'che*. Men and women would spend a lifetime honing their bodies and minds so that one day they could stand before the ancient wordweavers and have their chance at becoming *Redi'che*. Do you know how many survived the ritual? Half. Only half of those that attempted to become this," Pom lifted his sleeve to reveal swirling silver marks that covered the surface of his arm,"would see the next day. Sometimes, even less."

"I'm dead anyway at this pace. The wolves will be on us before long, that or something worse. You said so yourself. I don't have the strength to fight spirits, not like you. If I don't try this, then I'll never have a chance of even making it home, let alone making any kind of a difference once I get there."

Pom looked away, trying to come up with some kind of response. "I don't like it. There has to be another way," he grumbled, deep in thought.

"There isn't, Pom, and you know it."

"And if you die, what then? Do I leave you here in the Henis-a-paka? You don't know what that means for you. Your spirit will be trapped here, like the Varcuya, slowly going mad from the hopeless isolation. I would have to bind you, like Anishta."

"It's a greater risk not to try. This will work, trust me. I am a quick study, probably the quickest you will ever meet, and I've

bound a Song into myself before. You are the only person who can help me do it, if I'm to become what I need to be to survive."

The determination in Suqata's voice was unmistakable, even palpable.

"And what makes you think I would give you that kind of knowledge anyway? You are just a boy, playing a game with creatures and events beyond your depth. I promised Anishta I would help you return, not upend my whole basket of tricks for your benefit. Why should I help you?"

"You'll help, for the same reason that you saved me in the woods."

"Do tell, young one."

"You are lonely. The chance of hearing another's voice, even a pathetic human like me, is worth the effort. Am I right?"

"Bah! Foolishness. I am fine by myself. In fact, I prefer it. Besides, if I ever needed such companionship there are other spirits here, and I always have the wolves."

"Garro Knocta? And yet you would sit here and let the Varcuya use him like some kind of puppet. Come on, Pom, past all of the bravado, you do care for things other than yourself."

"You'd be hard pressed to prove it, fleshling." Suddenly Pom's eyes became silver once again, just as they had when he spoke to Anishta. "We have watched you for some time. Watched as you stood at the precipice of greatness and change, and saw you turn away. You are not ready for what you ask, Chinequewa. You are too weak."

"Then help me, Cora Vaco. You're the only one who can."

The old man cocked his head to the side and considered Suqata, taking his measure with those shining eyes, then clapped his hands one resounding time.

"Fine. I'll help you, but if you die attempting this, I will leave your body for Garro Knocta's children. No use letting all that young flesh go to waste."

Suqata laughed. "Of course. We wouldn't want that, would we?"

THE SONG CORA VACO TAUGHT Suqata was the longest and most intricate combination of words he had ever heard. Each rise and tempo shift meant something new, and had to be copied exactly or the effect would be disastrous. Proving his training and ability, Suqata learned the whole lay in just over an hour and when they were done, he began to Sing. Beneath the rise and the fall of his voice he could hear the old man speak.

"Are you ready to begin?"

"Yes."

"Good. Now concentrate, boy. Remember the night you bound the hiding *sen-wa* to yourself. Remember how it felt, and your thoughts when you attempted it. Remember."

Suqata closed his eyes, and suddenly he was twelve years old again, crouched in the shadow of Captain Graye, his practice sword clutched tightly in his hands. He felt the fear as if he was there again, and the same heady rush of excitement when he first felt the power hum through him. Then, he heard his own thoughts as the distant echo of someone else speaking.

"Change me, make me more," said a young voice, so faintly that Suqata barely heard it over the sound of his own Singing. "Change me," the voice said again. Such a simple statement that held in it a thousand small changes. Before Suqata knew he was doing so, the thought turned to words, spoken in the ancient tongue and woven into the Song.

In that instant, Suqata's body was ablaze with pain. More pain than he had ever experienced in his life. More than he had ever dreamed possible. As the Song took hold of him, he could hear himself scream as he had never screamed before, the sound of it muffled and distant as if it were coming from someone else far away. He watched the silver lines scrolling their way across his skin, lacing through his flesh like trickling mercury. All the while, there was always his voice, just there on the other side of knowing, Singing through the cloud of pain and confusion. It rang out with power and purpose, although his mouth no longer formed the

words. It was as though his voice was now its own thing, free of his control or direction. He lost all concept of time. It could have been days, or weeks, that he floated in that sea of sensation bound to the music and free of the world. Then, all went dark.

"WAKE UP, SUQATA," A VOICE whispered sharply, and Suqata's eyes were open. He still lay on the cave floor near the hot stone. As his eyes slowly found focus, Pom's grim face appeared hovering over him. "How do you feel?" he asked in a hushed voice.

SUQATA STIRRED, FLEXING HIS MUSCLES and hands. He was cold, but his clothes were drenched in sweat and his limbs felt strangely light and weak, like that of a newborn calf, but there was no pain, which was a pleasant surprise. He could barely move, so he lay there quietly and tried to get his bearings.

"I'm not dead," he said feebly, "though I feel like I should be. How long was I out?"

"An hour or so. The fact that you are even conscious astounds me," he said, looking him square in the eye in a disbelieving sort of way.

"Sorry to disappoint you."

"Much to the contrary. When I was young, I'd seen great warriors attempt what you have done, and those that didn't die would lie in a deep sleep, sometimes for months, before returning to the world. But you … you have proven a great deal of my notions to be wrong. Keep this up and I will really start to think you are special."

Suqata attempted a smile. "Must be nice to know you can still be surprised?"

"I generally don't like surprises. Cora Vaco, on the other hand … " Pom stopped in mid-thought, and Suqata knew the old man had said something he had not intended.

"You speak as if you are not the same being. Is that true?"

"Why are you always asking questions? It is not your concern."

"Please Pom," Suqata strained to sit up and face him. "There are secrets I need to know: about my people, and the *mahko*." Then,

gathering his courage, he said, "I want to hear them … from Cora Vaco the Crow."

Pom looked wearily to the young man and said, "Be careful what you wish for."

Instantly, his eyes shone silver and a satisfied grin crept across his face.

"I knew it wouldn't be long before you asked for me," Cora Vaco said with a mocking tilt to his head, "not long before you came to me with your questions."

Suqata was still very weak, but faced him. "The real question is, will you answer them?"

Cora Vaco perched there on the balls of his feet with a look of glee.

"Of course. I have nothing to hide. I will give you three." He held up three knobby fingers. "Three questions of an immortal *mahko*—a grand boon by any standard, so choose them carefully."

Suqata did not hesitate.

"How do I defeat the wolves once I return to The Hollow?"

"I do not know. Next question."

"Bastard, that's it!" Suqata huffed, "Some all-knowing spirit."

"I cannot tell you something I don't know, can I? Next question."

"Fine. Why is Pom enslaved to you?" Suqata asked.

A look of indignation played across Cora Vaco's face.

"Pom-poko-kuno is no slave. He is my friend, or as close to a friend as I have ever had," he said, pulling his cloak in over his arms. "I have lived since the One Voice sang me into existence. Cora Vaco, the Keeper of Ways, the Claw in the Night, the Storykeeper, and the Soul Speaker. I have more knowledge than man will ever learn, but in a way I have always envied you. Not for your treasures, or your creativity, but for your ability to change. Mankind is never the same thing twice, and in a lifetime, you change constantly from one day to the next. The *mahko* do not change. I have always been the same Cora Vaco, which can become boring after so many seasons. But one day, when there was nothing else left to lose, I made a bargain with my friend Pom. I would give him eternity, and in

exchange he would share his mortal form. Who knew what would come of the whole thing. Now we are neither man nor *mahko*."

Suqata looked at the person squatting before him, and considered what he had heard. "I don't believe you," he said in a low voice. "I can't imagine you giving up all that kind of power, or Pom sacrificing his life for your curiosity."

"There were ... extenuating circumstances. But enough of that, last question!"

"Fine. Where are my people? Where are the Chinequewa?" Suqata asked breathlessly.

"They have gone beyond the mountain, what's left of them anyway. One summer, I came to them in the forest, called by an old woman. Her voice was strong, and I was curious. She said that enemies had come to their valley, but her people no longer had the power to defeat them. The generations had made them weak, and she was the last of the wordweavers. She couldn't give their hunters the power of the *Redi'che*. She asked for my help, and in exchange she would give me something I have desired for a millennium. So, the deal was struck, and I gave the men of her village the power they sought, and one cold winter's night they descended on their enemies with strength and fury. Many died, and my price was paid."

"What was your price, Cora Vaco?" Suqata asked, but before the old man could speak, his eyes changed back and the *mahko* spirit was gone.

"You should get some rest," Pom said wearily as he looked to the cave opening. "We'll have to leave very soon."

Suqata was too tired to argue, so he laid he head down in the crook of his arm. He watched Pom until sleep took him.

"WAKE UP, SUQATA," POM HISSED.

Suqata sat up with a start. "What is it?"

"We have to move. The wind has shifted." Pom reached up and

tapped the side of his nose knowingly. "I smell something coming. Are you strong enough to move?"

Suqata flexed his hands, marveling for a second at the *sen-wa* marks that ran up his arms. "I'm as ready I'm going to be," he replied.

The weather had not changed outside of the cave, although it did seem darker. Old Pom pointed up the mountainside into the fog and said, "That is where we are going." Suqata followed his hand, not expecting to see much, but instantly his vision changed. It was like looking down a swirling tunnel that became shorter and shorter until he could clearly see a monolithic stone set deep in the ground, and covered with swirling symbols so intricate that the surface of it looked worm eaten. Just as quickly, his vision snapped back to normal and Suqata was left staggering.

"Careful there, boy," Pom whispered, "I don't need you falling down the mountain."

Suqata was speechless. "That was amazing," he said as he steadied himself against the old man.

"Yes, your senses have changed, amongst other things. It will take a while to adjust, but we don't have time to—"

In a second, Pom was gone in blur of claws and fangs, falling down from the cave opening.

The wolf-kin had found them!

"POM!" Suqata yelled, and jumped from the rock ledge onto the creature's back, the three of them landing with a crash in one of the brackish pools between the boulders.

"Hold him!" Pom cried out, and Suqata wrapped his arms around the creature's muzzle. It thrashed relentlessly, and he could feel the blast of its hot breath across his forearm, and the warm foam rushing from between its fangs. It thrashed with its free arm and tried to bite down, but Suqata squeezed tight. It struggled fiercely, raking its claws across air and flesh, but Suqata only squeezed harder and harder. Suddenly, he felt the beast's jaw dislocate with a loud pop. Pom did the rest, driving his carbato dagger into the wolf's chest. It fell over into the pool, dead.

"Are you all right?" Pom said. He pulled Suqata from the water.

"Yes." He stood up and realized his body felt different—stronger.

"Good. I didn't want to have to carry you ... "

Before Pom could finish, they both heard a disturbance in the distance. Together they climbed out from between the rocks. Down through the fog at the foot of the mountain, they could just make out a figure emerging from the dense tree line, its bristling silhouette heaving in the thick fog. It was the other wolf twin. Suqata reached for the hilt of his sword but found Pom's hand stopping him short.

"Wait, boy. Look closer," he said.

Suqata looked again, this time concentrating. His vision quickly changed, now focused in on the wolf. Suqata could suddenly see everything, from the steam of its breath to the wild, hunted look in its eyes.

"Something isn't right," he said aloud. "It's scared ... "

Without warning, it disappeared into the fog, followed by a horrible, primal scream. Suqata's vision snapped back to normal. Even from their high vantage, he and Pom could still see the wolf struggling, then torn asunder by the ghostly white hands of a Varcuya.

"Run, Suqata!" Pom called out. He pointed again towards their destination. "Run and don't stop until you reach the ruins."

As Pom bounded away, Suqata instinctually did the same. One jump sent him soaring through the air, and landing on the balls of his feet yards away.

"Amazing," he said eagerly. He summoned his strength and bounded off again. The sound of cold wind rushed past his ears and through his hair. It was like flying, but even in the midst of the exhilaration, Suqata knew that he was running for his life.

# CHAPTER 21
# THE RUINS

S UQATA BOUNDED OVER THE MOUNTAINSIDE LIKE A ZEPHYR, HIS MOVE-
ments more flight then leaping, until he landed atop the stone
monolith seconds behind Pom. The swirling, scroll-worked surface
felt strange beneath his bare feet, and he looked down onto the
plateau below them.

"Have we lost them?" he asked Pom. Suqata glanced back down
the mountain, searching for the Varcuya.

"Not yet. They'll show themselves again soon enough, but
they'll be wary about coming to this place."

Amidst the trees, as the clouds of frozen mist drifted aside,
tall carved totem poles were beginning to appear. They towered
up from the grey, their grim faces staring out into the endless sky
of the Henis-a-paka. Suqata couldn't help feeling like they were
watching him, their immortal gaze challenging him to come forward, friend or foe.

At their feet stood the remnants of stone walls and thatched
roofs, now fallen into ruin and forgotten. But even from their bare
bones, Suqata could see the remains of what was once a great city:
large courtyards with wide gardens, and paths and streets con-
necting the length of the plateau city like threads of a spider's web.
The city was tiered, with roughly cut stairs leading up through the
rows of destroyed buildings, some still adorned in elaborate relief
sculptures and *sen-wa* markings.

"Welcome to Tika-matu, Place of the Sky, as it was once called.
Men no longer even remember when this was a great city, let alone
its name," Pom spoke in a solemn tone. "There used to be such
life here. Music and songs like you have never imagined. And the
women." He smiled wryly, then bounded off again into the fog,
Suqata following right behind. When they landed together on the

dark pathway surrounded by thick brush and rubble, they quickly moved to the cover of a half-standing wall.

"This is incredible," Suqata said, "I never knew anything like this existed in the colonies. The captain always said that before the Kael came to these lands, there was nothing but ..." Suqata found himself stopping mid-thought, ashamed to continue.

"What, boy? What did your captain say was here?"

Suqata looked down at his feet. "Fools and forests. He said the place was nothing but fools and forests."

"Well, your captain is an idiot, isn't he?" Pom hissed, positioning himself so that he could easily peer through a rough gap in the wall. "This used to be a shining center of knowledge and trade for the First People, long before the Sundering."

"What happened to it?"

"It was destroyed, of course," he snickered, "but not by men from across the ocean. They came from here, from this very land. Oh, the destruction wrought by the misguided is the worst of all."

While Pom scanned the distance, Suqata examined the wall they hid behind. He ran his fingers over its rough surface and intricate tool marks. It was covered with deeply carved images of people in strange dress, all bearing the broad features of the northern tribes. Their hands were raised to the sky, and above them, figures of cloaked men ran effortlessly across the branches of trees, their bodies adornrd with *sen-wa* markings.

"The *Redi'che*," Suqata whispered. It was unlike anything he had ever seen in his short life.

Just then, he heard movement, a soft rustling of branches that quickened his heart and put all his senses at alert. One glance at Pom confirmed the old man had heard it as well. He now had his twin daggers drawn and held loosely in his hands. Suqata slowly reached for the hilt of his sword, but before he could draw it Pom motioned for him to be still.

"Something is off. Do you smell it?" he whispered, barely loud enough for Suqata to make out his words. Pom tapped the side of

his nose, and right away Suqata knew what was amiss. He smelled blood—a lot of it. It was very distinct now, its strong, coppery tang filling his senses. That was when the soft rustling of leaves turned into a loud crash.

"Come on, quickly now!" Pom said. He was off into the brush, with Suqata right on his heels. It didn't take long to see they were running towards the scent, not away from it. In a few seconds they could see the source of the noise and the blood. Lying in the brush was the body of the wolf called Smoke, covered in long, deep slashes from head to foot. The beast was enormous, with coarse dark fur stretched across lean muscles that rose and fell with each of its labored, shallow breaths.

"Cora Vaco?" it spat, slightly lifting its head from the ground. When its eyes met Pom's, the wolf growled, pulling back its lips to reveal rows of yellow fangs. Suqata's hand instantly went to his sword hilt but stopped just short of pulling the blade free. The wolf was laughing—thick and mirthlessly. "I have found you, Crow. Found you at last, just as my brothers asked. It's not too late."

Pom crouched down beside it without any sign of fear. "What a mess. You seem to have been through quite an ordeal, pup. So speak, why were you sent to find me? Why are you not too late?"

"You still draw breath, Uncle Crow. I have arrived in time. There are things I must tell you. Things you must know." A trickle of blood ran from the wolf's muzzle down into its fur as it spoke.

"Speak up. What must I know?"

"Of our betrayal!" The wolf growled, but this time it sounded more like a whimper. "My father has been betrayed. The shades have lied and betrayed the great Garro Knocta, and we shall all die for it."

Pom leaned in closer and laid his hands on the wolf's bloodied chest, and the creature shrank back in fear as the old man's eyes flashed silver.

"Be clear, wolf-kin. We have very little time, and more than our lives and your revenge depend on what you say now."

The beast gurgled another laugh, then spoke again. "Strange I should die here with you, Crow. When Father told us that the shades would teach us to take on the forms of men, all he could say to us for a time was, 'Now who is the fool, Cora Vaco?' The shades taught us their magic, and told us to go forth and take man's flesh for our own. The more of us that did this, the weaker the border between here and the Waking World would become. Soon, we would be free to go where we willed. So, one by one, we crossed over, some into the bodies of mortal wolves but soon some found men to possess. It took all our power not to lose ourselves. This was before the Varcuya learned of the girl. Then, nothing else mattered."

The girl.

Pom turned to Suqata when he heard this, and he watched as the signs of dread wrote themselves across his face.

"Auralyn is in danger," Suqata said. "She is Anishta's daughter, and she has a spirit Song bound to her body. Somehow, she was the one who sent me here."

"I know who the girl is. This changes everything," Pom said darkly. "Do you have any idea what this means?"

"It means, Cora Vaco, that the great Garro Knocta and my brothers are no longer needed!" The wolf spoke barely in a whisper now, and as his strength began to fail him, his eyes took on a haunted, distant look. "The Varcuya no longer need us to open the way. They watched as my brothers and sisters began to go mad, trapped in the men they possessed. They forgot who they were, losing themselves to man's emotions. Even Garro Knocta. The knowledge the betrayers gave us was incomplete. Now we will be destroyed along with the men when the Varcuya cross over to devour the Waking World."

In one last shuddering breath, the wolf spoke no more.

Then, a cold voice spoke out like a blast of winter wind.

"Do not weep for the creature. He has served his purpose, and now you shall follow it into death."

Suqata looked up from the fallen wolf to see the ghostly figure

of a Varcuya hovering but a few yards away. Its thin, emaciated limbs were outstretched, covered in the silver swirls of written *sen-wa* and *sen-tal,* while its white hair floated about its hollow face as if eternally immersed in frozen time. It turned its hollow glance to Pom, and the old man twirled his twin daggers, pointing at it with one of the blades.

"You and your kind have been very busy of late, wraith," he said, still spinning one of the daggers in his left hand. "All this work, and for what? To make fools of a pack of high-strung dogs? Very unsporting, don't you think, considering they are not very bright." His eyes darted quickly towards Suqata's sword hand. Right away Suqata knew what Pom meant for him to do.

"They are but a means to an end," it hissed. The Varcuya quickly shifted to the side with unnatural speed, causing Suqata and Pom to counter. "When the imbalance is complete, the fabric between the worlds will rip. A new Sundering! And then, FREEDOM! Oh how I have missed the warmth of blood, locked away here with nothing but spirit spawn to feed on. It will be good to taste it again."

"Well, I'm afraid you will have to wait a little longer. And please, watch what you say. You may spook the boy. I'm not sure how much you remember of being human, but frightened youths are prone to be ... unpredictable." Pom looked to Suqata and gave him a wink.

In a blur, Suqata pulled his rusted blade. He slashed out at the wraith, the sword leaving an arc of silver in its wake. The blade passed untouched through the Varcuya's gossamer flesh, as he had feared it would, but the distraction was just enough. Pom was gone, and where he stood now hovered the winged shadow of the Great Crow. It swooped down at the Varcuya, cutting through the chill mist. The creature turned to face it, but too late. Invisible blades slashed across its torso leaving blazing lines of green light.

The Varcuya screamed, like the howl of a hundred dying men, and Suqata reached for his ears, fighting to hold out the impossible pain. Another slash appeared as Cora Vaco raced in again for the kill. The best Suqata could do was watch as the two insubstantial figures, one glowing white and the other shadow black, rained down blows upon each other. He pulled his hands away from his ears and tried to Sing the banishment Auralyn had taught him that day in the field, but when the words took form in his mind and on his lips, he was struck down. It felt as if the Varcuya's scream were still with him, echoing into his mind. He tried to Sing again only to meet the same wall of pain, racking his body like physical blows knocking him to ground. He fought past the anguished wails, but when he finally looked up from where he lay, he saw his chance to act was gone. Cora Vaco was now struggling in the wraith's bony grip.

"That's it, fight me, Crow. Fight the dying of the light," it hissed. The shadow form was fading from around Pom, but it didn't stop him from plunging his daggers handle deep into the Varcuya's chest. Another mind-shattering scream followed and Suqata felt his insides explode with agonizing pain, threatening to spill out. He fought to keep his eyes open, fearing what would happen to Pom if he were to black-out. Even the ruined stones that lay beneath the wraith responded to the horror's anger. As it squeezed Pom's neck tighter, everything near it was cast in a shimmering layer of frost. Then, without the slightest sign of pity, it racked its claws across the old man's chest, covering its hands in red.

"You are almost mortal in this man's skin, Cora Vaco," the Varcuya said. "Your power is nothing compared to ours. Can't you feel it?" It slowly turned its attention to Suqata, flaring its hollow eyes with hunger. "Do you feel the power of my voice binding you? Without your Song, boy, you will die here with the crow—in this graveyard of man's lost potential. It's a shame you will never see the world we will make. It begins with your Orin's Hollow. With this girl, Auralyn. Then, nothing will be able to face us, and we will bring night everlasting to the Waking World."

Suqata tried to push his mind past the pain, past the sound of the creature's coiling, rasping voice, but every attempt brought

nothing. His power was beyond his reach. There was only one choice left to him.

"Wait!" he cried out, "I can't take it anymore. The pain. Make it stop. Please!"

The creature would have smiled, if had lips to do so. With Pom still hanging from its hand, now limp and barely breathing, the Varcuya moved in closer to Suqata. It slowly clawed at the air, feeling the power humming from within him, and it let out a moan of satisfaction, then spoke again.

"What do you wish, young one? Do you wish to be released from your misery?"

Suqata looked up, and his eyes met Pom's. Then, quite unexpectedly, the old man winked.

"Never. I just wanted you to move a little closer."

Pom's seemingly lifeless hand shot up and threw his remaining dagger towards Suqata. When the hilt found his hand, Suqata disappeared from sight.

*I have to time this just right.* He thought as he felt his body slip under the power of the Hiding Song. He held his breath and readied the blade in his hand. Before him stood the wavering, unrecognizable shape of the Varcuya and Pom. He knew he had only one chance at this. It had to be perfect. Suqata leapt high into the air behind the Varcuya. Then, holding the dagger in both hands, he released the Hiding Song as he descended. The jagged blade rammed its way home, and just as the cold air hit Suqata's lungs, he sang out clear and strong.

*"Qui vanoya u nash wunato, qui vanoya u nash wunato, qui vanoya u nash wunato!"*

The creature never had the chance to utter a word. In a brilliant flash of white and cold, it was gone and Suqata was flung to the ground, the smoking carbato dagger still clutched in his frozen hand, while its twin stood half embedded in the stony ground. Suqata's head was ringing, but he wasted no time in retrieving the weapon and scrambling over to the rubble where Cora Vaco lay. He gently

lifted the old man to his lap. Through his thin hands, Suqata could see the strange green slash the wraith had delivered across his chest and stomach, now covered in frozen blood and frost. He reached to touch it, but was met with Cora Vaco's hard stare.

"Leave it," he grumbled weakly, "no use both of us dying today." His words struck Suqata as surely as a fist.

"Tell me what to do and I'll do it," he said fiercely, "I'm not about to leave you here to die. You would get all the credit for the kill."

The old spirit laughed and small dots of blood coated his lips. It was a weak one, but honest.

"I don't think you have time to do anything but save yourself. Listen, Suqata, listen. More are coming. They're minutes away."

Suqata stopped and steadied his own heartbeat. He heard them, like the crisp crackling of frosted leaves. More Varcuya were gathering, and Suqata let his vision extend past the ruins and trees, each time he did, he saw another. There had to be a least a dozen. Pom reached up the grasped Suqata's shoulder. "Your time of sacrifice is at hand."

"OY UDAN KI-YI, HI-ASHITH MA-DI," the old man whispered the words, and the forest shifted around them until they were concealed.

"That should buy us some time. I would like to have done this another way. To have given you time to take in all that you must, but once again fate has taken time from us, Suqata." As he spoke, his eyes held a kind of sorrow Suqata had never seen in them. They slowly turned back to their usual icy-blue, but the sadness remained.

"What are you on about, Pom? We can still make it out of here together. You are the Great Crow, Cora Vaco. Every story I ever heard of you had you beating the odds, or outwitting all your enemies. You are smarter than fate; everyone knows that."

"Alas, that is where you are mistaken. No one is smarter than fate, not even the spirits of the ancient world. Only one of us was ever meant to leave this place, and that is you." Slowly, Pom

unclasped the dark, feathered cloak and forced it into Suqata's hands, who took it reluctantly. It was heavier than he had thought it would be, and the feathers were soft against his skin.

"Why are you giving me this?"

"Remember I said only a being of both worlds can pass between them? Only a man that has been touched by the *mahko* can see the way. You must become more than what you are, Suqata." Pom looked away. "You must take Cora Vaco into you and become the Great Crow. It is the only way."

Suqata let the cloak slip from his fingers to the ground. His breath became thick and labored, and he could suddenly feel the heat of anger rising inside him now, coursing through his veins. Some part of him wanted to drop Pom right there, like some creature that meant him harm, and just be done with it. Done with it all; to have come so far, and be so close to home, only to discover this was the key to his way. Suqata felt like a puppet on a string.

"Why do you tell me this now?" he said through gritted teeth. He felt as though his head might burst, but seeing the old man, broken in his arms, some of that self-righteous rage died away. "You should have told me, long before now. Why didn't you say something? Did you think I wasn't strong enough? Did you think my resolve was so weak? I am not afraid, do you understand, but I am tired of secrets. This is my choice."

Pom smiled. "You don't have time for this! Trust me when I say I know better than any living being what you are feeling right this second, and for that I am sorry. Let me offer you this knowledge; you were the price your people paid all those years ago, and only you have been destined for this moment. Deep down, some part of you has always known." Pom's hands began to tremble. "But beyond this choice, nothing is decided. You are now the master of your destiny, as you have only dreamed of, and the mysteries of the world are out there for you to discover. Your spirit is stronger than mine, and more independent. Cora Vaco and you will make a formidable pair. Together, there is nothing beyond your reach."

Just past the fog, Suqata could hear the moan of the icy wind following the Varcuya through the ruins. They had not picked up on their trail yet, but it was only a matter of moments. There just didn't seem to be enough time.

"Will I still be me?" he asked quickly. Pom's strength was obviously waning, and Suqata knew his time was coming soon.

"Yes, and no. It is a partnership, an open sharing of knowledge and experience. It will be hard to understand at first, but you will in time. You must." Pom reached down and picked up the cloak. He handed it again to Suqata, this time offering it. "Will you do this?" he asked, his voice catching slightly as he spoke. Suqata lifted the dark mass from Pom's hand and threw the length of it over his shoulders, clasping the feathered cowl into place.

"Yes. I will, Pom," he replied.

In that moment, many things happened. Pom's body went rigid in his arms, and suddenly Suqata could hear the distant sound of a Song so beautiful, so haunting, that he felt his heart ache with each word sung. They were combined into an intricate lattice of the ancient tongue, too complex for Suqata to decipher, and when the Song reached its peak, a dark shape began to form beside Pom. In seconds, it took shape, swirling and shifting until it became the dark outline of a large, menacing crow. It looked as if a patch of starry night had pulled itself from the sky and now stood before him, staring at Suqata with shining silver eyes, its head quizzically cocked to side. That was when Suqata heard it speak.

"It is time," Cora Vaco said. His voice rang with a power Suqata had never experienced, as raw and unadulterated as a crack of thunder on the horizon, and yet there was something in the sound of it that he did not expect: the sound of excitement. There was a rush of motion as the dark crow beat its wings, and in a blur of stars and shadow it flew straight into Suqata's body, leaving only a thin trace of darkness behind it.

"Pom, what just happened?" he asked, trying to catch his breath. "Is it over?"

"No, my boy. It is only just beginning," the old man replied.

In the distance, Suqata heard cries of victory on the wind. The Varcuya had discovered them, and were quickly approaching. Pom then pointed out into the fog, past the edge of the ruins.

"There," he whispered, "you will find an open cliff. That is your way." He looked up into Suqata's eyes and smiled one last time. "I'm glad you found me again, my boy. That day, when he came to take you, your Captain Graye, I thought you were lost to me. There was so much I had left to teach you, but time has never been our friend. You were my greatest student, and my friend. I am glad to have seen the man you have become." Pom-poko-kuno's features began to shift, changing from one face to another, some young, some old, until finally they became those of someone familiar. There, looking back at him with blind, empty eyes, was the face of his teacher.

"Hopano," Suqata said. He felt a single tear slide slowly down his cheek, falling on the old man's worn shirt. He searched without hope to find the words to explain how he felt at that moment, but when nothing seem appropriate he simply said, "I never got to say goodbye to you that day."

The old man's grip tightened on Suqata's arm for just a second. "You have now. *Namu nashta*, my boy, and farewell." And just like that, Pom-poko-kuno, who was Cora Vaco the Great Crow, who was the teacher Hopano, faded and was gone.

Suqata now sat alone, surrounded by the sound of his enemies' approach.

"The cliff is where your way lies," he whispered to himself. He gripped the carbato daggers in both hands tightly, and in a stir of mist he was off through the ruins. Suqata bounded over walls, past fallen towers, and through arches adorned with ancient stone faces. It didn't take long for the wraiths to sense his movements. Soon, they were on his heels, howling wildly into the emptiness. Suqata never looked back or broke his stride. On and on he ran, until the grey stones and tall stoic totems gave way to the trees once again,

and then even they fell away. Suqata found himself standing on the bald stone outcropping surrounded by grey. Beneath him was nothing, just an endless space of mist, but even without seeing it, Suqata knew that this was the place he was looking for.

"Nowhere left to run, fleshling," a cold voice hissed behind him, and Suqata turned to see six Varcuya hovering mere yards away. "You have killed one of us. We must make your death painful, and lasting."

"I'm afraid that will have to wait," Suqata said, glancing one more time into the grey abyss. "You see, I have an appointment with the wolves, and I dare not be late."

"Oh. Is that so? So sure are you," one of them replied, just as another moved forward threateningly. "Who are you to deny a Varcuya his kill, boy?"

Suqata spread wide his arms, a dagger in each hand, and closed his eyes. When he opened them again, they blazed with silver light, and he smiled knowingly at his enemies.

"I am Suqata, the Claw in the Night, The Storykeeper, The Soul Speaker, and the Keeper of Ways. You have no power over me."

With that, he fell backwards into the void, arms outstretched like great, black wings, and disappeared from sight.

# PART 5

# THE CROW'S FLIGHT

# CHAPTER 22
# THE WOLVES DESCEND

O BRIE'S BREATH FORMED SMALL GREY CLOUDS AS HE BREATHED SLOWLY and steadily. He then lifted his cupped hands to his mouth, hoping to strain out some of its precious heat. He longed to move and stretch, but feared he might make a sound and alert the men that searched for him. So, he continued to sit there, in the cold and quiet, and wait as his joints grew more numb with each passing hour.

This was by far the worst hiding place he had found since escaping the mad men the night before. It was a wooden supply shed about twenty yards from the mill loading dock. He had been hunkered down there since daybreak surrounded by the smell of salted fish, pickled in barrels, and stacks of hard-backed biscuits. He had tried them both and decided that going hungry for the time being might be in his best interest. Besides, he was only there out of necessity. This was the closest he had been able to get to the barges on the river. Now, he was only a few yards away from escape on one of them leaving Orin's Hollow. All he had to do was be patient and quiet. The patrols throughout town had been oppressively regular since Lady Auralyn was attacked, rounding up anyone they thought looked suspicious, with Obrie the kitchen hand at the top of their list. Right after Suqata, of course.

Sitting alone in silence was not Obrie's strong suit, and it took every ounce of his concentration to keep himself from whistling, humming, or just plain dozing off, but after a whole night of vigilance, sleep soon took him quickly and without question. Sleep brought dreams: terrible visions of the night at the mill. He could see Ashton and his men upon him, their eyes filled with hunger as he watched them shine in the moonlight. Then, as if they had walked fully formed out of some nightmare, they changed into monsters. He could see Suqata and Auralyn running, drawing the creatures away from him where he lay, and then onto the bridge.

There was a flash of white light, and suddenly Suqata was gone, leaving the girl alone with the bodies of her attackers. Obrie had tried to help. He ran to her side, calling out into the night for help. All he heard in response were the angry, raised voices of the guards. They found him standing over her and reacted, chasing him off towards the mill side of the river. He could still hear their calls in his head, and then the sound of a single shot over his shoulder sending tingles through his frame.

The phantom shot snapped Obrie awake from the dream with a start. His leg kicked out like he was still running and his foot hit the loose boards at the base of the shed wall with a loud crack. He shuddered at the sound.

"Damn," he whispered, freezing perfectly still. "Maybe nobody heard that?"

Almost in response, there was a resounding crash at the shed door. Then another. One more, and in shouldered two armed Black Guard.

"You there, get up! Keep your hands in front of you!" the first one growled as his partner held his rifle at the ready. Obrie held his hands up in the air so that both men could see, but couldn't move any further. He wanted to, desperately, but a day's worth of sitting in such tight quarters had rendered his leg useless. The guard took this as a challenge and grabbed Obrie roughly by the collar.

"Come on, big boy! Out into the day we go!"

The sunlight was almost blinding, reflected off the glistening mounds of fresh snow, and Obrie had to blink away tears that formed immediately. It was cold out, colder than he could ever remember being, and the afternoon light was quickly turning to evening, giving every surface an orange glow. Just yards away, though, he caught sight of something that made his heart sink. Where once he could see the rolling greenish-blue waves of the Shadow River, white capped and heaving with life, now lay a glistening expanse of ice. Nothing moved. The dock lay deserted, while the barges sat undisturbed, held tight by the river's frozen mass.

"What kind of witchery is this?" he whispered to himself. The Shadow River never froze, not in any of the years since Orin's Hollow was formed on its banks. The current was just too strong. But sure as day, there it was, and gone was his last chance of escape.

"On your feet, slave," the soldier said, pulling Obrie up to his full height and forcing him along, away from the dock and up the wood-plank steps to the street above. The Hollow was as quiet as the grave, every window shuttered and closed. Not even a footprint broke the even drifts of white that lay heaped against the doorways and corners. The festival lanterns were still hung, but were now frosted over and swaying heavily in the wind.

"Where are you taking him, Slater?" the rear guard said to the one holding Obrie's collar. "Lieutenant Dobbs said all detainees were to be brought back to the guard post for questioning. We're going the wrong way."

Slater turned to his comrade and flashed him a menacing glare. He then produced a length of rope from his belt and roughly bound Obrie's hands behind him. He was breathing hard with excitement, filling the air with clouds of steam, and there was an uneasy way to how he moved that made Obrie wary. He seemed ill fitted to his own skin, as strange as that sounded.

"C'mon, Ashley, let's take this filth into the alley there and be done with him," Slater growled. Obrie could hear the guard's teeth grinding as he spoke. "Captain said 'suffer not a witch to live.' This one fed us all for years, without anyone being the wiser. No telling the damage he's done. Let's just end him. We'll be heroes."

"I'm no witch!" Obrie interjected. There was obvious fear in his voice, but true to form he tried to make things light. "I may have been a little skimpy on the rabbit in the stew once or twice. Besides, you men needed more vegetables anyway."

Neither of them laughed. Instead, Slater struck Obrie hard in the face. "Be quiet, witch! Captain Graye told us all about you and your kind. He said you would try to confuse us, make things sound like they are not so. Test our conviction." He leaned in and stared hard into Obrie's watering eyes. "But I know the truth. You are dangerous. You are my enemy."

Obrie watched him in stunned silence. It wasn't until Slater gave him a triumphant smile that Obrie saw them: shining white eyes, like those of an animal in torchlight, and the beginnings of curved fangs descending almost to his gum line. Obrie felt his blood go cold.

"You are one of them, aren't you?" he screamed and fought to get free. "Let me go! I have done nothing. I won't tell anyone, I swear."

"What is he talking about, Slater?" Private Ashley was now uncomfortably toying with the hammer of his rifle, watching Slater. "We were not given orders to kill anyone," he said, "least of all this young'un. It's Obrie, for Providence's sake. We've known him since he could barely keep the kitchen fires lit. We are following orders. Sergeant Johnson and Patrick will meet us in the square soon, so stand down."

Slater's reaction was quick and vicious. He swung back hard with the butt of his rifle, meeting Ashley's head with a resounding crack. He crumpled to the ground like a rag doll, and a second after, Slater was standing over him with his bayonet tip raised to finish the job. Obrie didn't have time to think, everything was happening so quickly. He ran forward, leveling his shoulder at Slater, but was unbalanced in his attempt. He found himself sprawled on the ground beside his would-be savior.

"So, the kitchen boy wants to be a hero now?" Slater said, his eyes wild and glaring. "A little too late for all of that. This is over." He held the rifle bayonet like a great spear, ready to drive it through Obrie, when suddenly something else drew his attention.

The edge of the bridge was not far away, rising over the now gleaming surface of the river and flanked by nothing but empty air. Near its center, a rolling wind had begun to swirl, tossing shimmering crystal dust all about. Along with it came a growing sound, both sweet and melancholy all at once. It was the music of raised voices, and the distinct chime of distant bells. It grew and grew,

filling up the corners and spaces of the streets, until everywhere you looked was a blizzard of sparkling ice. The crystals swelled together and took on a lean form, twisting and darkening until it was no longer snow, but flesh, draped in a shadowy cloak. The sound of singing voices ended, leaving only the haunting ring of their passing, and before them crouched a man, his head bowed and his cowl drawn up so that his face was wrapped in shadow.

SLATER LEVELED THE MUZZLE OF his rifle at the intruder and pulled back the hammer with an even click. "What kind of sorcery is this? Who are you, stranger?" He was almost drooling with anticipation as he spoke.

The figure then stood up to his full height, letting the ragged, dark leather of his cloak fall closed in front of him. Then he raised his right hand before him and made a grasping motion, chanting strange words that shook the very ground beneath them.

*"Cha e anashi."*

Obrie did not understand, but somehow he could feel them move through him, like a wave on a still pool.

"Reveal yourself, wolf-kin," he said, this time in the common tongue, as he slowly pulled back his cowl. Obrie almost cheered when he saw his face, but found his happiness fade away just as quickly as it had sparked to life. Before him, cloaked and silent, stood his friend Suqata. His face was gaunt and hawkish, and his eyes burned with a cold light.

Before Obrie could say a world, Slater's body contorted and the guard let out a scream. He twisted again, and quickly the scream changed from one of pain to a howl of rage. When his convulsions were done, Slater was more beast than anything. He tore at his uniform as if he were trying to tear away the vestiges of humanity, flexing his now clawed hands. He lunged forward, bounding over Obrie at Suqata with the rifle bayonet.

"DIE, CROW!!!" he howled.

There was a flourish of dark cloak, sounding like wings taking flight, and Suqata disappeared, reappearing a few yards to the left of Slater. The wolf-kin slashed again, finding nothing. Suqata had moved again in the blink of an eye. He slashed again and again, never hitting his mark, but when Suqata appeared one more time Slater leveled the rifle and fired. The sound was deafening. When the acrid smoke cleared, Suqata was gone.

"Show yourself! Where are you hiding? Come out you ..." Slater's words stopped short. Suqata was standing beside him, seeming to have stepped out of the creature's cast shadow, with the blade of a bone dagger angled at his heart. Without a word, he slashed the blade across an expanse of exposed flesh. The cut was deep, though not a killing blow, but the effect was instant and miraculous. The blade gave off a hum that filled the cold air, and then a dark shape rose, ripped free from Slater's body. It lingered for a second, thrashing in the cold air, then disappeared, leaving the guard hanging in Suqata's grip, fully man once more.

Obrie was so engulfed in the fight that he totally missed the sound of approaching boots in the snow.

"Put him down, darko, or we will fire," called a voice from behind Suqata. Standing a few feet away were two more Black Guard, one with a raised rifle. The other, an officer by the look of him, had his saber drawn. "You are under arrest for assault on members of the Black Guard, and suspicion of witchcraft. Slowly step away from ..."

Suqata dropped Slater to the ground and left him dozing along with his comrade. Before the two newcomers could react, he sung out clearly the words, *"Cha e anashi."* The officer convulsed violently, bent double with pain, but when he looked up again, his eyes shone with the same rage as Slater's had only moments ago.

"Kill them!" he cried.

"These things are everywhere!" Obrie screamed as he scrambled to get out of the line of fire. The first soldier reacted, getting off a shot. Suqata dodged the bullet with just a bob of his head, then

sped forward with both knives drawn. The officer met his attack with cold steel, while the other swung hard with his rifle. It did not connect, but Suqata replied with a swift kick to the man's stomach, taking him down for the moment.

Soon, the sound of the officer's sword clanging against the hard bone daggers resounded off the nearby buildings like cymbal crashes. Suqata met each slash, deflecting them with powerful slashes of his own. Gone was any sign of finesse in their saber blows. These were the blind hammerings of a beast, and soon the officer's focus was lost. Suqata caught the length of the saber between his dagger blades, twisted, and snapped the sword just above the hilt. Abandoning the useless thing, the creature leaped forward with its claws, raking them through the ragged end of Suqata's cloak as he jumped high over the guard's head, his legs windmilling in the open space. Unbalanced and enraged, his hands came slashing out again, but not quickly enough. As Suqata landed, both daggers came down across the beast's back. There was a blood-chilling howl, and a shadow shape pulled itself free of the fallen officer. It lingered in the air for a moment, and from where Obrie lay he thought the shape looked distinctly like that of a wolf before it faded away. Suqata now stood alone, surrounded by the bodies of the Black Guard, all them unconscious, save for one. He lay groaning in the snow, taking his time to stand.

"What is going on here?" he said as he looked around at the fallen soldiers, "What kind of witchcraft is this?"

Suqata turned and said only one word.

"Run."

The command sent shivers through his body, and dutifully the Black Guard picked up his rifle and ran back into town without even a glance backward. Suqata then turned his attention to Obrie, who lay only a few feet away.

"Oh, Su. You are a sight for sore eyes," he said brightly, "Good thing you showed up when you did." There was a slight quaver

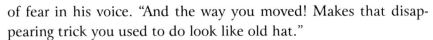 

of fear in his voice. "And the way you moved! Makes that disappearing trick you used to do look like old hat."

Suqata did not respond. Instead, he slowly tilted his head sideways and regarded Obrie with shining, emotionless eyes. His gaze held no pity or recollection of human things, and seemed to peer deep into Obrie's soul, searching through the secret corners of his heart.

"I know you?" Suqata said. His voice echoed in Obrie's ears. "You are familiar to me."

"I should think so. I'm your friend! We've known each other since we were boys, you still fresh out of the camps, and me still clinging to Johnny Boy's apron strings. Suqata, don't you remember?"

Suqata was still for a moment. He appeared caught off-guard somehow. Taking the pause as a good sign, Obrie stood up, and in a flash Suqata's blade was at his throat.

"You know me?" he said. The knife sat perfectly still, only inches from Obrie's Adam's apple.

"Yes! I told you, we are friends, Suqata, for as long as two people can be," Obrie tried his best not to stir. "Please, Su." Slowly Suqata's eyes returned to their blue-grey color, and the dagger began to shake in his hand.

"Obrie?" Suqata lowered the blade. His mouth was agape, and his face wet with tears. He stepped away, then dropped to his knees in the snow, and his friend was quickly at his side.

"Yeah boyo, it's me. You really had me scared for a moment there. It was like it wasn't you. I couldn't believe it, seeing you just appear out of the shimmering blue. Now here you stand, just as real and solid as day-old cheese, and looking pretty good for a dead man."

Suqata looked down at himself. His brow creased as he lifted the ragged cloak up to the light. He stared at the length of it for a time, examining the surface like he was seeing it for the very first time.

"I would be lying if I said I did it all on my own," he said in a whisper, more to himself than Obrie. "Wait a second. What did you mean by 'dead man'?"

"I meant that I thought you were dead. Last night I saw you and Lady Auralyn on the bridge, and Ashton and those others. I was a long ways off, but I could still make you out. Then there was a flash and you were gone. I thought for sure you were just done—burnt up like oil on the fire, but here you stand. And I am glad of it, especially since I thought I was losing my mind."

Suqata looked at Obrie in a puzzled sort of way, his eyebrows raised, then turned to take in his surroundings.

"You said last night?" Suqata's face had gone pale. "Obrie, how long was I gone?"

"A day, Su." He almost laughed until he saw the seriousness on his friend's face. "You've only been gone a day."

# CHAPTER 23
# AS NIGHT FALLS

S UQATA FELT A DULL THROBBING BEHIND HIS EYES. HE WANTED NOTHING more than to lie down and get some much needed sleep, but now was definitely not the time. He needed to hide, and quickly. It only took a few moments for him and Obrie to get off the street and out of sight, but with every door in Orin's Hollow closed to them, their options were pretty slim. It was Obrie who pointed out the nearby cellar door. Suqata broke the lock holding the two frozen wooden doors closed and they quickly crawled inside.

It was almost as cold in the stony cellar as it was outside, but the stacked crates, boxes, and dusty barrels that lined the walls gave them some insulation. Suqata sat down on one of the barrels and pulled his cloak tightly around himself. His body wouldn't stop shaking, even after the chill had started to fade. Obrie, however, kept himself busy by looking around for anything useful. After a few minutes he returned with a thick candle, which he lit with a tinderbox he kept in his pocket, and a jar of what appeared to be apple preserves.

"We are all neighbors, so I'm sure they won't mind if we help ourselves," he said. He scooped out two fingers' worth and happily slurped the sticky sweet mass from them, then offered the jar to his brooding friend, who shook his head and declined. And so they sat, quiet as strangers in the dark, murky space, until Suqata broke the silence.

"Thank you, Obrie, for assisting me back there," he said. He was aware that he sounded far more formal then he had planned. The fact was he was finding it difficult to even look Obrie in the eye. Only yesterday Suqata had thought his friend was dead after he left him at the mill. Even though he had hoped to draw the wolf-kin away from him, the knowledge still came with a twinge of guilt that Suqata was finding hard to set aside, even with Obrie sitting right in front him, hale and hearty.

"Thanks for what? You're the one that handled those monsters," Obrie said between mouthfuls. "Good thing too. I was just about to give them a piece of my mind." He smiled, but in a weary sort of way, and quickly his face took on a look of concern. "Where have you been, Suqata?"

The question was a simple one, and yet Suqata found it was impossible for his brain and mouth to come to agreement as to what to say. Obrie had grown up with the same stories as he had— tales of evil witches and shamans in the woods, waiting to take the innocent down into the dark for their own wicked ends. What would his friend say when he found Suqata was touched by the other world? Would he shun him and run away? Somewhere in the recesses of his mind, Suqata could almost hear Cora Vaco laughing at his turmoil.

"It's complicated," was all the reply he could seem to muster, and he knew it wouldn't be enough.

"Not even a hint then for your best friend in the whole world?" Obrie asked again, still licking his fingers.

"Let's just say that I'm not in a hurry to go back there. I've seen things, Obrie. Things that I would have never dreamed existed, or ever believed possible. And now, to be sitting here with you only a day after that flash on the bridge, I'm not sure of anything. I'm not sure I am the same person." Suddenly, Suqata felt an overwhelming anger wash over him, and he slammed his fist into a nearby barrel, smashing through the hard wood and metal band without much effort. He looked down at his unmarked fist and laughed mirthlessly. "I'm not even sure what is real anymore."

Obrie promptly handed Suqata the jar of preserves.

"That there is real, now isn't it, Su? It's sitting in your hand just as plain as day. And I'm real, too, you can bet your life on that. I know you've been through something rough, but last thing you need to do is start doubting what's right in front of you."

Suqata thought it odd, but the weight of that jar and its slick raised surface was actually reassuring. He was home, back in the world he belonged.

"So, you don't think me some kind of dark witch?" he asked.

"I was actually hoping for it. Those soldiers, or whatever they've become, weren't the friendliest bunch, if you didn't notice. We're going to need more than my good looks and your lovely singing voice to stay alive."

Suqata smiled with a little more assurance. "I think you may be right. There is someone here in town we need to talk to. He might provide the help that we are going to need, but first things first … "

"What's that?'

Suqata looked longingly at the jar of preserves in his hand.

"Where is my toast?"

Obrie's jaw dropped. "If I hadn't heard it with my own two ears, I wouldn't have believed it. Long-faced Suqata made a joke? Why do I have the strange feeling that tonight is going to be filled with surprises?"

JUST AS THE SUN WAS beginning to descend below the western tree-tops, Suqata and Obrie were making their way through the doors of Pious Higgins' church. Oddly enough, it had been left unlocked.

It was dark inside, and here and there Suqata noticed candles that had burned themselves down to lumpy pools of wax, and the dishes and cups from last night's festivities were still about. As they walked quietly under the high ceiling of the great hall and into Pious' living space, it was obvious nothing had been done to clean up since the celebration.

"It doesn't seem like Pious Higgins to not be home in the evening, let alone to have the place in such a state," Obrie said, examining a half-eaten cake left conspicuously on the mantel. "He has a servant named Thomas I think. He should have had all of this cleared away hours ago. Maybe they're gone?"

Suqata crouched down by the hearth and waved his hand over the still warm embers.

"No," he said, "the fire has only just burned down. Someone was tending to it up until a few moments ago." He then looked up into the high rafters. The last bit of light filtered through the colored glass from the ornate window at the front of the building, making geometric shapes stretch across the beams at peculiar angles. Suqata watched them for a moment, all the while feeling a sense of anticipation growing inside the pit of his stomach. He closed his eyes, letting his heart slow to a steady thrum, and listened to the sounds of the world. Beyond the surface of reality, there was something amiss: a sound in discord with the natural rhythm of things, but Suqata couldn't get a sense of where it was coming from. He pushed past that feeling for the moment, and there was something else of more immediate importance. He and Obrie were not alone in the priory.

Suqata raised his hand and pointed to the stairs across the room from the hearth. He climbed them silently, Obrie bringing up the rear. Once to the top landing they stepped out onto the balcony that overlooked the den below. There were two doors leading off to other rooms. Only one was closed. Before either of them could act, there was a rattle at its doorknob, and the door swung open with a loud clunk. Standing in the shadowed entryway was Pious Higgins in his full priestly robes, brandishing his walking stick overhead as if it were a broadsword.

"Back, demons of the abyss! You shall not take this servant of Providence without a fight!" he yelled, his eyes bulging and his breath coming in heaving bursts.

"Sir, stop! We aren't here to hurt you." Suqata held his hands out before him, palms up. "You know us, Pious Higgins. We were here in the priory only last night."

"Oh, what proof is that? We are dealing with evil from the beyond. The Black Guards I saw this morning were men I knew. Them, and their families, and yet they are still monsters!"

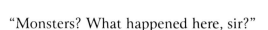

"Monsters? What happened here, sir?"

Higgins glanced at Obrie and back to Suqata as if he were suddenly unsure, but never lowered the walking stick .

"They came in the wee hours of morning, after the guests had gone home. Thomas and I were sharing in the last of the winter mead. It was quite good this year. Anyway, there was a commotion outside and when I took a look out the window I saw soldiers coming down the street with torches. Soon, they were slamming through every door in sight. Thomas and I walked through the chapel and out to the front doors. I demanded to know what was going on." As he spoke, Pious Higgins' hands began to shake, as did the walking stick in his hands.

"They said that there had been an attack at the bridge, and that the attackers were witches. They said Captain Graye and Governor Brockholm had ordered a town-wide search for others who might be harboring them, or hiding themselves. That is when they arrested Thomas."

"Why Thomas?" Obrie asked. "He's old and a tad gruff, but if he's a witch then I'm a radish."

"I don't know, lad. All I know is that Thomas was so frightened. He kept whispering a word. 'Lupo.' I don't know what it means. I tried to reason with them. Why would a servant of darkness hide in the house of divine Providence? I raised my voice and one of them struck me."

Pious Higgins moved forward into the waning light, and Suqata saw a large cut and bruise on the priest's forehead, and his wispy grey hair was stained red on his left side down to his ear.

"Where did they take him, sir?" Suqata asked.

"I don't know. They didn't say. As they were leaving the one who struck me turned and said, 'Such is fate of all fools who play with dark knowledge.' That was when I saw it." Pious Higgins' features were drawn, and his lip quivered when he spoke. "The torchlight fell across the man's face and I saw him for what he really was—some kind of creature, and his eyes flashed silver."

"Lupo," Suqata whispered. "Thomas was Inicowa tribe, from the southern coast, right? I've heard that word before. It means 'wolf.'"

"Why would he say that?" Pious Higgins was beside himself.

"Sir, take a good look at us." In a moment's flash, he reached out and grabbed the walking stick and held it tightly. "We are not monsters. We have come to help, but first we need you to calm down."

Pious Higgins released the walking stick with a sigh of relief. "Thank Providence," he muttered under his breath.

TOGETHER THEY ALL WENT BACK down to the parlor and took seats around the table while Obrie put on a pot of tea. Suqata got the hearth lit, and in a few minutes the priest was doing much better. He sat quietly and sipped at his tea, every few moments dabbing the wound on his head with a damp towel. Eventually the fear left his eyes and he looked to Suqata and Obrie questioningly.

"How is it that you two are the ones that come to my aid?" he said.

"The truth is, sir, we were coming for your help. Everything is upside down. As least we don't have to convince you of the danger now, but all of this only raises more questions. The mere fact that you can both see these creatures is a mystery at best."

"And why is that, dear boy?"

Suqata began to answer, but was unnerved to find that he didn't know where the knowledge had come from. Somehow he knew that normal men and women, those that lacked a natural connection to the *sen-wa*, would not be able to see the true nature of the wolf-kin. It was as if the thought had been placed in his memory ever so carefully without him being aware. The whole thing was unsetting, and Suqata could almost hear Cora Vaco's tittering laughter deep in the corner of his mind, mocking him.

"That does not matter right now," he said, pushing his unsettled feeling aside for the time being. "What matters is that you are aware. These creatures have infiltrated the Black Guard, and possibly the captain and governor as well, moving them along like puppets for some purpose unknown." Suqata looked to Pious

Higgins. "Something is coming. A terrible menace that has to do with the Winter Massacre and the Knights of Ascalion. You were there all those years ago—you can tell me what really happened."

"How dare you speak of that dark day!" Higgins barked, roused unsteadily from his chair. "The knights were soldiers of Providence! They fought back the darkness in this town's most trying times! What do they have to do with right now?"

"I don't know, but you have to listen to me! Now is not the time to fall back on old rhetoric. For years no would ever speak to me of the Winter Massacre, as if it was a secret that someone like me was never supposed to hear. Whatever happened that night has somehow stained this place, and opened it up to the evil that is here now, I know it. You need to tell me, and quickly!"

Pious Higgins looked aghast at Suqata, but immediately sat back down and crossed his trembling hands.

"We had no idea what they were planning," he said, his voice barely a whisper. "We thought they were our saviors. The whole town was so frightened of the Chinequewa, and the secrets they held in their woods. It only took a few rumors to get it started, and soon people were whispering tales of witchcraft and dark powers. I'm ashamed that I did nothing to stop it, but we had no idea what the knights would attempt."

Suqata could feel the anger rising in his chest, but kept it at bay.

"When they met with the governor and the town council, they told him that they had received a vision. They said they heard the voice of Providence commanding them to … destroy the Chinequewa village—down to the last man."

"And you believed them?" Suqata growled.

"Some believed that the knights were sometimes given visions, leading them to fight for the people. The war with Umbar began because of a vision the knights received three hundred years ago. Who was I to argue with a divine message!"

"And so they slaughtered my people, because of a voice they heard telling them to do so?"

"You have to understand, Suqata, back then we were so afraid. There were things in this new world that were as strange to us as any magic. Before we could reconvene, the governor had given them his blessing. Many died, but many escaped as well."

"That's why the Chinequewa came to Orin's Hollow?" Obrie said. He looked at Higgins like the man was on fire. "Revenge for you killing their people?"

"No, Obrie," Suqata said, laying his hand on his friend's shoulder. "They came for the knights. Whatever those men heard, it wasn't Providence. It was the same menace that guides these creatures."

Terror washed over Pious Higgins' face. "We need to warn the people of The Hollow," he said, combing his hands through his thinning grey hair, lost in his own thoughts. "And to think that Lord Brockholm is still holding his damned fool party tonight. The Black Guard has been rounding up suspected witches since last night. We have to do something."

"There is one thing too that you are forgetting, sir," Obrie said. "The soldiers have already spread the word that Suqata and I are witches. No one is going to believe us."

Suqata looked to the priest. "They don't have to believe us, Obrie, not if Pious Higgins does. He can warn them. You have to make them see reason. This whole witch scare is just a ruse to keep them blind to the real danger. A danger that is growing every moment that we don't act."

"What would you have me do, Suqata? I am not a soldier."

"You are their priest. Go tell them the truth." Suqata said, standing as he spoke. "They have more to fear from the Black Guard now than they do from any witch. They can't just close their doors and hope the danger passes—not again."

"My boy, they'll never believe it. The Black Guard has always been our sword and shield in these dangerous lands. No one will ever stand against them, not as long as we have no proof."

Suqata then quickly stood to leave. "This is your chance to make up for past failings, Pious. The people need you. And if they

need proof, we'll give it to them," he said. "Tonight when the moon is gone, something will change in The Hollow. A change so powerful that it will affect everything. At that time, the townsfolk will see the creatures for what they really are. You must have them ready by then. By midnight."

There was silence in the parlor for a long while. Then Pious Higgins laughed grimly and slammed his fist against the table.

"Well, better to face your destiny than run from it," he said; "it always seems to catch up to you in the end. Besides, I wasn't too keen on going to the governor's party anyway."

"Good," Suqata said, "Remember, don't let on that you are aware of them until midnight. There is a reason these creatures have been taking the others. It's to keep us blind to what they are up to. Obrie, help Pious Higgins scrounge up as much silver as you can find. It's the only weapon that will free those affected. Round everyone you know up here at the chapel."

"Where are you going to be?" Obrie asked excitedly.

"I have business at the manor."

Suqata nodded farewell to the priest and headed quickly for the kitchen door. Before he could leave, Obrie's hand was on his shoulder.

"You aren't telling me everything, are you, Su?" he said. His demeanor had changed, and now had an edge to it Suqata had rarely seen in him. The weight of Obrie's scarred hand felt like the weight of the world.

"Nothing you need to worry about."

"You've always had your secrets, and I've never wanted to pry. I always figured you would tell me about things sooner or later, but now is not the time for secrets. What aren't you saying, my friend? What are you afraid of?"

Suqata drew in a deep breath and felt his body ache, but he was ready and focused on what was to come. He did not turn, but spoke to Obrie over his shoulder.

"Have you noticed how many soldiers have been taken by the

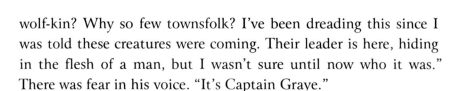

wolf-kin? Why so few townsfolk? I've been dreading this since I was told these creatures were coming. Their leader is here, hiding in the flesh of a man, but I wasn't sure until now who it was." There was fear in his voice. "It's Captain Graye."

"Are you sure?" Obrie said.

"Without doubt or hesitation," Suqata replied.

They both looked at each other, knowing what this meant. Captain Graye was a trained killer, never bested in battle. "Well, looks like you have your work cut out for you." Obrie grinned and patted Suqata square in the back. "But you've never shied away from a challenge."

Suqata smiled.

"So go on then," Obrie said. "But first, show me the trick one more time. You know, for old times' sake."

"Ok, but watch carefully." Suqata pulled up his cowl and began to count, snapping his fingers in time. "Three. Two. One." And in a blink, Suqata was gone.

"Good luck, Su." Obrie said before closing the door behind him.

As MIDNIGHT APPROACHED, COACHES BEGAN arriving at the manor drawn by long teams and driven by servants wearing their finest. Each coach stopped at the grand entryway in turn and the guests were announced. The manor was alight with hundreds of lanterns, and two large braziers crackled happily at the foot of the entryway steps. Also, in every shadowed corner stood a Black Guard with his rifle shouldered. Even at a distance, Suqata could feel the tension in the air. There was no cheer, or excitement like the festival in town, only the oppressive weight of impending events.

A hundred yards or so off, Suqata sat on a sturdy tree limb watching as the last of the coaches came down the icy path towards the manor. Suqata could feel something shift in the world around him. The sound he had heard earlier in town had grown stronger the closer he came to the house. He could feel the vibration of it in his very bones.

"I am coming, Lynn," Suqata said aloud, but his words were swept away in the night wind. He looked up to a solitary lit window on the top story of the manor. "I made a promise that I would protect you, and I plan on keeping it."

CHAPTER 24

# THE SUNDERING

S UQATA STOOD QUIETLY IN THE SHADOWS AT THE BASE OF THE MANOR'S northern wall. Tall hedges grew all alongside of it, and though the winter had thinned them out they still provided just enough cover. Auralyn's window was two stories above his head and clearly seen from a distance, so he waited patiently for the guards patrolling that part of the grounds to circle back to where he stood. He didn't have to wait long. He heard the steady crunch of snow under their boots far before he saw them, but as they appeared around the stand of dead hedges Suqata disappeared from sight.

They were in match step, rifles shouldered, and talking as soldiers do when working mundane tasks. Concealed within the Hiding Song, Suqata couldn't tell if they were wolf-kin or not, but it didn't matter. When he released his breath, he attacked, striking the first guard hard in the neck with the butt of his blade. The other turned to defend himself, but Suqata spun quickly around him, wrapping his arms around the guard's neck. He squeezed until the man made no sound, save for the steady grunts as he fought his grip. Enough applied pressure and Suqata knew he could have ended him right there, but instead he tightened his hold just enough. In seconds the guard went limp and fell unconscious to the ground with a dull thud.

Suqata pulled the two men into the shadow of the manor wall and placed them out of sight. Before he was done positioning them, he heard the sound of mocking laughter. Suqata turned, blades at the ready, and saw nothing. Aside from the unconscious guards, he was alone.

*Foolish, boy. Foolish, foolish,* a voice said. This time, there was no mistaking it. He could hear the voice as clearly as if it was whispering in his ear. *They will wake soon enough, and then you'll have more enemies to deal with. Best to finish them now and be done with it. What's best is best, is best.*

The voice was coarse, with a condescending tone that set Suqata's nerves on edge. He recognized it, closed his eyes and tried to will it away, but the spirit of Cora Vaco only laughed at the attempt.

*Not going to get rid of me that easy. We must work together, young Suqata, if you hope to live to see the morning. I have not waited for you all this time to see you skip, skip happily to your doom, doom, doom.*

"No killing, Crow. Not if I can help it." Suqata spoke the words ardently in his mind, trying to push Cora Vaco's thoughts aside. "These men are innocent of any wrongdoing. It is the wolves I'm after."

*And yet, these men were your jailers not a fortnight ago, were they not? Kept you a slave, they did, and you still spare them?* The spirit sounded angry at first, but slowly his ire seemed to subside. *Fine, let them live,* he said, *Spare who you will, but remember why you are here. The girl. If we cannot think of a way to end this before midnight, she will have to die. Your knife will taste her blood, of that you can be sure.*

"I am not your puppet, Cora Vaco."

Suqata took a long look at the soldiers, lying there at his mercy.

"It doesn't matter now," he said, "We have other tasks ahead of us." His words lacked the conviction he had intended, but with another mocking laugh Cora Vaco receded once again to the back of his thoughts, leaving Suqata in silence.

THE WINDOW WAS A GOOD twenty feet up, but that posed little trouble. With one leap, Suqata landed on the short balcony without a sound. He leaned his head against the cool glass and listened for a moment. When he was satisfied no one was stirring inside, he used his dagger to undo the latch. He eased inside, closing the balcony door behind him. Once his feet touched the cold marble floor, Suqata glanced quickly around the room. It was the same as when he and Auralyn had left for the festival. There was a fire in the hearth, and by Auralyn's seat was a tray of tea and one half-full cup beside it. At the foot of the seat lay a discarded blanket, and atop it sat the open leather tome that Auralyn always kept handy. Suqata walked forward and lifted the book from the floor. Tucked in the

spine of the book was the thin silver blade he had seen once before, but the tip of it had pierced one of the thin parchment pages.

"That is strange," he whispered. Suqata slid the blade out of the book and laid it aside. "Lynn treasures this moldy thing. She would never damage it. Not without reason." The page that was pierced lay open before him. On it was an in-depth description of the Ajanti Song, complete with woodblock prints illustrated in stark black and white. The images depicted a man overcome by the Song, and the animal spirit taking shape from the figure's chest. As he read, Suqata couldn't help but remember when Auralyn had sung it before him. He placed his hand over the center of his own chest where the spirit crow had come forth like some kind of ghostly omen.

"What were you up to, Lynn?" he thought, "why mark this page?" He flipped the pages backwards and forwards, always looking at the images, watching again and again as man and spirit were separated.

"That's it. Auralyn, you're a genius!"

Just as realization was sparked, Suqata heard a soft click from the other side of the room. The door to Auralyn's room opened just as Suqata vanished from sight into the Hiding Song, the airless space of it rushing in to surround him. He barely had time to take that crucial breath as Mistress Hodges walked in. She was carrying Auralyn's dress from the night of the festival and moving steadily around the room, picking through the disarray.

Hodges was wearing a dark blue evening gown that swept behind her. It was much nicer than her usual frock, and was complete with long white gloves that she seemed quite proud of. Her hair was done up in a round mass, topped by a jeweled comb with two tall, white plumes. The whole effect gave her the look of a self-important goose, and some part of Suqata wanted to laugh out loud despite the fact that he was still holding his breath. Even as the thought barely crossed his mind, Cora Vaco spoke again.

*Do not be a fool, boy. This one is dangerous. I don't like the way she moves. Get her out of the way, now!*

"You must be joking!" Suqata responded. The idea he was having an argument in his own thoughts was disturbing enough, but to consider what the old spirit was implying was even worse. "She is harmless. Look at her. Besides, what could I do to Mistress Hodges? She's just a pompous old woman."

*Think of something. You don't have much breath left.* The truth of that statement was becoming painfully obvious. Suqata could feel his lungs burning even as he stood there watching Hodges tidy up. He thought to make a move for the door, but she would most definitely hear him open it. Not to mention he had no idea what was waiting for him on the other side. Quickly he dodged around the divan and spun past the table, almost completely avoiding her as she continued to preen about the room. He was on his way to the door when he stepped on the train of Hodges' dress. The fabric pulled taut. When she looked down to see what she was caught on, she found herself staring at an empty footprint. Stealth was now no longer an option.

The boy released the Hiding Song and quickly moved forward, wrapping his arms around Hodges' neck and leveling the carbato blade at her wide throat.

"Scream, ma'am, and I'll have no choice but to use this. Don't make me have to do something we'll both regret," he whispered into her ear, and the housekeeper became still as stone. Her breath came in rapid gasps, so fast in fact Suqata feared she might swoon to the floor.

"I knew it would come to this," she whimpered. "I knew it the moment I set eyes on you. That steady walk, and those cold blue eyes. 'He's a killer,' I said, no doubt about it."

"This isn't what it looks like, Hodges. I don't want to hurt you," Suqata said, almost pleading.

"Well, what do you want then? Hmm? To take me for a midnight stroll?" She eyed the blade with bulging eyes.

"I just need to know where Auralyn is. Tell me where they've taken her and I'll let you go."

Cora Vaco's voice arose again in Suqata's mind, louder and fiercer than before. *No, fool. Do not let her go. End her now,* he said, but Suqata focused and pushed past his urging.

Hodges was beginning to tremble. "What do you want with her? Are you planning on killing her now and finishing what you started on the bridge? The captain said you might try something like this. Oh Providence, save us from the evil of witchcraft!"

"I don't want to hurt anyone, ma'am. You know me. I'm no witch!" Suqata said, but he knew he was well past convincing her of his intentions. "Just take me to where she is and Auralyn will explain everything. And don't try to alert anyone. I don't want this to go badly for either of our sakes."

Together, Suqata and Mistress Hodges left the room and walked slowly into the hallway. Though there were no Black Guards in the corridor, and every corner was brightly lit with branched candelabras emanating honey-colored light. Suqata whistled a slight tune and a quick wind swept through the hall extinguishing the flames, until only darkness remained.

*Nice trick, huh,* Cora Vaco whispered.

They walked slowly down the hall, Suqata listening intently for danger. When they approached the balcony that looked down onto the ground hall, Suqata heard the distinct sound of violin music and the chatter of voices. He peered down through the banister railings at the groups of party-goers standing about the mansion, all the men in their finest and the ladies adorned in long gowns of Nogran silk. The servants moved about them with trays of champagne and hors d'oeuvres. Everyone, visitor and servant alike, wore strained and wearied smiles. Even with the elegant atmosphere, this was a party that few truly wanted to attend.

*Not having much fun are they?* Cora Vaco said, and Suqata found himself agreeing with the intrusive voice.

Soon, the groups began to shift about, and the guests all applauded as Governor Brockholm walked proudly into the hall, chin held high with an undeniable swagger in his step. Captain

Graye and Auralyn closely followed him. The Governor was all smiles, shaking hands and meeting guests graciously, but the captain stood reservedly behind, his hand placed securely on Auralyn's shoulder. She was turned away from him, dressed in a beautiful pearl-white gown that caught the light along the trim, but it was her hands that gave her away. She held them tightly together, wringing them nervously. It was when Suqata finally caught a glimpse of her face that he knew something was wrong. Her skin was pale and taut around her mouth, and there were dark rings under her eyes as if she hadn't slept in days, but most telling was her expression. She looked about as if she was waiting for something bad to happen, for some calamity to fall.

*This is off. Bad for us. Very bad. We must leave. Now!* But Cora Vaco's warning came too late.

Mistress Hodges let out a scream from beside Suqata that could have broken glass! All eyes shot upwards to the balcony, and eight guards moved quickly into view.

"You there! Halt!" they called out, and raced up the stairs.

Suqata reached for the sword across his back but was knocked sideways by a solid blow to his head. He turned to see Mistress Hodges stand over him, her eyes shining silver in the light from beyond the railing. She licked her lips and grinned, revealing the tips of white fangs.

"Soft boy. Hodges never liked you anyways," she growled.

*Told you so.* Cora Vaco said mockingly.

Suqata was still a little dazed when Hodges launched her short, round frame into the air, springing forward like an uncaged animal. He staggered back, barely avoiding her slashing hands, then rolled into a crouched position.

"If you can hear me in there, ma'am, I am sorry," he said and lunged back at Hodges. As he did, his outstretched blade cut a perfect line across her chest, just over her heart. The knife hummed

violently as it split the air and flesh. Then, in a rush of black, the wolf-kin pulled free of her body. She collapsed unconscious into his arms, just as he heard the boots of the guards rushing towards him.

"Stupid, Suqata!" he said aloud. He'd fallen right into their trap. Within moments he had six Black Guard rifles aimed point blank at his head.

"Release her, boy! Don't make us fire," the lead guard ordered.

Suqata glanced past the weapons and measured his chances of escape.

"I'm sure none of you would consider letting me explain?"

"Why? You are outnumbered and outgunned, not to mention you have nowhere left to run. There are at least twenty more Black Guards between you and escape."

"Twenty? Truly? Well, in that case you have me cornered, sir," Suqata said with a grin. "Congratulations."

"So, surrender the woman now."

"Who? Oh, Hodges. Well, she and I were just having a bit of a chat. That is, we were until she sprouted fangs and claws and tried to kill me. Just give me a moment, please."

*That's it boy. Stall for time. You do have a plan for getting yourself out of this, don't you?* Cora Vaco suggested.

"Not exactly, no," Suqata replied aloud. It took him a moment to realize the guards were looking at with confused expressions.

*Well, you'd best get to it before these fellows fill you full of holes and metal bits.*

"I am. Give me a minute."

Once again the guards watched bewildered.

"I think the boy has lost his mind, sir," one guardsman said to the lead. "Let's put him down before he harms her."

Suqata's realized his time was up. Summoning all his strength, he Sang out with all his might. The Song was incredible, one part of it revealing the spirits, the other part binding them. With each word he uttered, Suqata could feel his spirit rise with the rhythm of his voice, flowing and ebbing around him like the current of

a white-capped river. All of the guards surrounding him doubled over in pain. While two even dropped to their knees, beneath the sound of Suqata's raised voice came the mournful howls of wolves ripping and tearing at their human shells. Suqata could feel his power waning, so before it was gone entirely he brought the Song to an end. The guards staggered towards him, their eyes filled with white-hot rage, all of them shining silver. Suqata held both daggers lightly in his hands and grinned at his enemies.

"Here I come," he whispered, and disappeared.

The next few moments were a blur for all that witnessed it. Before any of the spirit-touched guards could react, he was amongst them, appearing and disappearing in a flurry of his dark cloak. He struck down the lead within seconds, then two more, leaving them in heaps on the floor, the air filled with the shadowy remnants of the wolf-kin escaping their bodies. Each time his appearance was signaled by what sounded like the flutter of crow's wings on the wind.

Soon the downstairs guards joined the fray, while others whisked Lord Brockholm, Auralyn, and the captain through the ballroom doors. Their true natures were revealed, and the guards howled as they chased the guests from the grand hall, filling the air with the sound of panicked screams and chaos.

Suqata met the soldiers on the stairs, pulling his saber from the scabbard across his back. Musket fire reverberated in the space, as did the sharp clang of the rifle balls against Suqata's blade. He caught most, but one blasted through his defense, the lead shot burning its way through his upper thigh. Suqata screamed out in defiance and continued to fight his way down the steps. The last guard held his own for a moment, saber to saber, but was no match for the silver-endowed edge of the carbato blade. He fell in a dark haze as the wolf spirit tore its way free.

*Quickly, quickly, before he gets away with her,* Cora Vaco screamed.

Suqata looked at the wound in his leg. The hole was clean through the muscle, and all around it pulsed the strange, swirling *sen-wa* markings. The pain was almost unbearable.

"What's happening to me?" he said through clenched teeth.

*Your body is trying to heal, but you are losing strength as you lose blood. The Song on the balcony has overtaxed you. You won't have enough strength to Sing anything that powerful until you've rested.*

Suqata removed the saber belt from his shoulder, using it to quickly bind the wound . He stifled a scream as he pulled the leather strap tight, then looked pensively at the knives in his hands.

Suqata pushed open the double doors of the ballroom. As he strode inside, the room filled with candlelight that reflected eerily off the dark granite floor. It felt like standing in dark, still water. A strange glow filled the space, seemingly emanating from every surface, and with it came a resonance so strong that he could feel it in his entire body, as if the very earth was shaking with the sound of a hundred thousand voices beneath it.

A guard moved slowly out of the shadows behind him, closing the door. As he did, Suqata could hear him growl.

"They've been waiting for you," he snarled, and pointed to the far side of the room. Standing there were Captain Graye, Lord Brockholm, and Auralyn.

"Welcome, my boy," Graye said, smiling uncharacteristically. When he approached, Suqata caught a flash of silver-white from his eager eyes. "It's about time you showed."

# CHAPTER 25
# GARRO KNOCTA

"MOVE AND I KILL THEM BOTH," CAPTAIN GRAYE SAID IN A LOW, menacing tone, and two guards moved in closer beside Suqata, gnashing their teeth.

"What is the meaning of this, captain?" Lord Brockholm yelled as the guards holding him snapped and snarled into his ear like rabid dogs. Auralyn was being held as well, but from the look of her it wasn't requiring too much to restrain her.

"This is only the will of Providence, governor," Graye replied dismissively.

"Simply outrageous, man. Release us at once." Lord Brockholm struggled against his captor, though Suqata could hear an obvious tremble in the man's voice. "You have lost your hold on reality, and your mad search for witches in every shadow has brought you to this lunacy. I should have had you put in irons the moment this madness began." As he spoke, his eyes became wide. "You have the same evil in your heart as the rest of your precious knights— hidden behind a mask of righteousness! Ascalion is a curse on this land, and it ends tonight."

Graye laughed thunderously and Suqata could feel his blood freeze in his veins at the very sound of it.

"Old fool, what do you know of righteousness? I am of the dream of Ascalion fulfilled," he sneered. When he spoke, Suqata could hear the distinct echo of power, like a hammer striking smoldering steel, but with it came another sound—one like the howl of a dozen hungry wolves in the distance. Standing there before the governor, Captain Graye appeared to grow in stature. Gone was the lithe, muscular build of an older man, replaced with the power of one in his prime. The governor watched the transformation in horror.

"Get away from me, you monster!"

Graye leaned forward and took Lord Brockholm's face in his

hand. "Don't you understand this was all meant to happen? You have followed in my shadow this whole time, and yet you never saw where I was leading you. I don't care about witches or demons from hell, you fool. What I search for is power, and nothing more. The power over destiny—the same power my father sought for years before dying in this place. And now, at long last, everything is in prepared. It is as you say, m'lord, 'This all ends tonight.' But for the new world, this is only the beginning."

From where he stood at the entrance to the ballroom, Suqata could suddenly feel a shift in the world around him. First, the ever-present hum he had heard all night reached a deafening, peak. Then, there was a great rending of the air, and Suqata watched as the space in the center of the room grew brighter and brighter as a rift began to form right before his very eyes.

*They are coming, boy!* Cora Vaco yelled. *Beyond the tear is the Henis-a-paka, and the Varcuya are waiting. We are almost out of time!*

In pure desperation, Suqata tried the banishment again, gathering what was left of his strength into his voice. He Sang out clear, over the rush of otherworldly energy.

*"Uiek, kiyi, uiek nu tuyuk, uiek kiyi, uiek manas tuk!"*

The guard holding Auralyn writhed in pain and fell, clawing at itself as the wolf spirit escaped his body, but Captain Graye and the other held fast. The power of the song wracked through their frames, each line tearing away the illusion of humanity. When Suqata could sing no more, the two men turned to him. Their eyes shone even brighter, like shards of broken moonlight, and their faces had become more wolf-like, with raised brow ridges and snouts. Captain Graye's hair now hung loose to his shoulders and it moved wildly in the growing wind.

"You are weakening, Suqata," Graye said, showing his impressive fangs. "You have spent your power poorly, and now you have nothing left to face me."

Suqata held out his blade before him, twisting it in the light to show the ribbon of silver along its edge.

"I don't need the *sen-wa* to deal with you, Graye."

"Yes! That's the boy I know. So defiant at your core that you don't even know when you've lost. Can't you see? Nothing you do now can stop what is coming."

Suqata looked to the rift and then to where Auralyn lay. She was deathly still, haloed by the pulsating light, with Captain Graye between them. He would have thought her dead already, but beneath the thrum of power he could still hear her heart beating in sync with it. Lord Brockholm was beside himself, fighting desperately to move towards his daughter.

"You fiend!" he cried. "What have you done ... "

Abruptly, Captain Graye struck the governor hard in the stomach, and he folded over to the ground.

"Silence," Graye barked, then turned his attention back to Suqata. "Now, where were we?"

"Captain, you have to let the girl go," Suqata said. He kept his sword up and slowly inched towards Auralyn. "Can't you see it's killing her!"

"Sadly, yes, dear boy, but for a new world to rise some innocents must be sacrificed. Such is the way of things."

"No. This isn't you," Suqata said, "You've never been cruel, captain. The power of the *mahko* has driven you to this. Can't you see, you can't control it."

Suqata surged forward, slashing at where the captain stood, but in a flash he found his blade met. He had not even seen Graye pull his sword from its scabbard. Suqata recovered, thrusting forward, and once again their swords clashed, casting sparks into the glowing air.

"Good, Suqata. Excellent form," Graye said, smiling. "Again."

Suqata spun away then attacked again, this time taking a high strike. Graye swatted the blow away almost playfully. Over and over they met, swirling and spinning through the chaos like blurs of solid light clashing against one another.

"Good! Again!" he cried.

Suqata slashed again, this time disappearing into the Hiding Song for a split second before delivering another blow. As he reappeared, Graye reacted quickly, blocking his attack and sending Suqata flying backwards with a shrug of their met blades.

"Come now, boy. Your heart is not in the fight."

Suqata picked himself up quickly, ignoring the throbbing pain in his injured leg, and resumed an attack pose.

"Maybe it's not, sir," he said, circling into position again. "But I don't want to kill you. After everything, I don't want your blood on my hands. You have to release the power inside you—if not, Garro Knocta will kill you."

Captain Graye smiled only more fiercely than before.

"Is that what you think, Suqata? That I am not in control? I can see how you might make that mistake, with all of my men acting like fools with the wolf's power." Graye gestured to his fallen men. "But I am the master here, boy. Imagine the *mahko*'s amazement as he tried to subject me to his will only to find my resolve was iron. I was prepared for his assault, and now his strength is mine. Oh, I hear him now and again, raging against the borders of my mind, but to no avail. So his howls became less and less. Soon, Garro Knocta will be nothing but a memory. The *mahko* wanted freedom from his dreary prison, but now his power will serve a greater purpose."

Suddenly, Suqata understood.

"The voices," he whispered. "You said you heard a voice that day, before we met the governor. The same voice that led the knights to slaughter my people. You serve the Varcuya."

"Yes, my boy. I am the Servant of Ascalion, the Spirits of Eternity. I knew that the wolves would meet us on the Last Road that night and that they would bring their great power with them. The Varcuya prepared me to receive their gift. With it, they said I would shape this land in my image, into an orderly utopia, and fulfill the dreams of the knights that came before me. And when they come, I will be their emissary. Even now, I can hear them speaking." He turned to the fissure and stretched out his hand. "They are almost here."

Suqata stopped for a moment and focused his mind, listening for sounds beyond the surface of the world until he heard the voices he sought. They were cold, and evil, and full of malice. As he listened, his sword tip began to fall.

"When they come, they'll turn this world to ashes," he said.

Graye stood his ground. "You cannot shake my faith, boy. You and your kind will never understand the call of destiny. The Chinequewa knew what the Knights of Ascalion would bring to this land. They fought and died, but did not conquer. History only remembers the conquerors." As he spoke, Captain Graye raised his blade to attack. "There is only one way to true victory, and that way is never pretty."

Graye's saber descended with blinding speed, cutting a silver arc in the air behind it. Suqata had barely dodged the first charge when another slash came ringing against his battered blade. The two of them traded blows over the rumbling floor of the ballroom, both in lockstep like a vicious dance, the blue light of the growing rift reflecting strangely off of their flashing blades. Graye's blade found flesh, sending drops of blood spraying across the dark floor. The sword burned when it touched Suqata, and quickly he understood that he too now had a weakness to silver, as long as he was bound to Cora Vaco. Every second the rift grew, and the ominous voices of the Varcuya grew louder and more distinct.

"You're a great deal better than you ever let on," Graye said. "I think you've been holding back all this time."

Suqata slashed forward, just barely missing the captain's face.

"Well, I remembered how little you like to lose." Suqata touched the scar on his lip to drive home the point.

"Ah yes. Such a long time ago, and yet a defining moment in our relationship. Master and slave. It doesn't have to be that way anymore, Suqata. Ever since I heard the spirits speak to me, I've known I wanted you at my side. You are Chinequewa, and they respect your strength. Now that you've learned the true meaning of power, we can be equals, you and I."

Suqata almost stopped dead in his tracks.

"What do you mean?" he asked, even as Cora Vaco screamed in his mind.

"I mean that you are, and have always been, meant for greatness. I saw it that day at the camps, and I see it now. We are the same, you know? I was but a boy when your people swept into the valley. I watched as they killed my father before my very eyes. I was powerless to stop them. I knew that someday, I would find a way to never be powerless again. And then, when I met you that cold day, I thought to make an example of you. But you were not the enemy I sought. Instead, I saw myself in your distant eyes—the eyes of an orphan. Why do you think I brought you along on the Last Road that day? I hoped to share this power with the one man I knew was worthy of it. My student."

*Don't listen to him, boy. He wanted you dead and out of the way!* Cora Vaco screamed.

"How was I to know you had such power at your disposal already? Afterwards, I had to distance myself from you, but I never meant you any harm."

*He wanted you far away so he could master Garro Knocta.*

"But you disappointed me by putting your trust in this waif of a girl. Look at her! Brought down by her own foolish pride."

Suqata felt a fire inside himself stoked to life at the very mention of her name.

"You don't know her. You don't know who she is." His sword rang out as it met the captain's. He parried the attack, responding with a slash that tore through Suqata's cloak.

"Oh, I know her, boy. I've known her type for years. She is just the same as her simple father. People given wealth and privilege that have no idea what to do with it. Pompous, spoiled, worthless, and above all, weak. They would have come here and undone everything I built." He hammered at Suqata, raining down blow after blow. "The order. The serenity. A world where everyone knows their place. Can you believe he really meant to free the

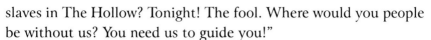

slaves in The Hollow? Tonight! The fool. Where would you people be without us? You need us to guide you!"

*Don't listen to him, Suqata. You are more than what he says.*

"Captain. Please. It doesn't have to end this way. You can end this madness now."

Their blades clashed hard together, and they met face to face in the light of the fissure.

"It is too late for all that, Suqata. The die is cast, and Providence will have its way," Graye howled in the deafening tempest, his eyes burning bright. "Come, boy. You know your place is at my side. You owe none of these fools anything—this girl, your people, or the spirits that taunt us both—not one of them! The fight is over, and you have nothing left to give."

Somewhere inside, Suqata knew that part of what Graye had said was true. His body was battered and bleeding, and almost all his power was drained. He had very little left to give, except for one, last thing.

"You're right, captain. This is over."

Then, with the last shred of power left in his bruised body, Suqata Sang out clear and strong.

*"Min aska to, min aska to, u gwa lay, u aye to."*

"Stop, boy! Stop this now," Graye cried, his voice cracking with rage.

But Suqata didn't stop. He Sang, without stopping to draw a breath. He Sang until his throat was raw. The words of the Ajanti Song poured from his mouth, taking form as the swirl of *sen-wa* and *sen-tal* symbols burned into the air. Suddenly the immense shape of a crow, now both smoky white and shadow black, ripped free of his body. He could no longer hear Cora Vaco's voice inside his head, and all around him spirit animals were taking form, pulling themselves from the bodies of the fallen and those still standing.

When the power of Suqata's voice subsided, Captain Graye lay on the ground fighting to contain the spirit energy that now spilled unchecked from his body.

"What is happening to me!" he cried, "What have you done,

boy?" But Suqata wasn't listening. He had already run to Auralyn's side and lifted her carefully into his arms.

"Lynn, wake up! It's Su. You're going to be all right now!"

When her eyes opened, Suqata could see they were filled with pain.

"Kill me, Suqata," she whispered, barely loud enough to hear over Graye's screams and the growing roar of the fissure. "It's the only way to end this. Do it now."

Suqata held her close.

"Never. Don't you dare give up. Not now. I know you have the strength in you. You can close the gateway. You've held this power inside you since you were a child, always keeping it in check. You can master it now. I didn't travel across worlds to watch you give up."

She smiled through gritted teeth and squeezed his hand as tight as she could, summoning the last of her strength. Auralyn then reached out her hand to the rift, and Suqata could hear the terrible voices of the Varcuya on the other side scream out, clawing their way toward the light of the Waking World.

She slowly closed her hand, and the tear in space began to inch closed!

"Come on, Lynn. You're almost there!" Suqata cried, but even then he could see her faltering. "Just hold on for a few more seconds."

That's when Suqata heard Graye's cries stop, and the rise of a rumbling growl that sent tremors through the floor boards.

He turned slowly.

Standing over the captain's still, unconscious form was the shadowy shape of a wolf the size of a warhorse. Like Cora Vaco, its dark shape was that of a patch of starry night that had been cut from the sky. Its ears were laid flat, while the hairs at the peak of its back stood straight and bristling. It stared at Suqata, who returned its gaze pointedly, afraid to turn away should the monstrous apparition lunge and rend him to pieces. It was magnificent, and mind-numbingly frightening all at once, and as it stalked forward it seemed to shift from walking on all fours to walking upright, depending on the angle that you looked at it.

The great beast approached Suqata and Auralyn, bent forward and sniffed.

"Cora Vaco?" he said. His voice hung in the air after he spoke, and he turned his head questioningly. "You smell like the crow," he growled, this time waiting for a response. Suqata was frozen, unable to articulate even the simplest of words.

"Don't eat him, brother. This mortal is bound to me," a familiar voice spoke out, but this time not from inside Suqata's head. There was a rush of feathers, and on Suqata's shoulder now sat the blackest crow he had ever seen, save for one white streak across the top of his head and its large, peculiar grey eyes. The two creatures looked at one another for some time, until the wolf finally spoke again.

"Much has changed here, in the Waking World, Crow," Garro Knocta said, "maybe too much for my children and me."

"It's not so bad. At least the food has gotten better," Cora Vaco said while preening his wings. The wolf growled in response, shaking the room.

"You mock me! I was slave to this man-thing's will. I should rend all of these puny creatures into nothing!"

Suqata pulled Auralyn close and fumbled to reach his saber. The large crow landed on the blade, glanced questioningly at him, then shook his beak.

"Brother, man is as he has always been. Always reaching for what he does not have, or understand. They are not our concern." Cora Vaco beat his wings and once again landed on Suqata's shoulder, looking off towards the rift. "The Varcuya, on the other hand, have crossed the line. This world may not be ours anymore, but it is definitely not theirs."

Garro Knocta set his eyes on the pulsating light, then lifted his head and howled. There was a rush of cold wind, and suddenly the room was filled with the dark, shadowy shapes of wolves. At least two dozen wolf-kin spirits now stood waiting—imposing, even at half the size of their master. They watched Garro Knocta with their silver eyes, their dark forms shifting about in anticipation.

"Come, my children," the great wolf laughed, and bowed his head ready to spring. "Let's not keep the wraiths waiting."

Then, like a black wave, they were off, bounding into the rift. For a moment, Suqata thought he heard the Varcuya scream in terror, but it was lost in the cacophony of the rift closing behind them. The last thing Suqata and Auralyn heard was Garro Knocta's booming voice.

"Farewell, brother. I will crunch your bones next time we meet," he said, and in a blinding flash they were gone.

AURALYN WOKE FEELING BEATEN AND bruised, but at the same time better than she had in a long time. Standing over her were her father and Lieutenant Dobbs, and she now lay on one of the couches in the grand hall.

"Oh my child, you are awake," Lord Brockholm said, almost overcome. He wrapped his hands around hers and kissed her forehead gently. "Thank Providence. I feared the worst when you would not stir."

"Papa," she said hoarsely, her throat dry and sore, "where am I? What has happened?"

"I am not completely sure, my dear. All we know is that it is over, just as sure as it started."

Auralyn looked to Dobbs, who smiled and tipped his hat. "Lieutenant, how is the town?" she asked. Some measure of her commanding presence was returning to her, and Dobbs smartly saluted as he spoke.

"The town is fine, m'lady. After whatever affliction ran its course, the Black Guard returned to their normal selves. It is really the townsfolk we have to thank. A large group was mustered together by Pious Higgins and your kitchen hand, Obrie, and together they were able to free those that the soldiers had rounded up. Once their numbers had grown, they were able to protect the rest of the town from the afflicted. There was very little loss of life, thank Providence."

"So the soldiers are … "

"Fine, m'lady, just fine. Most came out of it pretty quickly, while others are still getting their bearings."

"What of Captain Graye?" she asked, not disguising the anger in her tone.

"He is a different situation altogether," he replied uneasily. "We found him here in the ballroom, eyes as wide as open shutters, but it's as if he's not there at all. His mind is completely gone. Doctor says he may never wake."

As Dobbs spoke, a fog seemed to lift in Auralyn's mind and she suddenly felt a sense of panic.

"Suqata! Where is Suqata!" she said.

"Gone, m'lady. There was no sign of him when we found you."

Auralyn wanted to jump up, to run out and find him, but as she stirred she noticed something in her hand that she hadn't seen until just that moment. Lying across her chest, beneath her reposed hands, was a large black feather. She wearily lifted it up and twisted it slowly in the light. In it she could see an expanse of stars going off into infinity.

# CHAPTER 26
# THE FRONTIER

A URALYN RODE HARD DOWN THE DIRT PATH BESIDE THE FOREST EDGE, letting the wind play through her hair. The air was sweet with the smell of fresh-bloomed honeysuckle and the scent of wet earth beneath the tall grass. The townsfolk were calling it a miracle, the fastest onset of spring they had ever seen, and everyone was out basking in the glory of it. But not Auralyn. She had spent the last few days inside her father's office meeting with farmers, tradesmen, and mill officials discussing one thing, and one thing only. Now, after weeks of deliberation, Orin's Hollow had come to a unanimous decision. It was something she had to share with one person who was very dear to her.

As she approached the gated fence that led off into the woods, Auralyn slowed and came to a stop. She dismounted and patted Augustus on his neck.

"You really think he'll show this time," she whispered to him, to which he whined a response.

"Me neither, but it's worth a try I guess."

Auralyn walked up to the fence and stared off into the deep, green expanse of the woods. She could never have imagined this place held such beauty when she arrived here, even though the winter held its own beauty, too. She reached into her cape, which she wore over a simply made blue dress, and produced the crow feather. It was pristine, as always, and she held it lightly in both hands like a delicate treasure.

"Well. It's done. The act was signed into law today," she said aloud to the forest. "After the Night of Sundering, there really wasn't any path left to us. We could never go back to the way things were, and no one wanted to. So now, we start anew, everyone as equals. No slaves in these territories ever again. I sent Dobbs to the camps this morning to begin dismantling their operation."

There was a slight breeze that blew past Auralyn's face, and the faint sound of wings. Then, she heard a voice behind her, familiar and at the same time different than she remembered it.

"There's a man there called Snodgrass that is not going to like that. Not one bit."

He stood quietly by Augustus, stroking his nose gently as the horse nickered up against him. His hair had grown longer since she last saw him that night at the manor, and he seemed to be a bit taller and leaner. Still it was unmistakably Suqata.

"Oh, Su, you should have seen it," she said, fighting back tears as she slowly approached. She was almost afraid to spook him, as if he might disappear or fly away. Both were possibilities. "Best of all, it wasn't given," she continued; "the people of Orin's Hollow demanded it."

Suqata seemed to draw in a long breath and sigh with relief. "That's going to take some getting used to, for everyone."

"Well, we had to start somewhere," Auralyn said, crossing her arms.

He smiled. "You've been busy," he said, turning his head quizzically to the side.

"I guess you could say that," she said, "but not just me. You should see Obrie. He's become quite the celebrity in town. He's already talking about opening his own tavern, and serving the best cider in the colonies."

"That should please him," Suqata couldn't help but laugh. "He's always liked being the center of attention. But what about you? You look well. Radiant even. Has your sickness been giving you any trouble? Has your Song been draining you?"

She shook her head. "No. Not anymore. I worried about it returning, but it hasn't."

"Well, you needn't worry about it anymore. I brought this back for you." Suqata held out his hand. Lying on his palm was the white river stone he had given her. It was now wrapped in a band of silver and tied on a long leather thong.

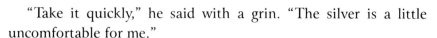

"Take it quickly," he said with a grin. "The silver is a little uncomfortable for me."

She did, and hung it around her neck, examining it in the light. The silver was etched with markings she didn't understand, but that were familiar all the same, and when it was against her skin it hummed like a small moth caught in her hands.

"It will protect you," Suqata said. "As long as you wear it, you never need to worry about the illness returning."

"Thank you," Auralyn looked up to her friend, now almost a foot taller than she, and smiled sadly. "Does this mean you are leaving again?"

"Not right away. There's still a lot I have to learn. Cora Vaco is bound to me now, and me to him, but it's not like I had expected. It is like my eyes are finally open, and the world I see is so much bigger than the one I knew. He still has a lot to show me. Not to mention that the ways between worlds have weakened. I have to keep you safe, as well as the rest of Orin's Hollow."

"But why you? Haven't you done enough?"

Suqata smiled and took Auralyn's hands in his.

"My people left me this task. Why, I don't know. All I do know is that it is up to me. I can't let them down. I am Chinequewa."

Auralyn felt warm tears trickle down the sides of her cheeks, and she turned away.

"So, no room in the new world for you and me," she said. Before she could react, Suqata swept her up in his arms and kissed her, full and long. He held her tightly to him, feeling the thrum of her heartbeat, and she his. When he set her down, breathless, he looked for a long time into her eyes.

"You are a part of me, Lynn. We will always be together," he said. Auralyn wrapped her arms around him and breathed him in. His scent was like the wind, pine smoke, and freedom.

"Always?" she asked.

"Always. I promised your mother I would keep an eye on you."

It took a moment for the realization of what he had said to

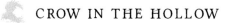 

seep in. Once it did, Auralyn looked up at Suqata, speechless, and he brushed her auburn hair from her eyes.

"It looks like we have a lot to talk about, m'lady," he said.

SO THEY HELD EACH OTHER, there at the border of the great wood. High in the king pines, Cora Vaco waited for his student, breathing in the smell of springtime—of rich earth, fresh honeysuckle, and fields of swaying grass. He was once again in the Waking World, and for the time being was content.

# THE OLD CROW

THE FIRE CONTINUED TO CRACKLE EVEN AFTER THE STORYTELLER'S TALE had come to an end. Many of the children now lay fast asleep in their parents' arms, which was as it should be. With full bellies and full hearts, very few ever reached the end of the story. There was no applause from the crowd, only smiles and handshakes all around.

"*Namu nashta*, dear ones," the storyteller said, and all replied in kind, "*Namu nashta*," and began to collect their belongings to leave. The storyteller was tired as well. He lifted his staff and began to stand when a small hand reached out to help him. Standing before him was a little girl, no more than seven or eight years old, wrapped in an old blanket from head to toe.

"Thank you, child," the storyteller said, standing to his full height.

"You're welcome," she replied. "I liked your story."

"It's not one I get to tell very often," he said with a wink, "but it's getting late, little one, and I think you should be off with your parents."

The girl smiled and shook her head. "I don't have any parents. I live with Mr. Menka, the baker. He's probably already sleep."

"Oh," the storyteller said. There was a silence between them as the little girl looked up at him with her big, blue-grey eyes, until the old man finally cleared his throat and asked, "Was there something you wished of me, my dear?"

"What happened to Suqata and Auralyn? And Obrie and Captain Graye? There's gotta be more to it, there just has to be!"

"Why? What makes you think there is more?"

"Because there is always more to a story. Nothing ever just … ends," she said, with all the conviction of someone four times her age. The storyteller wanted to laugh with joy, but didn't want to upset the serious little girl.

"You are right, of course," he said, "but in stories, as in life, there are chapters to be told. Sometimes peace reigns for years, and some-times only for a day. Soon, we are back again to the world of 'doing.'"

"So, what happened next?"

"That, young one, is a story for another day. One I promise to tell you, but you must be patient. Patience is a very important lesson, and one best learned earlier than later. Can you be patient, and await my return?"

The girl squared her shoulders and puffed out her little chest. "Yes. I can be patient."

The storyteller turned back towards the bridge and began to walk. As he approached it, he heard the girl call out.

"My name is Maylana, by the way."

The storyteller turned and bowed. "Farewell, Maylana. Until next time."

She skipped away into the night and the storyteller was once again alone. Or so he thought.

*So, meet anyone interesting this year?* Cora Vaco said.

The storyteller suddenly felt the crow's weight on his shoulder and gave the old spirit a grin.

"Perhaps. Now let us get home. We have much to do."

And in a gust of sparkling wind, he and the spirit left the Waking World, leaving only the ring of distant music behind them.

# SPECIAL THANK YOUS

THIS BOOK HAS BEEN A dream of mine for over five years, and it couldn't have come about without the help of my family, friends, and Kickstarter supporters:

Jared Noble
Beto Perez Jr
Thomas Taylor
Jason Young & Crissy Laubach-Young
Christopher D. Knox
K. Emms
Robin L Quinn
Sarah and Seth Roush
Matt Jardin
Sharon L. Parker
Andrew the Great, Esq.
The Upchurch Family
Ken Hunt
Aaron Hartwig
Larry Trombley Jr.
Don Ahlers
Jennifer L Penley
Jeff and Jacquelin Cayton

Chad & Deedee Hammons
Leon Skinner
Sam & Loraine Flegal
Henry Schubert
Jon Kroeker
Dwight and Alice Barfield
Azriael Phoenix aka Jason V. Parker
Marcus T. Parker
Lee Hulme
Margaret K.
Josh "the Awesome" Atchley
Donald Bryan Robison
George Parker
Joshua Rogers
Fell Merwin
BIG DADDY Uncle "G"
Mom and Dad

CPSIA information can be obtained at www.ICGtesting.com
Printed in the USA
BVOW03s1318220713

326161BV00001B/1/P